Gabriel's Promise

Sylvain Reynard

JOVE
New York

A JOVE BOOK
Published by Berkley
An imprint of Penguin Random House LLC
penguinrandomhouse.com

Library of Congress Cataloging-in-Publication Data

Names: Reynard, Sylvain, author.
Title: Gabriel's promise / Sylvain Reynard.
Description: First Edition. | New York: Jove, 2020. | Series: Gabriel's Inferno; 4
Identifiers: LCCN 2019031924 (print) | LCCN 2019031925 (ebook) |
ISBN 9780593097984 (paperback) | ISBN 9780593097991 (ebook)
Subjects: LCSH: Family secrets—Fiction. | GSAFD: Mystery fiction. | Love stories.
Classification: LCC PR9199.4.R4667 G29 2020 (print) |
LCC PR9199.4.R4667 (ebook) | DDC 813/.6—dc23
LC record available at https://lccn.loc.gov/2019031924
LC ebook record available at https://lccn.loc.gov/2019031925

First Edition: January 2020

Printed in the United States of America
3rd Printing

Cover art by LightField Studios Inc./Alamy Stock Photo

This book is dedicated to all those we have lost.
May they never be forgotten.

Prologue

1313
Verona, Italy

The poet paused, his quill hovering like an anxious bird over the vellum.

The words he'd placed in the mouth of his beloved were convicting. Even the ink condemned him.

In penning *Purgatorio*, he'd been forced to reexamine his life in the aftermath of her death. His tribute to Beatrice was both homage and penance. But this was not the end.

No, Beatrice's death was not the end of their love. He loved her still and in loving her would be transformed.

The bird of his quill returned to the vellum, giving voice to his loss. He had not been worthy of her in this life. But perhaps, in the next . . .

"Turn, Beatrice, O turn thy holy eyes,"
Such was their song, "unto thy faithful one,
Who has to see thee ta'en so many steps.

In grace do us the grace that thou unveil
Thy face to him, so that he may discern
The second beauty which thou dost conceal."

Here was his beloved now, beautiful and resplendent. Their love remained, but it had changed. And in changing, it deepened and became the stuff of eternity.

The poet looked out over the city of his exile and mourned for his home. He mourned for Beatrice and what had not been.

He hoped for what was to come. Her love had pointed him beyond herself, beyond their earthly love, to something transcendent, perfect, and eternal. He vowed, even as he purged his soul, that the words he penned would be prophetic and that all promises he made to her would be fulfilled. . . .

Chapter One

September 2012
Mount Auburn Hospital
Cambridge, Massachusetts

Professor Gabriel O. Emerson cradled his newborn daughter to his chest. He was reclined in a chair next to his wife's hospital bed, where she lay sleeping. Despite the protestations of the nursing staff, he'd refused to place the baby in the nearby bassinet. She was safer in his arms, resting over his heart.

Clare Grace Hope Emerson was a miracle. He'd prayed for her in the crypt of St. Francis in Assisi, after he'd married his beloved Julianne. At the time, he'd been unable to father a child, the result of his own self-loathing. But with Julianne at his side, as his Beatrice and his wife, he had prayed. And God had answered his prayer.

The baby stirred and moved her head.

Gabriel held her securely, his large hand covering her back so he could feel the rhythm of her breath.

"We loved you since before you were born," he whispered. "We were so excited you were coming."

In this moment—this quiet, tender moment—Gabriel had everything he had ever wanted. If he had been Dante, he was Dante no longer, for Dante never knew the pleasure of marrying Beatrice or of welcoming a child born of their love.

The poet in him reflected on the strange course of events that had taken him from the depths of despair to the heights of blessedness.

"*Apparuit iam beatitudo vestra,*" he quoted with sincerity, thanking God that he hadn't lost his wife and daughter, despite the complications during delivery.

The specter of his father intruded on his happiness, prompting a spontaneous promise. "I will never leave. I will be here with you both, my darling girls, for as long as I live."

In the darkness of the hospital room, Gabriel resolved to protect, love, and care for his wife and his daughter, no matter the cost.

Chapter Two

One week later
Mount Auburn Hospital
Cambridge, Massachusetts

I t began with an email.

It was a small thing—the checking of email. Perhaps it was one of the smallest, most inconsequential of actions. One tapped the screen of one's phone and email messages appeared.

A wise Canadian once wrote, *The medium is the message*. And in this case, the email and its contents were incredibly important.

There had been whispers.

The community of Dante specialists was not particularly large, and Professor Gabriel O. Emerson was well known. He'd been the top student to graduate from his program at Harvard, and in a very short time he made a name for himself at the University of Toronto.

Then he'd been besieged by scandal—a scandal involving his beloved Julianne, who also happened to be his graduate student. There had been an investigation. A tribunal. A ruling. A resignation.

The university kept the matter quiet. Julianne graduated and began doctoral studies at Harvard. Gabriel accepted a position as full professor at Boston University. They'd married on January 21, 2011.

But still, there were whispers. Whispers from a former graduate student named Christa Peterson, who claimed Emerson was a predator and Julianne was a whore.

Although Gabriel had done his best to silence Christa and to combat the rumors, the whispers continued. Now, a few months away from their second wedding anniversary, Gabriel kept his own counsel, not wishing to give voice to his worries. But in truth, he feared he'd tainted Julianne's career. At this time, the academic community was far more forgiving of its male senior faculty than its young female graduate students.

Gabriel knew this. Which was why he stared for some time at the email message he'd received.

The message was from a group Gabriel had heard of but never met. He read the message and then once more, just to be sure he hadn't misunderstood.

A strange feeling washed over him. His skin prickled. Something momentous was about to happen. . . .

"Gabriel?" Julianne's voice interrupted his thoughts. "Do we have everything? Rachel took home the flowers and balloons."

Gabriel opened his mouth to tell his wife about the email he'd just received, but was interrupted by the sudden appearance of Dr. Rubio, their obstetrician. She had a habit of popping up, like gray-eyed Athena in Homer's *Odyssey*. Dr. Rubio appeared, made pronouncements, and vanished, sometimes leaving havoc in her wake.

"Good morning." She greeted the Emersons with a smile. "I need to go over a few things before Julia and Clare are discharged."

Gabriel returned his cell phone to his jacket pocket. He'd received the scare of his life a few days previous, when he mistakenly thought Julianne hadn't survived the delivery. Anxiety still clung to him, like a hangover he could not shake.

Which was why, upon hearing Dr. Rubio's lengthy list of admonitions and instructions, he promptly forgot about the very important email and the absolute necessity of revealing its contents to his wife.

Chapter Three

W hat is she doing?" The Professor peered into the rearview mirror at his wife, who was seated behind him, next to Clare.

His handsome face was boyish and his blue eyes danced. He was finally bringing his family home from the hospital. He had difficulty containing his excitement.

"She's still sleeping." Julia bent over the baby carrier and lightly stroked the infant's cheek.

The baby's rosebud mouth pouted while she slept. Wisps of dark hair peeked out from beneath the purple knitted hat she'd received as a gift from the hospital auxiliary. She was a beautiful baby, with a button nose and pudgy cheeks. Her eyes were large and indigo blue, when she deigned to open them.

Julia's heart was full. Her baby was healthy and her husband was even more supportive than she'd imagined. It was almost too much happiness for one person.

"If she does something cute, let me know." Gabriel's tone was eager.

Julia laughed. "All right, Professor."

"I like to watch her sleep," Gabriel mused. He continued to drive the Volvo SUV at a snail's pace through the streets of Cambridge. "She's fascinating."

"You need to keep your eyes on the road, Daddy."

Gabriel flashed Julia a look.

"Since when do you drive so slowly?" she teased.

"Since everything I love is in this car." Gabriel's expression softened as he made eye contact with her through the mirror.

Julia's heart skipped a beat.

His enthusiasm for fatherhood had outstripped her expectations. She remembered the first night they'd spent in the hospital, after Clare was born. Gabriel held Clare all through the night and would not be parted from her.

Gabriel had said once that when he was an old man, he'd remember what Julianne looked like on the night they made love for the first time. She would remember the sight of her husband holding their baby on his chest for the rest of her life.

Tears filled her eyes and threatened to overflow. She bent over the baby in order to hide her reaction.

Gabriel turned the SUV onto their street—slowly, ever so slowly.

"What the hell?" His buoyant mood came to an abrupt end, rather like a ship hitting an iceberg.

"Language," Julia murmured. "Let's not teach the baby naughty words."

"If the baby were awake, she'd want to know what the hell was going on, too. Look at our lawn." Gabriel piloted the car toward the driveway, his eyes trained on the front of their property.

Julia followed his gaze.

In front of their elegant two-story house was a flamboyance of plastic pink flamingos. Plastic, shocking pink flamingos. A giant wooden flamingo stood next to the front door, holding a sign:

Congratulations Gabriel and Julia! It's a girl!

The smaller flamingos were so numerous Gabriel could barely see the blades of grass beneath them.

It was an infestation. An infestation of tacky, kitschy lawn ornaments, clearly chosen by a fiend with an extreme deficit of good taste.

"Holy shit!" exclaimed Julia.

"Language." Gabriel smirked. "I take it you weren't expecting this?"

"Of course not. I barely checked my email this week. Did you do it?"

"You think *I* did this?" The Professor was indignant. Surely Julianne knew his taste did not extend to plastic abominations of lawn ornaments.

But her comment reminded him of the email he'd received while they were still at the hospital. The contents of the message were urgent. He needed to speak to Julianne about them.

She distracted him by laughing. "Maybe the flamingos are from Leslie, next door? Or your colleagues at Boston University?"

"I doubt that. Surely they would have the good sense to send champagne. Or Scotch."

Once again, he prepared to tell Julianne about the email. But as he pulled into the driveway, the side door opened and Rachel, his sister, raced out.

She was smiling ear-to-ear and dressed casually in a white T-shirt, jeans, and sandals. Her long, straight blond hair spilled over her shoulders, and her gray eyes were alight.

"I guess we found the culprit of kitsch." Gabriel shook his head.

Julia touched his shoulder. "It was kind of her to do this. She's been going back and forth between here and the hospital, helping out."

Gabriel frowned. "I know."

"Even though you think the flamingos are tacky, you need to be appreciative."

He lifted his chin primly. "I can be appreciative."

"I mean appreciative in a believable way," Julia clarified.

When Gabriel's frown deepened, she unbuckled her seat belt and moved forward, pressing her lips to his cheek. "I love you. You're a wonderful husband and an incredible father."

Gabriel lowered his gaze and tapped his fingers against the steering wheel.

Julia tousled his dark hair. "Maybe we should keep a few of the flamingos? For the garden?"

Gabriel speared her with a glare.

"I'm kidding." She held up her hands in surrender. "Try to look happier than that, okay?"

"Fine." Gabriel exhaled beleagueredly. He turned off the car and climbed out.

"What took you so long?" Rachel gave her brother a perfunctory hug and opened the SUV's rear door. "We've been waiting all morning."

Gabriel leaned over the open door, watching as Rachel climbed into the back seat. "They had to check Julianne and Clare before discharging them. And they inspected the baby's carrier and car seat before we left."

"Well, that's good," Rachel replied. "But it shouldn't have taken three hours. How slowly did you drive?"

Gabriel brushed imaginary lint from his sport coat. Then he took a closer look at the back seat.

"Just a minute, Rachel," he cautioned. "I need to unfasten the baby carrier from the base."

"Hurry up. But go over to Julia's side because I'm not moving." Rachel leaned over her sleeping niece and her grin widened. "Hi, Clare."

Julia reached across the baby to touch her friend's arm. "I love the flamingos."

"I knew you'd appreciate them." Rachel beamed. "Dad was hesitant, but I thought they were hilarious. Even Scott chipped in."

"We need to take a picture of Gabriel with the flamingos and send it to Scott."

Rachel laughed. "Absolutely. He'll blow it up into a poster and hang it on his wall."

Julia removed the baby's knitted cap to expose the shock of dark hair. She pointed to the pink barrette she'd carefully fastened. "Clare is wearing the gift you brought us yesterday."

"It matches her pink sleepers." Rachel gently touched the baby's head. Her expression shifted minutely.

Julia studied her friend. A trace of sadness was present in Rachel's eyes, but only for a moment.

Rachel smiled at her sleeping niece. "I bought a few more hair accessories last night. Since she has so much hair, we'll have to style it."

Julia nodded. "Gabriel will have to carry her. I'm not supposed to lift anything over nine pounds because of the stitches."

Rachel glanced at Julia's middle. "That bites."

"No biting." Gabriel winked at his sister before helping Julia out of the car. "I'm glad you're here."

"So am I." Rachel watched as he carefully removed the baby carrier and turned toward the house.

"Not so fast." She followed him. "I want to carry her."

With eyes twinkling, Gabriel handed over the carrier, but not before instructing her to be careful. He greeted Richard, their father, and the two men stood next to the door, holding it open.

Julia accompanied Rachel into the house. "Thanks for staying. I know it was a bit longer than you'd planned."

Rachel held the baby carrier with both hands as they approached the kitchen. "I wasn't going to leave before you came home. Aaron had to work, otherwise he'd be here, too."

"It means a lot. I know you've been fielding phone calls and deliveries and everything else."

Rachel shrugged. "That's what families do, Jules. They take care of each other. I'm just lucky I had some vacation days left. Rebecca has been spoiling us with her cooking. You should see what she made for lunch."

"Good. I'm starving." Julia's stomach was already rumbling. She stepped into the kitchen.

The kitchen table was set with the Emersons' best china, silverware, and crystal. Pink helium-filled balloons were tied to Julia's chair at the foot of the table, and a huge arrangement of pink and white roses formed a centerpiece. Almost every surface of the kitchen was covered with food, flowers, or brightly wrapped presents.

"Surprise!" An older woman with short white hair and gray-blue eyes stepped forward.

"Katherine?" Julia fanned a hand over her mouth.

"I thought you were in Oxford." Gabriel shook off his surprise and greeted his former colleague with a kiss on the cheek.

"I was. I came to Cambridge to meet my goddaughter." Professor Picton embraced Julia and stepped back, her eyes sparkling. "Can I hold her?"

"Of course." Gabriel removed Clare from her baby carrier, pressing a kiss to her head before transferring her to Katherine's arms.

Clare opened her big blue eyes.

Katherine smiled. "Hello, Clare. I'm your aunt Katherine."

The baby opened her tiny rosebud mouth and yawned.

"Clare is a beautiful name," Katherine continued, undeterred by the infant's sleepiness. "I thought your parents might have named you Beatrice. But I can see you look more like a Clare."

"There's only one Beatrice." Gabriel placed his arm around Julia's shoulders.

"Oh, what fun we'll have," Katherine whispered to the child. "I'll teach you Italian and all about Dante and Beatrice. When you're old enough, I'll take you to Florence and show you where Dante lived."

The baby seemed to stare at her aunt. Katherine bent closer and recited,

> "'*Donne ch'avete intelletto d'amore,*
> *i' vo' con voi de la mia donna dire,*
> *non perch'io creda sua laude finire,*
> *ma ragionar per isfogar la mente.'*"

Gabriel recognized the lines from Dante's *La Vita Nuova*, as Katherine quoted his praise for the lovely Beatrice.

Julia stood, frozen.

Then suddenly, like an unexpected cloudburst at a picnic, Julia began to cry.

Chapter Four

The room grew very still.

Everyone looked at Julia, who clapped a hand over her mouth as she tried to suppress her sobs.

Richard, Katherine, Rebecca, and Rachel stood in shock, not knowing what to do.

"Give us a minute," Gabriel murmured, his arm still wrapped around Julia's shoulders. He led her into the living room to a quiet corner near the window.

"Darling, what's the matter? Are you in pain?" Stricken, he bent to look at her.

Julia closed her eyes as the tears flowed. She shook her head.

Gabriel pulled her against his chest. "I don't understand. Do you want everyone to leave?"

She shook her head again.

He rested his cheek against her hair. "I didn't know they were planning all this."

"There are twice as many balloons," she mumbled.

"Is helium dangerous for babies?"

"No. Yes. I don't know." She fisted his shirt. "That's not the point. There are twice as many gifts and flowers than what we had at the hospital. And there are flamingos on our lawn!"

"I can remove the flamingos, darling." Gabriel kissed her hair. "I'll do that now."

"This isn't about the flamingos." Julia dipped her hand in one of the pockets of Gabriel's jacket, eventually retrieving a handkerchief. She waved it in front of him. "I'm glad I bought you this."

She blew her nose.

"A gentleman always carries a handkerchief, for just such occasions." He caressed her back, his concern escalating. "You're upset about the flamingos, but you don't want me to remove them?"

"The kitchen is filled with presents. Katherine came all the way from England and quoted Dante!" Julia burst into tears again.

Gabriel frowned, for the sight of her tears pained him. "Of course there are presents. People give gifts to babies. It's a tradition."

"How many of my relatives are in the kitchen?" She dabbed at her nose.

Gabriel's heart constricted. "Your father and Diane wanted to be here, but Tommy is sick. You'll see them soon." He wiped Julia's tears away with his thumbs. "The kitchen is filled with family, our family. People who love you and Clare."

She swallowed hard. "I miss your mom. I miss . . ."

Gabriel winced. There was an ocean of pain in Julianne's unfinished sentence. She'd had an unhappy childhood with a mother who was sometimes abusive, sometimes indifferent.

"I miss Grace, too," Gabriel admitted. "I think we will always miss her."

"I've only been a mother for a couple of days, but I love Clare so much, I'd do anything for her. What was wrong with Sharon?" Julia whispered, clinging to her husband.

Gabriel gazed down at his wife. "I don't know."

His answer was true. How does one explain indifference and cruelty? He'd experienced both from his biological father. And eventually he came to realize that any attempt to explain such behavior was futile, because explanations often masqueraded as excuses. And he would not countenance excuses.

He placed his hands on her shoulders and squeezed. "I love you, Julianne. We love each other, and we love Clare. We didn't begin our lives with the best role models, but think of who we have now: everyone in our kitchen, and Tom and Diane, and Scott and Tammy, and everyone else we love. We get to create our own family, for Clare."

"She won't know what it's like to have a mother who doesn't love her." Julia's tone grew fierce.

"No, she won't." Gabriel's embrace tightened. "And she has a father who loves her and her mother very much."

Julia wiped her eyes with the back of her hand. "I'm sorry for ruining the party."

"You haven't ruined anything. It's your party. You can cry, if you want to . . ."

Julia laughed and it was like the sun coming out after the rain. Then, inexplicably, she lifted up on tiptoes to peer over Gabriel's shoulder through the front window. "Our lawn is covered in flamingos."

Gabriel's lips twitched. "Yes. Yes, it is."

"I kind of like them."

"I think you're sleep-deprived." He kissed her forehead.

"I don't know what's wrong with me. I want to laugh about those silly flamingos and I want to cry because we have such a great family. And I'm hungry."

"Dr. Rubio warned us your recovery would take longer because of the complications. You've been feeding the baby every two to three hours. Of course you're hungry."

"I want to put a flamingo in the nursery."

Gabriel's head jerked back.

A flamingo will ruin the aesthetic we've painstakingly created, he thought. *It's a crime against interior design.*

He changed the subject. "Maybe you should take a nap and I'll send everyone home?"

"That would be difficult. With the exception of Katherine, everyone is staying with us."

"Right."

"Now who's sleep-deprived, Professor?" Julia grinned and took his hand.

Gabriel rubbed his forehead with his other hand. "I'll book rooms at the Lenox. It's a nice hotel."

Julia looked up at his earnest blue eyes and worried expression. She squeezed his hand. "Don't send them away. I'm fine. Really."

Gabriel gave her a dubious look.

As she leaned against him, he was seized by the memory of her in the delivery room. She was lying on a gurney, pale and very still. The doctor had shouted at the nurses to escort him out of the room.

He'd thought she was dead.

He felt his heart stutter and placed his hand on his chest.

Julia peered up at him. "Gabriel, are you all right?"

He blinked.

"I'm perfectly well." He covered up his agitation by kissing her firmly. "I'm concerned about you."

Before Julia could respond, a throat cleared nearby.

They turned to find Rebecca, their housekeeper and friend, standing near the doorway. Rebecca was tall, with bobbed salt-and-pepper hair and large dark eyes.

She crossed over to the couple and gave Julia a concerned look. "Are you okay?"

"I'm fine." Julia lifted her arms at her sides. "Just weepy."

"Hormones." Rebecca patted her on the shoulder. "It will take time for your body to get back to normal. You may find your feelings going up and down."

"Oh." Julia's features relaxed, as if Rebecca's words were a revelation.

"I had the same experience when my son was born. I was laughing one minute, crying the next. But it settles out. Don't worry. Do you want to lie down? I can postpone lunch."

Julia looked at Gabriel. He lifted his eyebrows.

"No, I want to see everyone. And I want to eat." She looked longingly in the direction of the kitchen.

"Lunch is almost ready. Take your time." Rebecca hugged Julia and exited the living room.

"I forgot about the hormone fluctuation." Julia gazed up at Gabriel. "I feel lost."

"You aren't lost." Gabriel's tone was firm. He lifted Julia's chin and took her lips in a slow, sweet kiss. "We will never be lost, so long as we have each other."

Julia kissed him. "I'm so glad you're here. I can't imagine trying to navigate this by myself."

Gabriel pressed his lips together. Once again, he remembered the important email but decided it was not the appropriate moment to mention it.

He gestured toward the window. "We have a thousand and one flamingos on our front lawn. You're far from alone."

Julia looked up into Gabriel's very serious, slightly irritated face. And she burst out laughing.

Chapter Five

That afternoon, Gabriel glared at a myriad of metal attachments, screws, and plastic pieces, which were arranged with military precision atop the nursery carpet.

(It should be noted there were no flamingos in sight.)

He cast a baleful look at an empty box on which an infant swing was jauntily displayed and scowled again at the arranged pieces. "Son of a—"

A throat cleared behind him.

Gabriel turned to see Richard standing in the doorway, holding Clare.

The infant was fussing and Richard was doing his best to soothe her, holding her close and moving back and forth.

"Where's Julianne?" Gabriel approached the doorway and lightly touched the baby's head.

"Taking a well-earned nap. Clare is supposed to be napping as well, but she isn't settling. I said I'd walk her around and see if she'd nod off." Richard spoke in low, soothing tones while rubbing gentle circles on the infant's back.

"I can take her." Gabriel held out his arms.

"Oh, no. I'm eager to have as much time with my new grand-daughter as possible. We'll keep you company." Richard stepped nimbly around the many metal pieces and went to stand by the window. "How's it going?"

Gabriel gestured vaguely at the detritus on the carpet. "I'm wrestling a baby swing."

Richard chuckled. "I've done that before. And put together bicycles and impossible-to-assemble toys on Christmas Eve. My advice is to ignore your instinct to figure it out yourself and follow the instructions."

"I have a PhD from Harvard. Surely I can figure out how to put together a baby swing."

"I have a PhD from Yale." Richard's gray eyes sparkled. "And I know enough to read the instructions."

Gabriel smiled wryly. "Well, I can't have a Yalie outdo me." He stuck his head into the large box and retrieved a booklet of directions. He adjusted his glasses. "These are in Chinese, Spanish, Italian, and German."

"I put together one of those swings when Grace and I brought Scott home from the hospital. I'd been up all night and put the legs on backward. I couldn't figure out why it wouldn't balance until Grace fixed it."

Gabriel snickered and peered more closely at the booklet. "The Italian directions don't make any sense. They must have hired a first-year student to translate them. I shall have to write a letter to the company."

Richard regarded his son with barely disguised amusement.

"Perhaps you should assemble it first." He cleared his throat. "Scott's delivery was relatively easy compared to Clare's. Julia looked pale when I left her a few minutes ago."

Gabriel lowered the instructions. "I'll go check on her."

"Rachel was in there with her plumping pillows and drawing the blinds. But you should probably look in on her soon."

Gabriel rubbed his eyes behind his glasses. "The delivery did not go as expected."

Richard bowed his head so he could see Clare's face. Her eyes were closed. He slowed his movements, still rocking back and forth. "Julia will need care and lots of support. Are you on leave or—"

"Ah. Here's the English part." Gabriel hid his face as he pored over the instructions. "Yes, I'm on paternity leave."

Richard lifted his head. "Julia is supposed to resume her course-work next September, correct? And you'll be teaching?"

Gabriel bristled. "That's what I do."

Given the email he'd received that morning, it was extremely unlikely, if not impossible, that he'd be teaching at Boston University the following year. But he hadn't disclosed that fact to anyone, including Julianne.

He crouched down and began rearranging the pieces to the swing according to the printed instructions. "We're glad you and Rachel were able to stay. We intend to have Clare baptized this week at our parish. We're going to ask Rachel to be the godmother."

"I'm sure she will be delighted. And I'm glad we will be able to attend the baptism." Richard appeared disquieted at his son's transparent attempt at deflection. "How are you coping with everything?"

"I'm fine." Gabriel sounded impatient. "Why wouldn't I be?"

"Fatherhood is a great responsibility." Richard's tone was gentle.

Gabriel sat back on his heels, his focus on the carpet. "Yes." He blew out a breath. "How did you know how to be a father?"

"I didn't always. I made mistakes. But Grace was an incredible mother. She seemed to have the right instincts for parenting. I was fortunate to have excellent parents, as well. They died before you came to us, but they created a home that was loving and caring. I tried to do that with you children."

"You succeeded." Gabriel picked up one of the metal legs and turned it over in his hand.

Richard continued. "Parenting is a commitment. You promise to love your children, no matter what. You promise to keep them safe. You promise to provide for them, to teach them, and to guide them. And with God's grace, a lot of patience, and hard work, you keep your promises."

Gabriel hummed as he placed the metal leg on the carpet. He reached for the swing's motor.

Richard adjusted Clare so that she was sleeping on her back in his arms. "Are you worried about being a father?"

Gabriel shrugged.

"You chose Julia to be your wife. She's a lovely young woman and the perfect partner for you. You and she will figure things out. And I will be there for you and your family. I'm blessed every day by you children, and by Scott and Tammy's son, and now by Clare. How fortunate I am to be a young grandfather and able to enjoy my grandchildren."

Gabriel put the motor down and began fitting two of the larger metal pieces together. Richard settled himself in the large leather club chair that sat in the corner, still holding a sleeping Clare.

Gabriel's gaze lifted to his daughter and the sight of his father's hand wrapped protectively around her.

Richard still wore his wedding ring. Gabriel was tempted, sorely tempted, to tell Richard that he'd dreamt of Grace while he was in the hospital. But three years after her death, Richard still wore the marks of his sorrow, in the lines that had deepened on his face and the white hairs that had multiplied on his head. Gabriel would keep Grace's apparition to himself.

He connected the feet of the swing to the two upright pieces that would form the legs. "During the delivery, something went wrong. They sent me out of the room. They handed me Clare but wouldn't let me see Julianne. I thought she was dead."

"Son." Richard's voice broke.

Gabriel reached into his toolbox and retrieved a screwdriver. He began tightening the screws in the legs. "How do you manage?"

Richard touched Clare's head gently, so as not to wake her. "That's an apt description. I manage. But my life will never be the same."

"There's freedom in acceptance. I realize everything has changed and I've tried to adjust my outlook accordingly. But I still grieve her. I grieve the loss of her and what might have been. And as time goes by and the grief fades but doesn't quite disappear, I've learned not to fight it. I lost the love of my life, and I will always feel her loss.

"She appears to me sometimes in my dreams. But only when I'm in our house. I find her appearances comforting."

"I'm sorry I wasn't there for you."

Richard appeared confused. "But you were."

"Not really." Gabriel busied himself with the swing, spreading the legs and fitting the crossbar in order to steady it. "I was mired in my own selfishness."

"When Grace died, you came and sat with me on the ground."

Gabriel lifted his eyebrows.

"From the book of Job, in the Bible," Richard hastened to explain. "Job's friends hear of his suffering and they come to see him."

"Job's friends aren't exactly heroes," Gabriel objected. He attached the swing's motor to the legs and tested the structure to ensure that it wouldn't tip over.

"True, true. But when they saw Job sitting on the ground, they went and sat with him. And they didn't speak a word for seven days, for they recognized how great his sorrow was." Richard paused until Gabriel made eye contact. "When Grace died, you came and sat with me on the ground."

Gabriel didn't answer, his emotions swirling in his chest. He picked up a wrench and tightened the bolts that held the motor to the legs.

"I've spent hours reflecting on my loss. But also hours remembering happy times. And the conclusion I've come to is that the best thing we can do for one another is to be present and to be loving." Richard paused and pressed a kiss to the top of Clare's head. "When my granddaughter is fussy, I can hold her. When Rachel is grieving, I can comfort her. When my son and his wife need an extra pair of hands or an expression of support, I will be with them. Time, love, and support—that is the core of being a parent."

Richard smiled. "You're embarking on a new phase of life with your family. Yes, there will be challenges. But there will be time enough to worry about them as they come. Focus on the present and don't let your worries about the future rob you of your joy."

Gabriel busied himself by sliding the swing off the carpet and onto the hardwood. He sat back to appreciate his handiwork. "Well done, Harvard."

"Well done, indeed." Richard's gray eyes twinkled. "But you've attached everything but the swing."

Gabriel looked at the upright apparatus in dismay. He turned around and saw the swing piece reclining secretively behind him. He grabbed his hair with both hands. "Fu-u-u. . . . . dge."

"Welcome to fatherhood." Richard chuckled.

Chapter Six

Just before midnight, Gabriel walked through the darkened house with almost silent footfalls. That was his usual routine before retiring.

He checked all the doors to ensure that they were locked and proceeded to check the windows.

Gazing out the front windows at Foster Place, he noticed a car driving slowly. The car was black and unremarkable. But traffic was rare on Foster Place, because it was a cul-de-sac. There were two parking spots available on the street, and they were only available to residents.

The car slowed as it passed Gabriel, continued to the end of the cul-de-sac, and drove at a snail's pace past him once again. The front license plate was obscured by mud. The windows were darkly tinted.

He watched as the car turned onto the next street and he replaced the curtain, covering the window. He then surveyed the ground floor.

Some months previous, Julianne had decided to decorate the house with lanterns, each of which held a flameless pillar candle. The candles shone gently, casting warm, rolling waves. She'd placed the lanterns strategically—one in each room, one at the base of the staircase and one at the top, one outside the nursery on the second floor, and one outside the guest bathroom. The candles were set to illumine at dusk and shine until morning.

Gabriel took a moment to admire the comforting glimmer of the lanterns, marveling at how they kept the darkness at bay. In his heart, he praised Julia's foresight. No one would stumble on the stairs or on their way to the nursery. It was a small thing, perhaps, to light a lantern. But in Gabriel's mind the gesture seemed all the more significant, as he considered what that evening would have been like if Julianne had not survived the delivery.

Gabriel's prayer was spontaneous, like his overwhelming gratitude for his family. Like the way Julianne loved him.

Satisfied his home was secure, he climbed the staircase. He stopped by the nursery and switched on the light. The new baby swing stood proudly in the center of the room, which was crowded with gifts and baby clothes. Richard had displayed Clare's name in large white letters above her closet.

Gabriel smiled and switched off the light.

In the master bedroom, a fanciful night light projected pink stars on the ceiling over Julianne's side of the bed. He could see her curled into a ball beneath the covers. The playpen stood almost within arm's reach of the bed. Clare was swaddled in soft material, lying in a bassinet that was securely resting atop the elevated floor of the playpen.

He touched Clare's head lightly, so as not to wake her. "Daddy loves you."

Then he turned to his sleeping wife and pressed a kiss to her hair. He took a moment to survey his surroundings, especially the large reproduction of Henry Holiday's painting of Dante and Beatrice that hung on the wall opposite the bed. Once again, he stared at Beatrice's face, noticing the shocking resemblance between his own brown-eyed angel and Dante's beloved.

Then his gaze moved to the large black-and-white photographs he'd taken of himself and Julia since they'd been together. There were others, of course. Stacks of photos lined his office, documenting Julianne's beautiful form throughout pregnancy. And there were a hundred digital photos of Clare saved on his computer that had been taken in the hospital.

But for now, at least, he looked with fondness at the old picture of Julianne's graceful neck and his hands holding up her long brown hair. And then the photo of her sitting on the edge of the bathtub, her beautiful back and the side of one of her breasts exposed.

Longing stirred within him. Longing for the connection of their bodies, something that hadn't been possible the past few weeks. Love had taught him patience, for he would not be so selfish as to press his wants on her now. But Professor Emerson was not a patient man. Nor was he naturally inclined to be celibate.

The more he thought of his wife and her lush and beautiful body, the more his longing grew.

He rubbed at his eyes. *A few more days. I was celibate for months before Julianne and I were married. Surely I can survive a few more days.*

Groaning, he crossed to his side of the bed near the window. He was used to sleeping naked, but that was no longer appropriate. With the scowl of the oppressed, he pulled off his T-shirt and threw it, leaving him clad only in pajama bottoms. Then he pulled back the covers.

He sprang back with a curse.

There, resting on his pillow, was a large, plastic flamingo. It was staring at him with a crazed smile on its face.

He swore.

A giggle sounded from the other side of the bed.

Gabriel switched on the lamp and glared at his wife. *"Et tu, Brute?"*

"What?" Julia rolled over to face him, feigning drowsiness. But she couldn't maintain a straight face.

Gabriel grimaced. He picked up the accursed lawn ornament with two fingers and regarded it distastefully.

Julia laughed. "Oh, come on. That was funny."

He wrinkled his nose and placed the flamingo on the floor. Then he pushed the creature aside with his foot. "I hope you cleaned it after you pulled it out of the dirt."

"Maybe." She gave him a saucy wink.

He examined his pillowcase, his hands going to his waist. "We're going to have to strip the bed."

She flopped back against the mattress. "It's late. I washed the flamingo before putting it on your pillow, I swear."

Gabriel gave her a dubious look.

She patted the sheets on his side. "Look, nice and clean. Come to bed. It's been a long day."

He gazed from his pillow to her tired but hopeful face and cast his eyes heavenward. He shook his head. "Fine. But I'm stripping the bed tomorrow morning. And I'm bleaching everything."

Gabriel removed something from the drawer in his nightstand and hid it in his hand. He left the light on and crawled under the covers. "Rachel must have put you up to it."

"No, it was my idea." Julia yawned.

He pulled her toward him and kissed her temple.

"I love to hear you laugh," he confessed. "And to see you smile."

Julia snuggled against him. "I'm sorry for the tears earlier. I'm just tired and overwhelmed."

"I'm worried about you."

"I'm fine."

"There's no reason for you to be tired and overwhelmed. You have me."

She rested her head against his bare shoulder. "Good, because I need you. And Clare needs you, too."

Gabriel hid his face in her hair. "Every day is a gift. I vow not to waste them."

"Me, too."

He felt for her right hand. "I wanted to give you something at the hospital, but we didn't have a lot of privacy. Then I wanted to give it to you when we got home, but the timing wasn't right."

Julia lifted her head. "What is it?"

He placed a small robin's-egg-blue box in her hand.

She sat up immediately. She undid the white ribbon bow that was wound around the box and opened the lid. A smaller velvet box was nestled inside.

Gabriel took the smaller box and opened it, presenting it to her.

Inside the box was a ring, which featured a large oval ruby flanked by two round diamonds. The setting was platinum and reminiscent of Julianne's engagement ring.

He removed the ring and grasped her right hand, slipping it on her fourth finger. "This is a gift to commemorate the great gift that you've given me. The ruby represents you, the heart of our family, and the diamonds represent me and Clare. Together, we form a family."

He leaned down to press his lips against the base of her finger.

"It's beautiful," she whispered. She gazed at him in wonder. "I don't know what to say."

Gabriel's eyebrows moved together. "Do you like it?"

"I love it. It's gorgeous. But most important, I love what it represents." She stared at the ring. "And it fits."

"I had to approximate the size based on your other rings. But it can always be resized." With his thumb he moved the ring back and forth on her finger, experimentally.

"It's incredible. Thank you." She kissed him once again.

Gabriel took the boxes and ribbons and placed them on his nightstand. He switched off the light. "When is the baby's next feeding?"

"Soon. I set the alarm on my phone."

Gabriel settled under the covers and brought Julia into his side. "Wake me when you're finished, and I'll change her. Then you can get back to bed sooner."

Julia hummed and lifted her right arm, examining her ring in the semidarkness. "I'm exhausted."

He chuckled. "Then go to sleep."

"Now I'm wired. It's the flamingo's fault."

Gabriel laughed. His wife giggled in response.

When their laughter abated, Gabriel found himself staring down into her large, expressive eyes. Something passed between them.

Impulsively, he shifted her to her back. He traced her eyebrows with his fingertip. *"Beatrice."*

She sighed when his lips met hers.

The electricity between them had not abated. Gabriel took his time, allowing his mouth to worship hers.

He deepened the kiss, his hand stroking her hip over her nightgown.

As his tongue gently teased hers, she made a noise in her throat. Gabriel felt encouraged and continued to dance, his lips firm and insistent.

His hand slid up her side and hovered over her breast. His eyes held a question.

"Your gift deserves a celebration," she whispered. "I've missed you."

Gabriel smiled widely, his hand hovering like a bird over her breast.

Julia's expression changed. "But it's too soon. My breasts are sore and I'm sore around the incision and farther down."

Stricken, Gabriel lowered his hand to rest on the mattress, near her hip. "I'm sorry."

Julia's palm moved to his thigh and began to slide upward. "I can look after you."

Gabriel caught her wrist. "Another time." He lifted her wrist to his lips and kissed the pale skin that stretched over her veins.

Julia sighed the sigh of the exhausted and frustrated. She slid her head across the pillow until it rested next to his shoulder. "Are you sure?"

"I'm sure. What can I do for you?"

"Nothing." She forced a smile. "I'll be fine in six weeks."

Six weeks? What fresh hell is this?

Gabriel blinked slowly. Somewhere in the recesses of his memory he recalled Dr. Rubio's Athena-like pronouncement that intercourse had to be delayed. But the duration of the delay hadn't truly penetrated his consciousness.

"I would if I could." Julia sounded apologetic. "I'm sorry."

Her earnest tone roused him from his reverie. "You have nothing to apologize for." He kissed her lightly on the nose. "Here." He slid his arms under her body and gently assisted her in rolling onto her side, facing away from him.

He spooned behind her, sifting his fingers through her hair. He felt her body begin to relax beneath his touch. "I'll rub your back."

His hands slid sensuously over her shoulders and down her back. Skin to skin, he caressed her. And where he found tension, he massaged. "How does this feel?"

"Great." Her body sagged against the mattress.

"And this?" He focused his contact on her right shoulder.

"It feels good."

"Then just feel, sweetheart. I'll stay right here. Right here." He pressed a slow, chaste kiss to the area between her shoulder blades and felt her shiver beneath his lips. "I'll be good. I promise."

He knew her body. He knew how to build the pleasure in her, and how to make her toes curl. But in these moments, his sole purpose was to care for her and help her fall asleep.

She moaned softly, her eyes closed.

His hands slipped down to her lower back. He kneaded the muscles carefully, and whispered his fingers across her skin.

Julia's breathing evened out and soon it was clear she'd fallen asleep.

Gabriel continued to caress her, but more lightly. *"Thy love is better than wine,"* he spoke in the darkness. "I'll never get over my desire for you."

With a final caress, he kissed her shoulder and carefully rested his hand on the curve of her hip. He sighed and lifted mournful eyes to heaven. "Give me chastity, Lord, at least for the next six weeks."

Chapter Seven

An infant's cry split the silence.

It took time for Gabriel to shake off his sleep, like a swimmer struggling to reach the surface. Julia rolled over next to him. He heard her fumbling with her cell phone.

She groaned.

"Is it time?" His voice was gravelly with sleep.

"Not for an hour." Julia sank back against the pillow and covered her eyes with her hands.

"I'll go." Gabriel pushed back the covers.

"No, I can do it."

"Just rest. I'll check on her."

Gratefully, Julianne pulled the covers over her head.

Gabriel crossed to the playpen and lifted a crying Clare into his arms. The baby quieted for a moment as he held her to his bare chest. But then she continued.

He walked swiftly to the nursery, murmuring and jostling her gently in his arms. She continued crying, even after he switched on the light. He hadn't discerned her different cries. Not yet. All crying sounded the same to him and so he wasn't sure what she was communicating.

He placed her on top of the change table and unswaddled her, carefully removing her sleeper. The baby cried louder.

He made shushing noises as he removed her diaper, which was wet. But she cried on, even after she was clean and dry.

Puzzled, he dressed and swaddled her, cradling her against his bare chest. Again the baby paused her crying as soon as she touched his skin. When she continued, he cleared his throat and attempted to sing.

The baby continued to cry.

"My singing isn't that bad," he protested. "I can carry a tune."

He sang more loudly, swaying back and forth across the carpet, like a dancer. When he ran out of verses to "You Are My Sunshine," he made up new ones.

He was just about to take the baby to Julianne for feeding when he placed his hand on the baby's head, stroking her hair. Clare stopped crying.

Not wishing to tempt fate, Gabriel kept his hand where it was and continued singing. When he removed his hand, she began crying again.

He placed his hand back on her head and the infant quieted.

Gabriel's sleep-addled brain moved slowly, but eventually it occurred to him that perhaps the baby was cold. He retrieved the purple knitted cap Clare had been gifted at the hospital and placed it on her tiny head.

The baby moved a little and closed her eyes, resting her cheek over Gabriel's heart.

He stopped singing but continued dancing slowly back and forth. He worried that if he placed Clare in the playpen, she'd start crying again. Julianne would have to feed her soon, anyway. She deserved a few more minutes of rest.

He dimmed the nursery's chandelier and settled himself in the large armchair in the corner, propping his feet up on the ottoman. He held Clare to his chest, the way he had the first night in the hospital.

"I have no idea what I'm doing," he whispered to the sleeping infant. "But I promise to learn more songs."

Chapter Eight

G abriel stood in the master bathroom, shaving. His dark hair was damp, his blue eyes bleary behind his glasses. He was clad only in a white towel, which he'd wrapped around his hips. He paused as Julianne entered the bathroom, closing the door behind her.

"Where's the baby?" he asked.

"Rachel is changing her and then she's going to take her downstairs." Julia yawned.

It was early morning, but the household was awake. Rebecca had already started breakfast and the scent of coffee and bacon wafted up the stairs.

"Did you sleep well last night?"

Julianne flushed a little. "Yes. Did you?"

"Tolerably." He took her hand and pulled her into his arms. "Is the timeline really six weeks?"

"I'm afraid so. But the timeline is about what my body can sustain, not yours." Julia kissed him firmly. "I'll see that you're *well* looked after."

Gabriel opened his mouth to protest, and then shut it abruptly. His lips widened into a wolfish grin.

She lifted her right hand and wiggled her fingers. "And thank you for this. It's even more magnificent in daylight."

"You're welcome." He kissed her, his mouth lingering against hers.

"I need a shower." She pulled back.

He kissed her forehead. "Now's your chance."

She hugged him around the waist before crossing over to the linen closet.

Gabriel pretended to continue shaving, regarding Julianne through the mirror.

She retrieved a pair of thick white towels, hanging them on a hook near the walk-in shower. Then she opened the shower door.

Gabriel turned around in anticipation.

Julia shrieked and leapt backward, bumping into her husband. He grabbed her by the shoulders, steadying her.

"*Et tu, Brute?*" She gave him an accusatory look.

"Oh come on." He squeezed her. "That was funny."

Julia shook her head and crossed back to the shower. Inside, a plastic pink flamingo wearing a shower cap grinned up at her.

"I hope you cleaned it when you pulled it from the ground."

"I didn't need to." Gabriel smirked as he returned to his shaving. "I used the one you cleaned."

"The shower cap was a nice touch." Julia switched on the shower and carefully removed her nightgown.

"I thought so." Gabriel turned and regarded her over the rim of his glasses. "Are you going to shower with the flamingo?"

"I get lonely in the shower." She gave him a heated look.

Gabriel watched as she removed her belly band and underwear, his gaze fixating on her stitches. In only a few days, her abdomen had contracted dramatically, making the slight smile of the cesarean section visible.

She entered the shower and closed the door.

Gabriel removed his glasses and leaned against the vanity as Julia stood below the spray. She brushed the water from her eyes and reached for a bottle of shower gel. Then she stopped.

She looked down past her abdomen and appeared to be inspecting her stitches.

"Is something wrong?" He lifted his voice above the din of the falling water.

When she didn't answer but remained frozen, he slid open the shower door. "Julianne?"

She was gazing down, motionless.

He followed her gaze and saw a swirl of red in the water that rushed about her feet.

Gabriel panicked. "Julianne?" he repeated, more urgently.

She lifted her gaze and made eye contact with him, her expression strangely unseeing. Then her eyes rolled back in her head.

Gabriel jumped into the shower, still wearing his towel, and caught her as her knees buckled.

"Julianne!" He scooped her up, feeling her body go limp in his arms.

Not knowing what to do, he ran to the bedroom and placed her on the bed, covering her with a sheet. "Julianne? Julianne!" When she didn't respond, he skirted the bed and raced to his nightstand. He'd just unlocked his cell phone when he heard her murmur.

"Gabriel?" She squinted up at him, a confused look on her face.

He sat next to her. "How do you feel?" He touched her forehead, searching for a sign of fever, but her skin was cool.

"I don't know." She looked down. "Why is my hair wet?"

Gabriel's expression tightened. "You fainted in the shower."

"Really?" She touched her forehead. "I feel like I just woke up."

"I'm calling the hospital."

"No, no hospital." She lifted the sheet, her arm shaking. "I'm getting the bed wet."

"Fuck the bed." Gabriel's blue eyes blazed.

She gazed at him and her fuzziness dissipated. "I had a dizzy spell in the shower a few days ago."

"Why didn't you tell me?" Gabriel's tone was sharp.

"I told the nurse. It's the stitches. I have to check the incision but it makes me sick to look at it."

He leaned over her. "Why didn't you say something?"

"It didn't occur to me. I'm fine."

Gabriel huffed. "You are not fine. What are we supposed to be checking for with respect to the incision?"

She grimaced. "Signs of infection or the wound reopening. The area around the incision is numb. It feels weird."

"We should have the numbness checked." His grip on her hand tightened. "I saw blood in the shower, before you fainted."

"Blood?" Julia's eyes widened and she began shaking.

Gabriel wrapped his arms around her. "Stay with me."

After a moment, she blinked rapidly. "I feel like my blood sugar dropped. Maybe that's why I fainted."

Still holding her, Gabriel opened the drawer to her nightstand. He rummaged around and retrieved a bar of chocolate.

"How did you know about my secret chocolate?" She eyed him suspiciously.

"I pay attention." He opened the chocolate bar, broke off a piece, and handed it to her.

She hummed as the sweetness spread over her tongue. "I've been bleeding since the surgery. The doctor said it's normal."

"Again, Julianne, why didn't you tell me?"

"I did. Remember last night? I told you there was—" She stopped, confused.

"We need to call the hospital."

Julia screwed her eyes shut. "Fine. Call the hospital. But I don't want to go back."

While she continued to eat her chocolate bar, Gabriel called Mount Auburn Hospital and was transferred quickly to the labor and delivery unit. He wouldn't leave Julia's side but spoke in low, calm tones so as not to upset her. It was clear from his body language that he was not happy with what he heard.

When he ended the call, he tossed his phone aside. "I think we should take you to the emergency room."

"Is that what they said?"

"No." He scowled. "They're telling me bleeding is normal but to monitor the output. And to check you for fever, which I already have. They say numbness around the incision is normal and will go away. Obviously, they don't know what they're talking about."

"Okay, but I don't think two first-time parents know more than labor and delivery." She lifted her hand and Gabriel took it once again. "I remember being in the shower and I remember seeing blood. That's why I fainted."

Gabriel scratched his half-shaven chin. "When was the last time you fainted? I remember you feeling woozy in my study carrel back in Toronto. There wasn't any blood."

"You startled me. And it was hot in there."

"It certainly was." Gabriel leaned down to kiss her forehead. "You swooned in my arms, which was greatly enjoyable."

"Naughty professor."

"Absolutely. I am, in fact, a very naughty professor. But not when you're ill." He brushed her hair away from her face. "Now, are we going to the emergency room?"

"I need to finish my shower." She peered down at the sheets in dismay. "We need to wash the sheets."

"I'll look after it." He stood and paused, still holding her hand. "And I'll help you shower."

She looked up at him with such relief it almost broke his heart.

She slid to the edge of the bed. He helped her to her feet and escorted her back into the bathroom.

The shower was still running and the shower doors were fogged. Gabriel quickly removed the pink flamingo (which had showered enough) and placed it next to the bathtub. Then he divested himself of his wet towel before helping Julia into the shower. He followed, closing the door behind him.

She looked up at him wistfully. "It's been a while since we showered together."

"We need to remedy that. And I need to buy more chocolate body paint." Gabriel hazarded a small smile, but it didn't reach his eyes. He was scrutinizing Julia like a mother hen.

He lifted her hand and placed it on his hip. "So you don't fall over," he explained.

Julia rubbed her thumb over his damp skin.

He positioned her so she was under the spray, wetting her hair once again. His thumb gently stroked her forehead, as light as a blessing, before his fingers sifted through her dark brown strands. Then he squeezed shampoo into his palm and began to apply it to the crown of her head.

"Roses," he breathed.

"It's new." Julia spoke with her eyes closed, leaning into him.

"I miss the vanilla."

"The shower gel is vanilla."

"Excellent." Gabriel's gaze darted to the tiles beneath their feet, looking for blood. He was relieved when he didn't see any.

He was leisurely in his movements. He massaged her scalp and lovingly worked the shampoo to the ends of her hair.

Julia lifted her other hand and placed it on his hip, clutching him for balance. Her nose came in contact with his pectorals and the delicate strands of hair that covered them. She nuzzled him.

After he rinsed her hair, he used her vanilla-scented soap to gently caress her shoulders, her swanlike neck, and her swollen breasts.

She opened her eyes.

"Are you still sore?" His thumbs hovered a respectful distance from her nipples.

"A little."

Gabriel withdrew his hands to her waist, allowing the water to stream down her front, rinsing her breasts. He bent forward and kissed across her collarbone and down to her chest, studiously avoiding her nipples.

He poured more soap into his hands and lathered them, then washed her abdomen before examining her stitches. "They're holding. I don't see any problems."

His hand drifted down to her tangle of curls, but he didn't move between her legs. "And here?"

"Just be very gentle."

Delicately, he washed in between her legs, staring watchfully into her eyes.

"This reminds me of Umbria," she whispered. "On our first trip to Italy, you washed me in the shower."

Gabriel's eyes smoldered. "I remember."

"I was awkward."

Gabriel frowned and withdrew his hand. "I never thought of you as awkward. You'd been hurt, Julianne. It took time for you to get used to me."

"I don't know how you put up with me."

Gabriel looked pained. He washed his hands quickly before taking hers. "It's you who put up with me, Beatrice. Never forget that."

He pressed a kiss to the center of her palm. "I'm the one who left you in the orchard by yourself. I'm the one who forgot you and treated you abominably until I remembered. And still, you think..." He shook his head. "I was haunted by my share of ghosts our first trip, and then after, when we returned to Selinsgrove."

Julia winced, remembering a particularly painful conversation they'd had in the woods behind Richard's house.

"You're still here." Gabriel's eyes met hers. "And so am I, which is why you have to let me take you to the hospital. You burst into tears yesterday and you fainted this morning. It may be postpartum hormones, but it may be something more."

"I just got home." She pressed her cheek to his chest. "Don't make me go back."

He placed his hand at her lower spine. "Will you at least speak to Rebecca? She's a mother. I want to hear what she thinks."

"All right."

"Also, I'd like you to consider taking a maternity leave from Harvard, effective immediately."

Julia stepped back. "No. I'm starting my maternity leave in January."

Gabriel gazed down at her intently. His jaw clenched.

She removed her hands from his hips. "I've already missed a week of classes. I told Greg Matthews I'd be back as soon as possible."

"*Julianne,*" he murmured. He was trying hard, desperately hard, not to tell her what to do. It was obvious she should begin her maternity leave immediately. She would be in no shape to take classes.

But he was trying to convince her to go to the hospital, which was more important at the moment than the timing of her maternity leave.

Julia looked at his somewhat grim expression. She knew he was biting his tongue. "If you take me to the hospital, who will look after Clare?"

"I'll ask Rachel to look after her while we're gone."

"I haven't pumped any milk."

"You can feed her again before we go and if we aren't home in time, we'll have Rachel and Richard bring Clare to the hospital."

Julia gripped his arm. "I'm not leaving her."

Gabriel arched his eyebrows. He began formulating a series of arguments calculated to convince his wife of the foolishness of her demand but abruptly stopped. "Fine. We'll take her with us."

"Good."

"Good," Gabriel repeated, rather woodenly. He reached for the soap and carefully turned Julia around. Then he continued to care for his wife, trying as hard as he could to mask his anxiety.

Chapter Nine

You should see a doctor." Rebecca's face was creased with concern. She and Julia were speaking privately in the kitchen.

"Gabriel is overprotective." Julia peered across the room at her husband, who was holding Clare.

"In this case, with good reason." Rebecca placed a pair of oven mitts on the counter, next to the stove. Her Bostonian accent became more pronounced as the creases of worry in her face deepened. "Fainting isn't normal postpregnancy. You don't want to be holding the baby and pass out."

Julia went very still. The thought hadn't occurred to her.

Rebecca continued. "A quick trip to the hospital will put everyone's minds at ease, including yours."

Julia chewed at the inside of her mouth, watching her husband with their baby.

"First, you need to eat." Rebecca pointed toward the kitchen table. "Have a good breakfast, take some snacks with you. But you should go to the emergency room."

"Agreed." Rachel approached the women from the other side of the room.

"Okay." Julia rubbed her eyes, suddenly very, very tired.

Rebecca patted Julia's arm and returned to the oven, where she'd been warming a breakfast casserole.

"Holy cow! What's that?" Rachel grabbed Julia's hand.

"Gabriel gave it to me."

"Look at the size of it!" Rachel cursed under her breath. "It's beautiful. Wow."

Julia grinned at her friend and the pair walked over to the table.

"So?" Gabriel's gaze fixed on his wife as she sat next to him. "What's the verdict on the hospital?"

"We'll go after breakfast." Julia extended her arms in order to take Clare.

"You eat, I'll hold her." Gabriel rearranged Clare in his arms and the baby opened her blue eyes.

"Why, hello there." He smiled, bringing his face closer to hers. "Good morning, Principessa."

The infant closed her eyes and yawned. And then she looked at her father.

Julia felt something warm and solid in her middle as she examined her husband. He wore a look of complete devotion as he stared down as his little girl. He was already wrapped around her finger.

Rachel cleared her throat. "That's a beautiful ring Jules is sporting."

Gabriel beamed with pride as his wife held up her hand for Richard to see it.

Rachel continued. "Apart from the trip to the hospital, what else is on the agenda for today?"

Gabriel answered without taking his eyes off Clare. "I'm hoping someone will address the flamingo infestation on my front lawn. The neighbors have been duly notified of Clare's birth. In fact, I think the Russians can see the infestation from space."

Julia snickered into her orange juice.

"We paid for a week. The infestation isn't going anywhere." Rachel gestured with her orange juice. "Next?"

Gabriel muttered something under his breath, but the edge of his lips turned up.

"Katherine is supposed to be coming over for lunch, but we'll be at the hospital." Julia retrieved a pile of napkins from the sideboard and passed them around. "Should I call and cancel?"

"No," said Rachel. "She can have lunch with us. I think she's hilarious."

"She's remarkable," Richard agreed, arranging his napkin.

"Breakfast is served." Rebecca approached the table, carrying a large, hot dish with oven mitts.

Richard suddenly thrust back his chair and stood. "That's heavy. Let me help you."

Rebecca seemed surprised by his actions. She blushed a little as he took the oven mitts and the dish from her hands and placed it on a heatproof trivet on the table.

Rachel blinked her gray eyes, slowly. And then she stared. The air around her seemed to turn to water, muting sound and causing all physical movement to slow down.

Richard resumed his seat while Rebecca served breakfast.

When she served Richard, he leaned over and said something to her and she laughed.

Rachel blinked again and turned her head in order to examine Gabriel and Julia. They were oblivious.

Rachel's eyes narrowed on her father.

A minute later, everyone at the table turned to look at her.

She bristled. "What?"

Gabriel cleared his throat. "I just said that we're having Clare baptized this week, before you go home and Katherine returns to Oxford."

"Great." Rachel's shoulders straightened.

"I hope Aaron will come." Julia shifted closer to Rachel, a wide smile on her face. "We want you to be Clare's godmother."

Rachel nodded, but her expression grew clouded.

"Please eat while it's hot," Rebecca admonished with a smile. She turned to Richard. "I'll make a fresh pot of coffee for you." She took his mug and returned to the kitchen.

"Thanks, Rebecca." Julia lifted a bite of casserole to her mouth and began eating.

"Rachel?" Gabriel interrupted her thoughts.

"You're having Clare baptized Catholic, but I'm Protestant."

"So?" Julia exchanged a look with Gabriel, who shrugged.

"We'll make an appointment with the priest." Gabriel sipped his coffee cheerfully. "And we'll tell him not to bring up the Council of Trent."

"Whatever that means." Rachel rearranged the food on her plate, but not a morsel entered her mouth.

❖·❖

"My assistant sent over a copy of your chart and we rushed your blood work, so I have those results as well." Dr. Rubio, Julia's obstetrician, bustled into the examining room.

"I'm glad you were the obstetrician on call." Julia sat nervously on the examination table, dressed in a hospital gown, while Gabriel cradled a placid Clare in his arms.

Dr. Rubio was an accomplished obstetrician of short stature who had dark hair that was striped with gray and dark, lively eyes. She was originally from Puerto Rico and was much tougher than her small frame made her appear. In fact, she had often clashed with Professor Emerson during Julia's pregnancy, particularly over the medical directive that he not perform oral sex on his wife. (He had accused her of going to an anti-oral-sex college. She had cursed him in Spanish.)

"So, what's happening?" Gabriel's tone was grim.

Dr. Rubio sat in an available chair and faced Julia, holding her chart. "Your stitches are healing nicely and the lochia discharge is normal. I know you tend to faint at the sight of blood, and that may have played a role this morning.

"You have fibroids, as you know, and one of them was cut during your cesarean section. Because we had to give you a transfusion, I rushed your blood work just now in case you had a reaction. But your blood work looks fine."

Julia breathed deeply. "What about the fibroids?"

"We'll continue to monitor them, but as I told you, we aren't inclined to remove them unless they become a problem. However, I'm concerned about your weight."

Julia touched her slightly rounded abdomen. "My weight?"

Dr. Rubio leafed through the chart. "I reviewed your weight gain during your pregnancy. You've lost quite a bit of weight since the delivery, much more than normal. Breastfeeding uses up an extraordinary number of calories. Are you eating well?"

"She's hungry all the time," Gabriel interjected. "She seemed extra hungry this morning after she fainted."

The doctor ignored Gabriel and focused on Julia. "Are you trying to lose weight?"

Julia shook her head. "When I was in the hospital, I ate what they gave me. And I've been eating at home. I tried my jeans on yesterday and they fit, so I'm back to my normal size."

"Some women are like that, but it's rare." Dr. Rubio withdrew a pen from her lab coat and began writing on a prescription pad. "I'm going to refer you to the hospital dietitian. I think you aren't eating enough or you aren't eating the right kinds of food, and so breast-feeding is playing havoc with your blood sugar."

She signed the referral with a flourish and handed it to Julia. "If the dietitian can't fit you in today, she'll schedule an appointment. In the meantime, be sure to eat a healthy, balanced diet. Don't skip meals. Don't skimp on the protein or carbohydrates, but don't eat a lot of sugary foods or drinks. Try to snack regularly so that your blood sugar doesn't crash. If you pass out again, come to the emergency room immediately."

"Okay." Julia sighed with relief.

Dr. Rubio studied her patient for a moment. "How are you feeling emotionally?"

Julia picked at the paper that covered the examination table. "I've felt a little overwhelmed."

The doctor nodded. "That can happen. But remember to check in with yourself and if you are sad or anxious for a couple of days, come back. If you're having thoughts that scare you, come to the emergency room immediately."

The doctor gave Gabriel a significant look.

A muscle tightened in his jaw. He gazed at Julianne protectively.

"It was good to see you again." Dr. Rubio smiled and closed Julia's chart. "I'll have my secretary schedule a follow-up with you in a couple of weeks. I'm so pleased to see that your baby is doing well. Have you scheduled a checkup with your pediatrician?"

"Yes," said Julia. "At the one-month mark."

"Excellent. I'll see you in a couple weeks, but don't hesitate to reach out immediately if something doesn't feel right. Until then, take care." The doctor took her leave and exited the room.

"She doesn't like me." Gabriel practically growled.

"How can anyone not like the handsome and famous Professor Emerson?" Julia teased, smiling.

"You'd be surprised," he muttered. He transferred Clare to her baby carrier, carefully adjusting her hat. "I didn't know about the baby's checkup."

"It's in the calendar on my phone." Julia began dressing.

Gabriel reached out and placed his hand against her cheek.

She lifted her face.

"Copy me on all the appointments—both yours and the baby's." His blue eyes were intense.

"Of course." She brushed the edge of his palm with her lips. "I just hadn't gotten around to it. I haven't even checked my email this week."

Gabriel started, for this remark reminded him of something. Something contained in an email.

He cleared his throat. "Julianne, I need to tell you that—"

A loud wail interrupted him.

Julia bent over the crying baby. She placed her hand on the baby carrier and began rocking it back and forth.

Clare opened her eyes.

"Let me do that." Gabriel rocked the baby carrier as Julia dressed.

She checked her phone. "It's time for me to feed her again. Maybe we can find a quiet corner somewhere."

"Of course." Gabriel lifted the baby carrier and escorted his wife into the hall.

This time, he didn't forget about the important thing he needed to tell her. This time, he simply chose to tell her later.

Chapter Ten

C an I bring the rocking chair in here?" Rachel asked Julia. "Or are you going to bed?"

"Bring the chair. I haven't had a chance to catch up with you, since we spent most of the day at the hospital." Julia was holding Clare in her arms. Rachel had just changed the baby and placed her in a clean sleeper before returning her to her mother.

Rachel set the rocking chair near the bed and retrieved her niece. As she rocked slowly, the child stared up at her in silent fascination.

Rachel smiled and gently stroked the baby's cheek.

Julia paused in front of her dresser, admiring the large wedding portrait of her and Gabriel in Assisi. The picture was positioned next to an older photo of them dancing at Lobby, a club in Toronto. She touched Gabriel's face, his intense expression. No other man had ever looked at her like that. Gabriel's attention was fixated and razor sharp. And that had only been the beginning. . . .

With a secret smile, she opened her jewelry box and retrieved her wedding ring and engagement ring. She compared the pair with the ring Gabriel had given her the night before. It was uncanny how the three somehow matched.

"You took your other rings off?" Rachel sounded incredulous.

Julia slid the rings onto her left hand. "My fingers swelled. I was worried they'd get stuck."

"Really weird things happen to pregnant women."

"Tell me about it." Julia plucked at the hem of her blue dress. "Sundresses and yoga pants are so comfortable, I may never wear jeans again."

"I think Gabriel might have something to say about that."

Julia flicked her hair over her shoulder. "I do what I want."

"Sure you do," Rachel teased. She took a closer look at her friend as she stood by the bed. "Turn sideways."

"Why?" Julia turned, looking down at her dress. "Is something wrong?"

"Your bump is gone."

Julia pulled the material taut over her stomach. There was a roundedness to her abdomen, but it was slight. "I'm wearing a band. It covers the incision and helps with the stitches."

"You're basically the same size again."

Julia frowned. "That's why my obstetrician sent me to the dietitian this afternoon. Breastfeeding burns a lot of calories, apparently."

"And gives you spectacular cleavage!"

Julia laughed and entered the closet. "Which won't last forever. But I'll enjoy it while I can."

She changed into silk pajamas and a robe and reentered the bedroom. She plumped the pillows on her bed and reclined, facing her daughter and her friend. "How was your day?"

Rachel touched the baby's head. "Fine. I catalogued all the gifts and flower arrangements for you."

"Thank you. Gabriel ordered birth announcements with a photo of the three of us. I was going to send them out with thank-you notes."

"I can help. Gabriel's sister Kelly sent a silver frame and a piggy bank from Tiffany. I've never seen one before."

"She's very generous," Julia mused. "She helped Gabriel connect with other members of his family. Their grandfather was an important professor at Columbia. Every fall they have a special lecture in his memory. We missed it because of Clare's arrival. But I think Kelly and her husband are coming to Clare's baptism."

Rachel's grin faded.

Her reaction did not go unnoticed. "We wanted to ask you to be Clare's godmother privately. I didn't mean to put you on the spot during breakfast."

Rachel lowered her head, allowing her long blond hair to partially shield her face. "Do you think Dad has been acting weird lately?"

"No, what do you mean?"

"He practically knocked over a chair this morning trying to help Rebecca with the casserole." Rachel was indignant.

"Richard is chivalrous. You know that."

Rachel tossed her hair, exposing her face. "I don't like how she was looking at him."

"I didn't see anything inappropriate," Julia said slowly. "Richard probably enjoys having someone his own age to talk to. But he's still grieving your mother."

"I thought Rebecca lived in Norwood."

"She did. She rented out her house to move in with us. It's only temporary."

Rachel made a derisive noise but didn't reply. She continued rocking, looking down at her sleeping niece.

Julia took time to choose her words, fearing she was going where angels refused to tread. "If I saw something romantic in the way

Richard looked at Rebecca, I would tell you. But I haven't. Were they acting weird while we were at the hospital?"

"No." Rachel continued rocking and her shoulders softened. "Maybe I'm just seeing things."

"Richard spends a lot of time by himself. I know my dad and Diane have socialized with him, but they have their hands full with Tommy."

"Dad moved to Philadelphia to be closer to Aaron and me, but we didn't see him much. So he quit his job at Temple and went back to Selinsgrove. He's been teaching a class here and there at Susquehanna, but other than that . . ." Rachel's voice trailed off. "You're right. He probably needs to get out more. I'll speak to Aaron about going home more often."

Rachel gazed down at the baby and lightly kissed the top of her head. "I love you, little Clare. But I don't think I can be your godmother."

Julia's eyebrows lifted. "Wait. What?"

Chapter Eleven

I f anything were to happen to you or Gabriel, I would raise Clare
as my own. I hope you will appoint me and Aaron as guardians."
Rachel's expression was determined.

"Of course. We've already discussed it." Julia's mind spun.

"But I did some reading online. At a Catholic baptism, one of the
sponsors has to be Catholic. I can be a witness as an Episcopal, but
you need a Catholic to be the sponsor. Since I'm a woman, the
Church would require the sponsor to be a Catholic male."

"I didn't know that." Julia's voice grew small. "I thought all
they'd care about was that you agreed to raise Clare in the Church."

"I would, but I can't be the official godmother. I could be a witness if you appointed a Catholic godfather."

Julia groaned. "There isn't anyone. Just my dad, but—"

"I get it," Rachel interrupted. "I'm glad you and your dad are getting along better, but I can see why he isn't the best choice. My dad
is Episcopal, and so are Aaron and Scott."

Julia covered her face with her hands. "I'm an idiot. I didn't know this. I thought we could pick who we wanted."

"Here's the thing: I'm honored you asked me. I can be Clare's unofficial godmother and her zany aunt Rachel. But you're going to have to choose a Catholic for the ceremony."

Julia dropped her hands. "Our priest is cool. I could ask him to make an exception."

Rachel began rocking more vigorously. "No. Honestly, Jules, I'm kind of upset with God at the moment. So I'm not comfortable taking on the responsibility of Clare's spiritual guidance, anyway."

Julia studied her sister-in-law. "Do you want to talk about it?"

"I still believe, but I feel I've been treated unjustly. My mother died unexpectedly. I want to have a baby, but can't." She heaved a great sigh. "It would be hypocritical for me to stand up as a godmother when I have so many doubts."

"I think God wants us to be honest, even in our doubts."

"Yes, well, I don't just have doubts; I have grievances. Why don't you ask Katherine to be the official godmother? She said she was Catholic."

"She's been dropping hints since we announced my pregnancy." Julia gave her friend a rueful smile.

"See? She's into it. She'll be perfect as the godmother."

"What about you?" Julia crossed the room to her friend.

"I get to be Aunt Rachel." She leaned down and kissed the baby's forehead. The baby crinkled her brow but kept her eyes closed.

"I'll talk to Gabriel." Julia paused. "How are you doing? Really?"

"I went off the fertility medication, but you knew that."

"How are you feeling about that?"

"Physically? I'm fine. But I'm in sorrow, Jules. I really wanted to have a baby, but that won't happen."

"I'm so sorry." Julia touched her friend's shoulder.

Rachel stroked the fine hair on Clare's head. "Aaron told me he didn't care if we had a baby. He's more concerned about me."

"He loves you like crazy."

Rachel kept her gaze fixed on her niece. "My life hasn't turned out the way I expected. I thought I'd have my mom forever. I thought she'd be with me when I got married, and when I had babies."

Julia made a noise and put her arms around her friend.

"But I just keep going, you know? There has to be a way forward. Aaron and I talked about adoption. Maybe that's something we can explore."

"Of course. And Gabriel and I will help, if we can." Julia held on to her friend, a tear coursing down her face.

Although Rachel was very brave, there were no words that would heal her wound. No magic that would alter the circumstances.

"I want permission to spoil this child." Rachel lifted the baby and placed her against her shoulder. "I want to start by buying a large and extravagant toy or contraption that will take Gabriel days or even weeks to put together. And I want you to film the entire process."

Julia laughed. "Permission granted."

Chapter Twelve

J ust before midnight, Julia sat in the nursery, feeding Clare.

Gabriel was situated in the rocking chair, watching over his family. He was touching his wedding band, turning it round and round on his finger. Although his focus was primarily on his current conversation, in the back of his mind nagged an important piece of information he'd yet to share with his wife.

Julianne had wanted to delay having a family. Yet here they were. And Gabriel's news was going to change everything.

He shook himself from his reverie. "I spoke with Father Fortin today. Rachel is correct—the official godparent has to be Catholic. We could baptize Clare in the Episcopal church."

"Rachel says she would feel hypocritical being an official god-mother."

"I could speak to her."

As if in reaction to her father's words, Clare finished feeding. She gazed up at her mother.

"Let me." Gabriel stood and crossed to Julia, taking the baby into his arms. He retrieved a clean flannel cloth from nearby and placed it on his bare shoulder, carefully positioning the infant over the flannel.

The child wriggled in his arms, protesting noisily until her father's hand rested on her back. Gabriel began to pat her.

Julia rebuttoned the top of her silk pajamas. "I think we need to let Rachel be. She's dealing with a lot and I don't want to pressure her into doing something she's uncomfortable about."

"But Rachel's doubts are serious," Gabriel observed, swaying on his feet. "Someone should speak to her."

Julianne's gaze alighted on his tattoo, which was visible atop his exposed left pectoral. "Rachel's doubts are caused by suffering. She's missing Grace, and grieving the fact that she can't have children, and now she's afraid of losing Richard. She seems to think Rebecca has her eyes on him."

"Nonsense." Gabriel followed Julianne's gaze. Under her inspection, the tattoo seemed to burn against his flesh. He found himself lost momentarily in a memory—a drug-and-alcohol-infused haze of loss that precipitated the tattoo. The pain that accompanied the remembrance was dull, not sharp. But it was pain, nonetheless.

He kissed the baby's head and focused his eyes on her mother. "A brown-eyed angel spoke to me in my grief. She helped me."

"She helped you by loving you and by listening. That's what your sister needs. She needs you to love her and to listen. Words won't heal her sorrow."

Gabriel pressed his lips together. His inclination was to argue with people until they accepted certain conclusions. Julianne was much more Franciscan in her charism.

"All right," he conceded, rubbing Clare's back. "But Rachel isn't going to lose her father. She's seeing ghosts."

"I disagree." Julia's expression grew grave. "Rachel's problem is that she isn't seeing ghosts."

Gabriel's dark brows knitted together. There had been times in his life when the supernatural had intruded. Seeing Grace and Maia at the house in Selinsgrove was one of those times. But he'd never mentioned the appearance to Rachel.

Richard had confessed to seeing Grace in his dreams. But Gabriel was fairly certain Richard had never mentioned those dreams to Rachel, either.

Gabriel changed the subject. "I'm fond of Katherine, as you know. Should we ask her?"

"I think she's a good choice."

Julianne paused to stare at her husband. His dark hair was tousled, his chest was bare, and he was wearing tartan pajama bottoms.

He adjusted Clare so that he was holding her in front of his body. And he smiled down at her, murmuring quietly.

Julia lifted her cell phone and began snapping pictures.

Gabriel grinned and moved Clare back to his right shoulder. As if on cue, Clare spat up, absolutely missing the flannel cloth and baptizing Gabriel's shoulder and neck instead.

Julia continued taking photos.

"We aren't filming a documentary," Gabriel grumbled. "Must you immortalize every moment?"

"Yes. Yes, I must." She mimicked his displeasure with a laugh and snapped away.

Gabriel retrieved a second flannel cloth and began mopping himself with one hand, while holding the contented baby with the other.

"You'd never laugh at Daddy, would you, Principessa?" The baby made eye contact with him and an understanding seemed to pass between them.

"Of course not." Gabriel brought his nose to his daughter's. "That's my girl."

Julianne captured the moment. Professor Emerson in a suit and tie was certainly attractive. But a shirtless Gabriel crooning at their baby was beauty itself.

"We need to put Clare to bed." Julia walked to Gabriel and kissed him firmly. Her lips found his ear. "So we can go to bed."

Gabriel lifted his eyebrows. "Are you . . ." His gaze drifted down to her lower abdomen.

"I am as I was." She placed her hand at the back of his neck. "But I'd like to do something for you. Something creative."

"Yes, Mrs. Emerson. I've always been very impressed by your—ah—*creativity*." He gave her a heated look. "But you fainted this morning."

"That's true." She kissed him again. "But I'm eager to look after my handsome, sexy husband."

Julia winked and exited the nursery.

Gabriel danced a little jig with the baby. "Your mother is very beautiful, Princess. And tonight, Daddy is getting lucky. Let's get you cleaned up and put to bed."

He placed the infant atop the changing table and retrieved a pair of surgical gloves that he kept in a box nearby. Rachel had mocked him mercilessly about them. But he would not be deterred.

He undid the lower snaps of the baby's sleeper and slipped her legs free. Then he began to undo her diaper.

"*Stercus,*" he exclaimed.

The color of the *stercus* in question was not one with which he was familiar. It defied description, definition, and the laws of nature. In fact, the Professor hypothesized the waste to be the product of a changeling, since nothing so foul could ever have been emitted by such a sweet and angelic being.

He gazed longingly at the doorway, as if hoping a certain brown-eyed angel would come to his rescue.

She didn't appear. And it was possible she was beginning certain sensual activities already. By herself.

There had been a time when he, Professor Gabriel O. Emerson, would have simply rewrapped the infant and returned her to her mother. For a fleeting instant, the Professor contemplated doing just that.

But Clare was his daughter. She was the fruit of his union with his beloved Beatrice and a miracle, besides. It would not be fitting to expect Julianne to do everything, including the removal of nuclear waste.

No, the Professor was now responsible for the little life that looked up at him innocently, absolutely unaware of the noxious emission she was now inflicting on her paternal parent. He would not fail her.

He held his breath and completed the various steps of removing the toxic substance, cleaning the baby thoroughly, covering her with some kind of ointment, and providing her with a new, pristine diaper.

Throughout the procedure the baby sought his face. He smiled and sang a little, wondering if his new foray into the music of Nat King Cole would be more to the princess's liking. He sang the words to "L-O-V-E" quietly, after apologizing for his initial Latin profanity.

Gabriel deposited the waste in the diaper pail, resolving to eradicate it from the nursery and his household as soon as possible.

Waste did not belong in pails. Indeed, waste did not belong on his property or anywhere near civilized humanity. To think otherwise was simply barbarous, in his estimation. But he was conscious, all too conscious, of the beautiful creature who was waiting for him in bed in the next room.

In haste, he snapped off his surgical gloves and placed them in the pail, as well. Then, just as a precaution, he carefully cleaned his unsoiled hands not once, but twice, with antibacterial wipes.

With the air of a saint who'd just completed a lengthy task of self-mortification, Gabriel redressed the baby and swaddled her competently in a large piece of flannel. Then he cuddled her to his chest.

He sang the first verse of "Blackbird" by the Beatles, rubbing circles on her back.

"Much better now." Gabriel kissed the baby's head. "What do you think of Daddy's new music? We're improving, aren't we?"

When the baby yawned indifferently, he kissed her and carried her into the master bedroom.

Chapter Thirteen

Two days later

O h, my gosh!"
     Gabriel's ears pricked up.

"That's fantastic."

Gabriel paused his tooth brushing, eager to hear more of the sounds emanating from the bedroom.

"Oh, my goodness!"

"Yes, yes, yes, yes!"

The cries coming from Julianne's lips signaled pleasure. But they puzzled Gabriel, since he was not the agent pleasuring her.

He leaned backward, peering through the doorway that led from the en-suite into the bedroom, eager to see what she was doing.

She was standing by the bed, scrolling on her cell phone.

Gabriel scowled, wondering who was eliciting such a reaction from his wife. He spat out the toothpaste, rinsed his toothbrush, and stalked toward her.

Julianne collided with him in the doorway, her dark eyes dancing. "You'll never guess who emailed me."

The Angelfucker, Gabriel thought, but did not say.

He plastered a restrained smile on his face. "Who?"

"Professor Wodehouse."

"Don Wodehouse? Of Magdalen College?"

"Yes!" Julianne held her cell phone aloft and danced in a circle.

Thank God it isn't the Angelfucker.

Gabriel took her hand. "Why did Wodehouse email you?"

"He's hosting a workshop on Guido da Montefeltro and Ulysses. It's by invitation only and he's invited me."

"That's great. When is it?"

"Early April, between Hilary and Trinity term. He's hosting it at Magdalen and it's funded by a research grant he was awarded."

Gabriel squeezed her. "Who else was invited?"

"Cecilia Marinelli and Katherine. But it looks like Professor Wodehouse is directing it." Julia scanned the recipient list. "No Professor Pacciani. No Christa Peterson, either."

"Thank heaven for small mercies."

"Paul was invited, along with a bunch of people I don't know."

The Angelfucker strikes again.

"Norris was invited." Gabriel sniffed in mock umbrage. "But not Professor Emerson?"

Julia looked up at him. She bit her lip.

"Don't." Gabriel's thumb tugged on her lower lip, freeing it. "I'm proud of you. You impressed Wodehouse when you gave your paper at Oxford. You earned the invitation."

"I'm sorry you weren't invited." Julia looked unhappy.

Gabriel kissed her forehead. "Don't be. This is great news. Wodehouse is not easily impressed."

She studied her husband's features. "And Paul?"

"Paul does good work." Gabriel wore a pained expression, as if he were struggling to be positive. "Katherine probably invited him. Although I'm not sure why, since he doesn't really work on Guido or Ulysses."

"I want to go."

"Of course. Email Wodehouse and tell him."

"What about Clare?"

"We'll come to Oxford with you." Gabriel smiled. "Rebecca and I can take care of Clare."

"Thank you." Julia brushed her lips against his. "By April, Clare should be sleeping through the night. I hope."

"Cecilia will see your name on the recipient list, but you should email her. And send an email to the chair of your department."

"What about my maternity leave? I contacted Greg Matthews and Cecilia yesterday, telling them I wasn't coming back this year. Won't they be upset I'm missing classes next semester, but going to the workshop?"

Gabriel snorted. "I'm sure Cecilia supported your invitation. Greg Matthews will send out an announcement to your department, bragging about you."

"I hope so." Julia pushed her shoulder-length hair behind her ears.

Gabriel took her hand. At six feet, two inches, he was much taller than she. His large hand toyed with her wedding rings. "I've been worried about the aftermath of Toronto and how it would affect our careers."

"Sweetheart," Julia whispered. "I didn't know you were still worrying."

"You had enough on your mind. But Wodehouse's invitation shows you are already making a name for yourself, even as a graduate student." Gabriel's blue eyes glittered. *That's my girl.*

Julia beamed. "Thank you."

Gabriel twirled her in a circle and dipped her, her laughter ringing out. "I had an interesting email this week, as well."

"What?"

Gabriel retrieved his cell phone from his nightstand. "You may want to sit down."

"Why?" Julia sounded alarmed. "What happened?"

Wordlessly, Gabriel scrolled through his email and handed the phone to Julia.

She read the screen.

And then she brought the phone closer to her eyes and read it again. And again.

"Holy shit." She lifted her head, her mouth hanging open. "Is this—is this what I think it is?"

Chapter Fourteen

G abriel took the phone from Julia and quickly put on his glasses. He read aloud,

"The University Court of the University of Edinburgh is pleased to invite you to deliver the annual Sage Lectures in Literature in 2013. The Sage Lectures were founded in 1836 at the bequest of Lord Alfred Sage. The Lectures take place annually, usually in the second term.

It is customary for the Sage Lecturer to arrive on campus in the first term of the academic year and then remain in residence while delivering the Lectures in the second term. We invite you to be our Sage Lecturer in residence during the 2013–2014 academic year."

He scrolled down. "Compensation, accommodation, airfare, publication, media, et cetera."

Julia sat on the edge of the bed, stunned.

Gabriel peered over the rim of his glasses. "Darling?"

"The Sage Lectures," she whispered. "I can't believe it."

"I can barely believe it myself. I must be one of the youngest lecturers they've ever invited."

"When did they email you?"

"The day we left the hospital."

"Why didn't you tell me?"

Gabriel frowned. "You were upset that day. I was going to tell you the following morning, but then we were at the hospital."

"You could have told me last night." Her tone was reproving.

"I was waiting for the right moment. I haven't answered them. I haven't spoken to my chair or to anyone from Boston University. I wanted to discuss it with you first."

Julia closed her eyes and touched her forehead. "I don't see how this is going to work."

Gabriel froze. "Why not?"

"Because I'm in coursework next year. Clare and I will be here in Cambridge, but you will be in Edinburgh."

"You can take a leave of absence and come with me."

Julia's eyes flew open. She stared at him in shock.

Gabriel scratched at his chin.

Julia stood. "I didn't want to take a maternity leave in the first place. I can't take another leave of absence, especially if I attend the workshop at Oxford this coming April; I'll never finish my program."

"Your advisor is the one who suggested the maternity leave." Gabriel adjusted his glasses.

"I don't think she envisioned me taking almost two years off."

Gabriel studied his wife. "This is a once-in-a-lifetime opportunity. I can't just say no. It would be like turning down the Nobel Prize."

"I know the significance of the Sage Lectures." Julia's tone grew steely. "It's an incredible honor. But I can't just say no to Harvard again, not after how hard I've worked."

He held up his hands. "I'm not going without you and Clare."

"Then you're declining the invitation?"

"Of course not." He sounded impatient.

"Then what are you going to do?" Julia's hands went to her hips.

"There has to be a way for me to accept the invitation and for you to come with me." He passed a hand over his mouth. "I thought you'd be happy for me."

"I am." She heaved a great sigh and her hands fell away from her hips. "But I don't want to be a single parent for that long, Gabriel. I can't do this alone."

Gabriel removed his glasses. He looked very, very determined.

But instead of arguing with her, he did something most unexpected. "The email I received instructed me to keep the invitation confidential. I'm not going to do that."

"Why not?"

"Because we need some advice. Katherine was the Sage Lecturer once, twenty years ago. I'm going to call her." Gabriel pulled his wife into his arms and hugged her. "We'll find a way."

Julia returned her husband's embrace, wishing she shared her husband's optimism. But she didn't.

Chapter Fifteen

Later that morning

Assistant Professor Paul V. Norris sat in his office at Saint Michael's College in Vermont, staring at his computer screen.

He was already a few weeks into his first academic job. And he was working hard—preparing lessons, attending new faculty orientation meetings, and trying to figure out where the land mines were located in the Department of English and how he could avoid them. But the email he had just received made everything else seem irrelevant.

"It was the best of times, it was the worst of times," he quoted to himself.

There, in his Saint Michael's inbox, was an email from Professor Wodehouse of Magdalen College. Among the short list of email recipients, he spied a certain Julia Emerson. But thankfully, no Gabriel Emerson.

Studentfucker.

Paul winced. He didn't like thinking of Emerson and the beautiful former Miss Mitchell together in any capacity. And certainly not like that.

He knew they were married. He knew they'd just had a daughter. The night before, Julia had sent a mass email announcing the birth of Clare and sharing a photograph.

The photo was only of Clare. Even to Paul's eyes the infant was beautiful. She had wisps of dark hair peeking out from underneath a purple knitted cap. But he'd wished Julia had sent a photo of herself.

He wondered if she'd attend the Dante workshop in April. He wondered if he should email her to find out before making his own decision.

"Hi, Paul."

Paul heard a female voice over his shoulder. He turned in his chair and saw Elizabeth, one of the new faculty in Religious Studies, standing at the threshold to his office.

Elizabeth was gorgeous. She had bobbed, curly dark hair, dark eyes, and unblemished brown skin. She was Cuban American and hailed from Brooklyn.

Paul had already discovered that Elizabeth liked to play Cuban music in her office. Loudly.

She gave him a wide smile and adjusted her rectangular glasses. "I'm going for coffee. Do you want to come with?"

"Um . . ." Paul rubbed his chin. He cast a conflicted look at his computer screen.

"Are you okay?" Elizabeth hovered in the doorway. "You look like you've seen a ghost."

"Sort of." He sighed and looked up at the ceiling. Of course he wanted to see Julia. That was the problem. He'd finally moved on from her and started dating Allison, his ex-girlfriend, once more. And now this . . .

"Maybe I should bring you a coffee." Elizabeth interrupted his musings. "What do you take in it?"

"I take my coffee black—like death." He stood, bringing his six-foot-three frame to its full height. He towered over Elizabeth's waifish five-foot-three frame.

She stood in the doorway, watching him.

He closed his laptop and grabbed his keys. "Coffee is on me. I've just been invited to a workshop in Oxford."

"That's great." Elizabeth clapped her hands in excitement.

It had been a long time since someone had applauded for Paul. He couldn't help but notice.

He pulled self-consciously on the front of his shirt. "The workshop is in April, in the middle of our semester. The powers that be won't let me go."

Elizabeth gave him a puzzled look. "Of course they'll let you go. It's Oxford. It's good press for the college."

She gestured to the hall. "While you're buying my coffee, we can put together a campaign strategy. I have some ideas."

Paul surveyed her enthusiasm and found himself returning her smile. He followed her into the hall.

Chapter Sixteen

"Gabriel cannot decline the Sage Lectures." Professor Katherine Picton, currently of All Souls College, Oxford, lifted the elegant china teapot from its silver tray. She served Julia and Gabriel before serving herself.

The trio were seated next to a roaring fire in the lobby of the Lenox Hotel. The Lenox was one of Gabriel's favorite hotels in the region, and Katherine shared his opinion.

She added a slice of lemon to her Darjeeling and sipped. Tea was the sustenance of the British Empire and made the entire world England, including the Back Bay area. And it was, she thought, not only a civilized beverage, but a fortifying one.

She gestured to the plates that were spread across the low table. "Please enjoy a scone. They're excellent."

Julia and Gabriel exchanged a look. They did as they were told.

Clare was sleeping peacefully in her car seat on the couch next to Katherine. She'd insisted the baby be placed next to her. "The Sage

Lectures are a feather in your cap, Gabriel. They will launch you to greater opportunities. I can't imagine you'd want to be at Boston University forever?"

Julia gaped.

Gabriel looked down at this tea. "The cross-appointment between Romance Studies and Religion isn't ideal."

"Of course not." Katherine put her tea aside and briskly buttered a scone before adding strawberry jam. "On the other hand, Julia, you can't keep delaying your doctoral program forever. You need to get on with it."

Julia closed her mouth.

"I take it you two have come to ask for advice?" Katherine probed. "I shouldn't want to presume."

"We'd be grateful for any suggestions you might have. Of course, we will need to talk further." Gabriel gave an encouraging smile to Julianne, then regarded Katherine.

Seeking advice from Professor Picton was a tricky business. (It was, perhaps, like seeking advice from the queen of England. If one didn't follow the advice offered, Katherine would not be amused.)

"You could ask the University of Edinburgh to delay your appointment, so that Julia can complete her coursework and pass her examinations. Then you can all go together." With one hand, Katherine balanced her plate, and with the other, she adjusted the blanket around the sleeping baby. She gave a small nod of satisfaction to the infant.

"That's a good idea." Julia sounded relieved.

"But I advise against it." Katherine tasted her scone again.

"Why?" Julia persisted.

"The world of academia is notoriously small. It's also petty." Katherine focused her shrewd gaze on Gabriel. "If the University of Edinburgh feels slighted, they'll withdraw their invitation altogether and, further, word will get out that you're difficult. I'm sorry to mention it, but there remains the circumstances surrounding your departure from the University of Toronto."

"It's no one's business," Gabriel gritted out. "Besides, Julianne and I are married now."

"I'm not defending the old windbags, Gabriel, I'm simply telling you how things are. You're a white male, which means the patriarchy of academia is slanted in your favor. But it also means the University Court at Edinburgh will not be impressed with your desire to sacrifice their prestigious invitation in order to stay at home in America with your wife and child."

Gabriel had just taken a sip of tea. It went down the wrong way and he began to sputter.

"Good gracious." Katherine peered over at him. "Are you all right?"

Gabriel nodded, lifting his linen napkin from his knee and dabbing his face. When he had composed himself, he spoke, "That's outrageous. Being with Julianne and Clare is my first priority. Do they believe I would just throw away this opportunity for nothing?"

"That is what they will hear. They will decide you aren't serious, or they'll dismiss you as a millennial, or whatnot."

Gabriel nearly swallowed his tongue. "I'm not a millennial. I'm too old to be a millennial."

Julia gave him a hard look, feeling remarkably conspicuous.

"Optics matter, and to deny that is foolish." Katherine's demeanor was implacable. She lifted her chin at Julia. "Not that there is anything wrong with being a millennial, provided one has intestinal fortitude and a good work ethic, as you do."

Julia was hardly mollified.

Gabriel put his tea aside. "What do you suggest?"

"Harvard is the path of least resistance. Julia has the support of Cecilia and I will ensure she has the support of her chair, Greg Matthews." Katherine's eyes twinkled. "You have my support as well, Julia, since I will be joining your department next year."

"I don't understand." Julia tried to look anything other than fearful.

"You need to take your coursework in the fall, and write your area exams in the winter. My recommendation is that we arrange for you to take your coursework at Edinburgh in the fall and write your area exams after the Sage Lectures in the winter."

The Emersons exchanged a look.

"Would that work?" Julia sounded dubious.

"It's worth a try." Katherine drank her tea. "I know the Dante specialist at Edinburgh. He studied with Don Wodehouse. Coincidentally, he'll be attending the workshop Don has organized at Magdalen in April."

"What about Harvard?" Gabriel interjected. "There's no guarantee Edinburgh will offer the courses Julia needs in the fall semester."

"We need to look into it. And we'd need to make the case to Cecilia and Greg that this opportunity will be worth it. But here's something you must remember." At this, Katherine leaned forward and lowered her voice. "You cannot underestimate the vanity and ego of certain institutions. Harvard will no doubt make much of your appointment as Sage Lecturer, Gabriel. You'd be their most distinguished alumnus in the humanities in the past twenty years. It's in their interest to support you and Julia.

"And, Julia, your involvement with Don Wodehouse's workshop and the opportunity to study abroad at Edinburgh will certainly set you apart from other doctoral students. Harvard wants its students to enjoy an international reputation." Katherine's eyes gleamed. "I'm itching to walk into Greg Matthews's office and take credit for the idea, but I won't. You should speak to Cecilia first."

"Edinburgh instructed me to keep the invitation secret," Gabriel explained.

Katherine sipped her tea contemplatively. "I see the point. My advice is to accept Edinburgh's invitation. Once you're announced as Sage Lecturer, Harvard should fall into line."

Julia looked over at her husband. "If we could work things out with my supervisor . . ." She wore a hopeful expression.

"Then we'll all move to Edinburgh together." He pressed his lips to Julia's cheek.

"Now that's settled, I have a gift for the baby." Katherine retrieved a large gift bag she'd placed on the floor next to the couch. She handed the bag to Julia.

Julia was surprised by the weight of it. The bag was much heavier than it looked.

"Open it," Katherine commanded.

"You've already given us so much," Gabriel protested.

She waved a wrinkled hand. "Let me be the judge of that."

"But we also came here to ask you something." Julia prompted Gabriel with a nudge of her elbow.

Gabriel leaned forward. "Katherine, Julianne and I would like to ask you to be Clare's godmother."

"Yes," Professor Picton responded without hesitation. So quickly, Julia barely had time to look from Gabriel to Katherine.

"You don't want to think about it?" Gabriel regarded his elderly colleague with amusement.

"No. I should like nothing more, as long as we won't be treading on anyone else's toes." Katherine gazed down at the baby and adjusted the blanket once again.

"Then we're agreed. Thank you, Katherine." Gabriel squeezed Julia's shoulders.

"I'm the one who should be thankful—to be the godmother to a child born of two extraordinary people. I expect great things from you, Gabriel.

"And you, Julianne. Only twenty-six years old and already making a name for yourself. Don Wodehouse mentioned your paper as the motivation behind his workshop on Ulysses and Guido. You challenged his reading of the Guido case and he's still pondering it."

She smiled. "Few people have ever successfully challenged him. He's notoriously obstinate."

Julia's cheeks grew rosy. "Thank you."

"It's time to open the gift. Go on, now. I'm aging as we sit here." Katherine nodded at Julia.

Carefully, Julia removed a brightly wrapped present from the bag. She unfastened the ribbons and slid her finger beneath the taped edges of the paper. Beneath it was a carved wooden box.

Julia placed the box on the coffee table. When she lifted the lid, she gasped.

Gabriel gave Katherine an incredulous look.

"Pick it up and look at it." She chuckled merrily.

Gabriel gently lifted the worn leather cover of the object.

Reading the title page and the following *incipit*, he sat motionless. Amazed.

"As you can see, it's a fifteenth-century manuscript of *La Vita Nuova*," Katherine announced. "It also includes some of the minor poetic works. It's a copy of one of Simone Serdini's manuscripts."

Gabriel leafed through it in wonder. "However did you get this?"

Katherine's smile faded. "Old Hut."

Julia watched as Katherine's happiness was replaced by a look of regret. She'd loved Professor Hutton, her supervisor at Oxford, but he had been married. As Katherine had admitted once to Julia, he had been the love of her life.

Her expression brightened. "Old Hut found it in a bookstore in Oxford, years ago."

"Really?" Gabriel's eyebrows lifted.

"It was a remarkable find. He had it authenticated by a private museum in Switzerland that owned other, similar manuscripts."

Gabriel cleared his throat. "Do you remember the name of the museum?"

"The Cassirer Foundation Museum. Near Geneva."

A look passed between Gabriel and Julia.

Katherine continued. "The manuscript belonged to Galeazzo Malatesta. Galeazzo was married to Battista da Montefeltro. Her great-great-grandfather, Federico I, took over Urbino after Guido's death."

Julia reached for the manuscript but stopped short of touching it. "I can't believe it."

"Battista joined the Franciscan sisters after her husband died. She was a remarkable scholar in her own right and the grandmother of Costanza Varano, who was one of the most revered women in the midfifteenth century." Katherine nodded at Julia. "Your interest in Guido and the Franciscans persuaded me that this manuscript belonged in your home. This is a gift for my goddaughter, but I don't mind if her parents read it."

Katherine laughed at her own joke and sat back, taking great pleasure in watching Julia and Gabriel fawn over the gift. "There's some interesting marginalia and a few illuminations. You may find something relevant to your research, Julia."

"Thank you." Julia stood and hugged Katherine.

Gabriel repeated the gesture.

"Not bad for an old spinster." Katherine's voice was gruff. She tried to hide her sniffling by pushing the Emersons aside and pointing out some of the interesting features of the manuscript.

Julia and Gabriel pretended not to notice the sudden wetness on her cheeks.

Chapter Seventeen

The sound of a baby's cries split the night.

Julia groaned and reached for her phone. It was amazing how Clare had adjusted to the feeding schedule. She was right on time, her cries of hunger anticipating Julia's alarm by only a few minutes.

Julia switched the alarm off and closed her eyes, just for a moment.

Gabriel was asleep next to her, his face half-buried in a pillow, his arm slung over her abdomen. In fact, he was snoring—the obnoxious sound fortuitously muffled by the pillow.

He'd had a busy day. He'd responded to the University of Edinburgh, accepting the position of Sage Lecturer. They'd cautioned him to keep news of his appointment secret from everyone except his employer until the formal announcement and gala, which they wanted to schedule as soon as possible.

He and Julia had hosted a celebratory lunch with Richard, Rachel, and Katherine. Popping champagne and ginger ale, Gabriel lauded Julia's invitation to the Oxford workshop, which she had accepted that afternoon, explaining to the family what a tremendous compliment it was.

Gabriel spent most of the afternoon in his home office, fielding phone calls and going through his files. He was supposed to announce the topic of his lectures, at least in very general terms, at the gala. The Professor, as usual, was not a person who would leave things to the last minute.

He'd tumbled into bed just after the late-night feeding. And now he snored. It appeared the Professor could sleep through Clare's cries.

Julia could not. She swung her legs to the bare floor and winced.

Her right leg felt as if it were asleep. She flexed it, steeling herself for the pins and needles she was sure to experience as her circulation corrected itself. Instead, the pins and needles never came.

She leaned over, poking her bare leg with her thumb from knee to ankle. She could feel the pressure, but the feeling was dull. Her lower leg remained numb.

She moved her leg. She had full range of motion of leg, ankle, and foot. She could wiggle her toes. But the nagging, dull numbness persisted.

Clare's cries had abated, but it was still time to feed her. Julia stood, putting most of her weight on her left leg, and limped over to the baby. She lifted Clare and kissed her, then moved uncertainly to the nursery, taking care to stay close to the wall in case she fell.

She did not wake Gabriel.

❈✻❈

There was a part of the very, very early feedings Julia enjoyed. She liked the quietness of the house. She liked holding and bonding with her baby. But she found it difficult to stay awake.

Rachel had bought her a large, crescent-shaped pillow and for good reason. One day in the hospital Julia had almost dropped the baby while falling asleep during a feeding. Rachel had intervened at just the right moment. Ever since, when Julia felt especially fatigued, she situated the pillow around her waist and was sure to rest the baby securely atop it.

Clare rested comfortably against her mother, feeding, while Julia stared blankly at the breastfeeding app Gabriel had downloaded on her phone. The app charted feedings, helped her remember the side on which to begin, and so on.

Julia wondered what it would be like in a year's time, when they were in Scotland. Clare would be weaned by then. And Julia would be taking classes.

Without a doubt Gabriel, as Sage Lecturer, would be deluged with meetings and invitations. Undergraduate and graduate students alike would clamor for his attention.

He was an attractive man with a lively, sharp intelligence. Many women found his personality sexy. And the Paulinas, Professor Pains, and Christa Petersons of the world had either seduced him or attempted a seduction.

It wasn't that Julia didn't trust her husband. She did. He'd been faithful to her since their relationship began in Toronto. But Julia didn't trust the women around him. She didn't trust the creeping separateness that came from living apart, which was why she didn't want to stay in Boston if he was in Scotland. But the idea of him being separated from Clare for so long and at such an early age weighed on her the most.

Commuting couples were not uncommon in academia. The University of Toronto had had several. Indeed, in Julia's department at Harvard there was a professor whose wife taught at the University of Barcelona and lived in Spain with their children. Still, a commuter marriage was not what Julia wanted; it was not what she wanted for Clare.

Julia knew the pain of being separated from Gabriel. When he'd been disciplined by the University of Toronto for violating the non-fraternization policy, he'd cut ties with her. She'd spent a long time mourning his absence, wondering if she'd ever see him again. Even now, the separation marked her. She didn't want to go through something like that again.

Julia said a silent, spontaneous prayer of thanks for Katherine Picton's wisdom and support. She'd become godmother to the entire family.

"Here." Gabriel stood in front of her holding a tall glass of iced water.

Julia startled. "How long have you been standing there?"

"Not long." He placed the glass in her hand and collapsed in the rocking chair. "You're supposed to drink a large glass of water every time you feed her."

"I know." Julia drank the water gratefully.

Gabriel yawned and rubbed his eyes. "Why didn't you wake me?"

"You were tired."

"So are you, darling." Gabriel lifted a child-sized wooden stool and placed it in front of Julia. He perched precariously atop it, his legs so long that his knees huddled awkwardly against his chest. "I just received another email from Edinburgh."

"They're up early."

"Indeed. They want to schedule the announcement and gala as soon as possible."

"Would you go by yourself?"

Gabriel breathed deeply. He touched the calf of her left leg. "No. I want you and Clare to come with me."

He slid his hand down to her foot and lifted it with both hands. Then he began to rub the sole of her foot.

"I'm not supposed to fly until six weeks after my c-section. I don't think Clare should be exposed to an airplane full of germs before some of her vaccinations, either."

"But you'd come with me if we waited until the twenty-first of October?" Gabriel's voice was low, cautious.

Julia thought for a moment. "Yes. I probably won't be able to go to the gala or any events, unless Rebecca comes with us. But we could try to make it work. Do you think Edinburgh would be okay with me joining you?"

"They'd better be." Gabriel's expression grew dangerous.

Here was the Professor in his natural state, fierce and protective, proud and determined, like a dragon defending his gold.

Julia decided to lighten the mood. "I'm sure the female population of greater urban Edinburgh will be delighted to see Professor Emerson walking the streets of the city pushing a stroller. In a kilt."

Gabriel scowled. "Nonsense. No one wants to see me in a kilt."

Julia smothered a smile. "You'd be surprised."

He gazed into her eyes, his blue irises piercing through her façade. "Is that worrying you? The female population?"

Julia wanted to lie. She desperately, desperately wanted to lie. "A little."

"I'm with you—in Cambridge, Edinburgh, everywhere." Gabriel's thumb traced a meridian down the center of Julia's sole. His eyes focused on hers.

"I don't want to commute," Julia said in a small voice. Her eyes grew watery.

"I was going to say the same thing." Gabriel met her gaze, blinking rapidly. He tried to switch his attention to her right leg, but she waved him off.

"Clare is just finishing." Julia turned off the breastfeeding app.

Gabriel stood and lifted the baby into his arms, kissing her cheek. He retrieved a cloth from the changing table and placed it on his shoulder. He patted the baby's back and swayed on his bare feet, waiting for her to burp.

Julia's heart skipped a beat.

"I'm so proud of you," she whispered.

Gabriel gave her a questioning look.

"Being appointed the Sage Lecturer," she explained. "As well as being a good father and a good husband."

"I'm far from good," Gabriel murmured. He averted his eyes, almost as if her praise embarrassed him. "Mostly I'm selfish. I'm selfish about you and I'm selfish about Clare."

"I wonder what the University of Edinburgh will think of having a father in residence."

"If they say anything, I'll sue them for discrimination." Gabriel's face indicated he wasn't kidding.

Julia adjusted her nightgown and stood on her left leg, taking great care to hide her physical trouble from her husband. Her right leg still felt numb.

Gabriel bent down and kissed her. "Why don't you go to bed? I'll rock Clare back to sleep. She likes to hear me sing."

Julia laughed. "Who doesn't?"

She placed their foreheads together. Then she returned to their bedroom, limping as soon as she was out of Gabriel's sight.

Chapter Eighteen

A few days later

On the day of the baptism, Rachel and Aaron stood next to their car in the driveway, speaking with Gabriel.

"Just follow us into the parking garage and we'll walk to the chapel together."

"We'll keep up." Rachel glanced in the direction of the front lawn. "Looks like the flamingo company came to take them away. Except for one."

"What's that?" Gabriel moved so he could see the flower beds in the front yard. Next to a large hydrangea stood a pink plastic flamingo, wearing a pair of black sunglasses.

He turned accusatory eyes on his sister. "Did you do that?"

"I deny everything." Rachel pushed past Aaron to open the car door.

"Will it be here when we get back?" Gabriel lifted his voice.

"Of course. And if it finds a girlfriend while we're gone, you may have little ones all over your lawn. Again." Rachel laughed loudly as she got into the car.

Gabriel muttered a curse as he gazed out at his beautiful front lawn. He was just about to return to his SUV when he turned his head, facing toward the street that ran perpendicular to Foster Place. A black Nissan with tinted windows was idling just beyond the intersection.

Gabriel approached the sidewalk and began walking in the direction of the car.

The driver placed the car in reverse just as Gabriel began to approach it. Breaking into a jog, he reached the intersection in time to see the car speed off.

He was not able to get the license plate number.

*

"What name do you give your child?" Father Fortin addressed Gabriel and Julia.

They stood at the front of St. Francis's Chapel with Katherine Picton. Gabriel held Clare in his arms.

This was the Emersons' parish. They could have attended church closer to their home in Cambridge, but there was something about the chapel and the Oblates of the Virgin Mary who served it that made Gabriel and Julia feel at home.

He and Julianne replied to the priest in unison, "Clare Grace Hope Rachel."

A murmur lifted from the pews, as Gabriel and Julia's family reacted. Richard, who sat near the front row, could barely contain his emotion, while Rachel's solemn expression morphed into a grin.

Julia had dressed the baby in Rachel's christening dress—a long, white silk-and-satin garment that was embroidered with flowers and had short sleeves—and a lace-edged bonnet, tied with a long pink ribbon.

Clare looked like a princess. Gabriel had taken hundreds of photographs of her before they left the house, posing her alone and with her family.

As the baby began to frown, Julianne held a pacifier at the ready.

"What do you ask from God's church for Clare Grace Hope Rachel?" Father Fortin asked.

"Baptism." Again, Gabriel and Julianne replied in unison.

The priest asked if they understood their duty as parents, and they affirmed their understanding. Then he addressed Katherine, who pledged her commitment as godmother.

Gabriel took his role as a father very seriously. Even now, as he stood before the congregation and before God asking for his child to be baptized, he meditated on the myriad promises he was obliged to make and to keep, as he sought to parent this little life.

After a few words, Father made the sign of the cross on the baby's forehead, inviting the three adults to do the same. The family made a short procession to the dais, where the Scripture was read and the homily was delivered.

Gabriel found his mind wandering, even though his gaze was fixed on Clare.

He thought about his own spiritual journey. He thought about his struggle with addiction and the loss of his first child. His hand itched to touch the name that was inked on his skin.

He thought about Grace and her love for him—a love that gave rise to adoption and a family. A love that had been reciprocated over time.

He thought about Richard and his siblings. He thought about Rachel and her own recent struggles. He thought about how he was surrounded by family. Scott, Tammy, and Quinn sat in a pew with Richard, Rachel and Aaron, Tom and Diane Mitchell, and their son Tommy.

Gabriel's biological sister Kelly sat with her husband in the pew across from Scott. Rebecca sat with them. A select group of friends and fellow parishioners sat farther back.

For someone who had spent a lot of his childhood alone and lonely, Gabriel was surrounded by a large family. And Katherine, one of the greatest Dante specialists of her time, who had somehow adopted him and his wife, agreeing to pass along her support and love to Clare.

The baby fussed in his arms, and Julia gave her the pacifier. She gazed up at her mother and settled, her sky blue eyes open and curious.

Gabriel hadn't thought he'd ever have another child. In fact, he'd had a medical procedure to ensure it would never happen. Then everything changed. Everything had changed when a brown-eyed angel in jeans and sneakers had sat beside him on a back porch.

Gabriel recalled his time in Assisi, during his separation from Julianne, and how he had encountered grace and forgiveness in St. Francis's crypt. He remembered his earnest prayers that Julianne would forgive him and marry him. That God would bless them with a child.

He held in his arms a miracle—the extravagance of grace that had been bestowed on someone who was proud and sometimes angry, intemperate and addictive, lustful and profligate.

Forgiveness was not for the sinless or the perfect. Mercy was not for the just. He had to learn to name and acknowledge his own shortcomings before he could receive the remedies. The remedies themselves challenged him to treat other needy souls with mercy and compassion. Julianne was a shining example of that.

As the priest began the homily, Gabriel glanced over at the relics that were situated at the front of the church to the right of the altar. One of the relics belonged to St. Maximilian Kolbe, a Franciscan friar who was executed at Auschwitz. He had volunteered to die in the place of another man, a man who had a family.

In the face of such bravery, such sacrificial love, Gabriel felt very small. He was no saint, nor would he ever become one. As he held his daughter in his arms, he resolved to do better. To love his daughter and his wife to the best of his ability and to become a man of character, whom his daughter would look up to and admire.

Clare dozed in his arms, still enjoying the pacifier. The priest ended his homily and led the congregation in a series of prayers.

※×※

Julia snaked her hand inside the crook of Gabriel's elbow, leaning against him. Instinctively, he pressed his lips to her temple.

She was keeping a secret. Although she justified her silence by hoping that the numbness in her leg was temporary, her conscience rebelled.

Her heart was full. And as was usual for her during such moments, she grew very still, pondering what was happening.

She was a wife, and now a mother. She was a student and a prospective professor. She was a daughter and a sister. And, like Gabriel, she had been plagued by loneliness and alienation in her younger years but was now surrounded by a large and loving family.

She felt the responsibility of her many blessings keenly. And she resolved to love and protect her child to the best of her ability. She squeezed Gabriel's bicep—a gesture of affection—and smiled up at him.

※×※

Gabriel returned her smile, grateful that he had a partner, a wife, as he embarked on the journey that was parenthood. And such a partner.

Julianne had always had an attractive figure, but she was even more beautiful now. Her cheeks were lightly flushed, and her chestnut hair was soft and falling in gentle waves to her shoulders.

Her curves were more pronounced on her slim frame. Her indigo-blue dress accentuated her cleavage. Gabriel tried to avert his eyes but failed. She really was magnificent.

Gabriel reflected on his hunger—a hunger not just for her body but for her. When he was tempted to feel shame for the way he desired her, he noted that God had made her beautiful. God had joined them together. An entire book of sacred Scripture was devoted to the pleasures of physical love.

"Behold, thou art fair, my love; behold, thou art fair." And I will never see anything on this side of Heaven more beautiful than you.

Julianne was obviously tired. He saw that she was favoring her right foot. But before he could consider the cause, he was distracted by her plain, low-heeled shoes. She had an entire closet filled with extravagant high heels, many of which were, in Gabriel's mind, works of art. But she hadn't worn them. Gabriel shook his head at the lost podiatric opportunity. Perhaps her feet still felt swollen.

As the baptism proceeded, the baby frowned and lifted her fists but didn't cry. Soon the priest was anointing her head and the final aspects of the rite were completed.

There were many mysteries in faith and in life. Marriage and family had always seemed mysterious to Gabriel. Yes, the links between people existed and they were, perhaps, the strongest bonds in the known universe. But how they emerged and persisted he could not exactly say. He couldn't describe his love for Julianne, although he'd tried. He couldn't describe the joy and delight he had in Clare, although he would endeavor to do so. Metaphors like light and riches and laughter came to mind.

Julianne's hand found Gabriel's and squeezed. The two of them joined the congregation in reciting the Lord's Prayer, adding their thanks for their family and Katherine, but especially for Clare.

Many thoughts and emotions cascaded through Gabriel's mind, along with the resolution to stay close to his wife and child.

Chapter Nineteen

L ater that afternoon, Gabriel made a telephone call to Julianne's
uncle Jack.

Jack Mitchell was a private investigator who had helped Gabriel on
more than one occasion, particularly when Julianne's ex-roommate
had threatened to post compromising videos of her on the Internet.

Gabriel described the black car that he'd seen in the neighborhood and asked Jack to look into it. Jack grunted and agreed, complaining that Gabriel's description wasn't much to go on.

Now Gabriel approached the threshold of his bedroom, holding
a pair of champagne flutes. From the doorway, he could hear Julianne softly singing.

He peered into the room and found her holding Clare against her
shoulder and dancing.

Julianne was singing a nursery rhyme to Clare, who appeared to
be dozing. The baby's head was uncovered and her hair was damp
from her bath.

Gabriel was surprised at how curly the baby's hair was.

Her mother's movements slowed as she came to the end of the song. She kissed Clare's cheek and placed her on her back in the playpen.

Gabriel watched as Julianne retrieved a stuffed lamb from a nearby chair and pressed a button on its back. The muffled sound of a human heartbeat lifted from the toy.

Gabriel craned his neck and saw her put the toy in a corner of the playpen.

He entered the bedroom and placed the champagne flutes on a nearby table before closing the door.

Julia lifted her head and smiled. "Hi."

"How was the bath?" Gabriel handed her some ginger ale.

Julia took the glass eagerly. "Good. It amazes me how her hair curls when it's wet. You and I don't really have curly hair."

Gabriel chuckled and clicked his glass of ginger ale against hers. "To Clare Grace Hope Rachel Emerson."

"To Clare Grace Hope Rachel Emerson."

Julia sipped her drink and sighed happily.

He took her hand and led her to a large, leather club chair that sat near the window. She put their drinks on the side table and sat on his lap.

"It was a long day." He positioned her so her side nestled into his shoulder.

Julia winced as her right leg ached.

"Is something wrong?" Gabriel's blue eyes examined her.

"Just stiff," she lied. She retrieved their glasses.

He fastened his arm around her. "How are your feet?"

She wiggled her left foot. "They're fine. I knew we'd be standing a lot today, so I didn't wear heels."

"Ah." Gabriel resisted the urge to complain. He opened his mouth in order to suggest a private viewing, but Julia spoke first.

"Rachel is very happy we added her name to Clare's."

"Yes." Gabriel frowned, thinking of his sister and her woes. "I tried to talk to her today but she wouldn't engage."

"She was probably worried about spoiling the party."

"Hmmm." Gabriel did not sound convinced.

"Everyone around her has a baby, when she's the one who really wanted to be a mother. She needs time to grieve."

"Humph." He sipped his drink.

Julia tapped the slight divot in his chin. "Don't *humph* me, Professor. Grieving is a process."

"You are not wrong." Gabriel kissed her nose. "But I was trying to help by speaking to her today and she shut me out."

"She needs time to process what has happened."

"I suppose so." Gabriel changed the subject. "Let's talk about the abomination that's now standing in our front garden."

"I have no idea what you mean." Julia hid her face behind her champagne flute.

"You know exactly what I mean, Mrs. Emerson. We can't have kitsch in the front yard."

"I think it's funny."

Gabriel shook his head at her. "I have to admit, the sunglasses were a nice touch."

"Thank you." Julia bowed slightly. "Katherine's gift to Clare is incredible. It's interesting she went to the Cassirers in order to research the manuscript."

"Yes. I haven't spoken to Nicholas since I told him we were going to loan the Botticelli illustrations to the Uffizi. He joked about a family myth that said the illustrations must be kept secret." Gabriel sipped his drink again. "Which reminds me, *Dottor* Vitali called the day before yesterday. He wanted to know if we would consider extending the exhibition."

"What did you say?" Julia finished her ginger ale.

"I said I had to speak to you. I'm inclined to refuse."

"Darling." She put her glass aside. "What are a few more months?"

"They've had them long enough. They are precious to me."

"Okay, Gollum." Julia kissed him to soften her criticism.

Gabriel glared, his blue eyes razor sharp. "What if they get damaged? Or lost?"

"From the Uffizi?" Julia laughed. "They're guarded day and night. They're safer in the Uffizi than they are in your study."

Gabriel rubbed his chin. "Vitali said that the exhibit was bringing in a great deal of revenue. It's helping the gallery finance the restoration of *Primavera*."

"See? It's a great benefit. You know how I feel about that painting. Maybe we can see the restoration while it's in progress."

"Vitali won't refuse you." Gabriel sighed. "All right. I'll tell him we will extend the loan until next summer."

"The end of the summer," Julia amended. "You know that the summer is their busiest time."

"Fine," he grumbled. *"Humph."*

Julia laughed and kissed his frown. "Thank you."

"The president of Boston University wrote to me, congratulating me on the Sage Lectures. He's scheduling a reception after the gala in Edinburgh."

"That's great, sweetheart."

"Edinburgh tells me I'll be expected to say a few words after they announce me in October." Gabriel's eyes fixed on hers. "Will you come to my talk?"

"Of course. So long as Rebecca agrees to watch Clare."

Gabriel's shoulders relaxed. "Good. We'll leave for Edinburgh the third week of October, but it will be a short trip."

"We need to be home for Halloween."

Gabriel looked puzzled. "What's so important about Halloween?"

"We need to take Clare trick-or-treating."

Gabriel's eye twitched. "Can we take a baby trick-or-treating?"

"Sure we can. Why not?"

Gabriel nodded slowly, as if the wheels of his mind were turning. "We need to choose an appropriate costume."

"For her or you?"

"Very funny. Although I'm more interested in seeing you in costume." He licked his lips.

Julia grinned. "All right, Professor. I'll see what I can do."

"Good." He cleared his throat. "Edinburgh pays its Sage Lecturers a large sum of money. The chairman of my department, along with the dean, has granted me a research leave for next year so that I can relocate to Scotland. But they'll still pay my salary.

"I don't need two salaries. We live very comfortably, so I was thinking . . ." He paused and searched Julianne's eyes.

"The orphanage in Florence." Her brown eyes lit up. "They do so much with so little. Imagine what they could do with a year of your salary."

"I confess I had thought the same thing. I could continue on my salary from BU and donate the Sage money. It would allow the orphanage to help more children."

"The Italian government won't let us adopt a child until we've been married for three years. I know we spoke of adopting Maria." Julia appeared saddened.

"I hope for her sake a family finds her before that." Gabriel's arm tightened around Julia's waist. "But if we're agreed, I'd like to donate to the orphanage."

"But quietly." Julia rested her head on his shoulder. "I'd rather no one knows but the orphanage and us."

"Of course. Elena and her team do good work there. I'm glad we can support them."

Julia yawned.

"I'm supposed to announce the subject of the Sage Lectures at the gala in Edinburgh," Gabriel continued. "My book on the seven deadly sins is almost finished. But I've decided to write something else for the lectures. I considered writing a book-length comparison of the relationship between Abelard and Héloïse with that of Dante and Beatrice. But again, I think I'll save that. For the Sage Lectures, I want to focus on *The Divine Comedy*, while bringing in sections from *La Vita Nuova*. What do you think?" He turned his attention more fully to his wife.

Julia made a noise that could only be described as a snore.

"Darling?" Gabriel touched her face, but she was fast asleep.

He smiled, gazing from one sleeping female in his arms to the other, who was fast asleep in her playpen. In this house, he was surrounded by women. And he'd never been happier.

"All right, little mama. Time for bed." He lifted her into his arms and carefully carried her across the room. He placed her under the sheets and studiously tucked her in.

He brushed the hair from her forehead and stroked her cheek with the back of his fingers.

"I'm glad you're coming with me to Scotland." He kissed her tenderly and switched off the light.

Chapter Twenty

Richard entered the kitchen just as Rebecca finished cleaning up after dinner.

"Would you like to join me on a walk?"

If Rebecca was surprised by his invitation, she hid it well.

"I'd like that." Her tone was bright as she removed her apron. She hung it on a hook inside the pantry.

Richard gestured in the direction of the hall and she preceded him, patting her salt-and-pepper hair and straightening her dress.

He opened the side door for her and the two stepped out into the late September air.

Rebecca was tall at five foot eleven. She was almost as tall as Richard. Her features were plain but her eyes were pretty and so was her smile.

Richard situated himself so that he walked on Rebecca's right, next to the road.

There were no signs of fall, at least not yet. The temperature was still warm in the evening. Although the cul-de-sac of Foster Place was thickly settled with older houses built very close together, it was quiet.

"Have you always lived in New England?" Richard began the conversation. They left the cul-de-sac and turned right on Foster Street.

"Always. My family is from Jamaica Plain, but my husband and I moved to Norwood when we got married. He passed away twenty years ago."

"I'm so sorry." Richard's tone was sincere.

"He was a good man. When he died, my mother moved in with me and my son. I cared for her until she died. Gabriel hired me a few months after that."

"I'm sorry you lost your mother. I'm very grateful for how you've looked after my son and daughter, and now my granddaughter."

Rebecca smiled. "I'm the kind of person who needs to look after someone else. My son took a job in Colorado and moved away. My daughter lives in Sacramento. It made sense to rent out my house and move in with Gabriel and Julia. But he's on the lookout for an apartment for me in Cambridge. Eventually, they will need their own space."

Richard nodded thoughtfully.

She turned her body toward him. "And you're a professor?"

"That's right. I taught biology at Susquehanna University, but I retired when my wife died."

"I'm sorry." Rebecca made eye contact with him.

"Thank you." He sighed. "I'm afraid I made rather a mess of things. I retired from Susquehanna and took a research position in Philadelphia, so I could be closer to my daughter and my son, Scott. But I never saw them. I found I missed the house I shared with my wife. So I resigned my post and moved back. Now I'm teaching one course a semester at Susquehanna as a professor emeritus."

"I can understand you wanting to stay in the house," Rebecca commiserated. "I can't bring myself to sell our home in Norwood, although I know I'll have to sell it eventually."

Richard's handsome face looked weary. "Do you mind if I ask you a question?"

"Not at all."

"Does it get better?" Richard's gray eyes were earnest.

Rebecca looked up at one of the many trees that lined Foster Street. "I know what you want to hear, because it's what I wanted to hear when I lost my husband. You want to hear that time heals and grief disappears.

"I'll be honest with you—grief doesn't go away. You will always miss that person, because you loved her and you miss her company. My husband has been gone for twenty years and I still miss him every day. And every night." She smiled ruefully. "But the pain lessens over time. I'm able to talk about him and look at photos and remember the good times. But it was a process."

Richard looked stricken. "I had hoped you'd tell me it would get better."

She placed a comforting hand on his arm. "Some things get better. But for me, the grief is still there.

"I've found a second family with your children. I get to borrow books from Gabriel's library and make my favorite family recipes for him and Julia. Now I get to help with the baby and make sure Julia takes care of herself. It feels good to be needed. I have a role. I have a purpose."

Richard stuck his hands in his pockets. "Yes, it's good to be needed."

"Your children need you. They need you in some way to be both parents for them, and that's difficult."

"Yes." Richard seemed to be processing her assessment.

"Life won't be the same, but it can still be a good life. Spending time with family and friends is important."

"I agree."

The pair continued walking in silence.

At length, Richard spoke. "Thank you, Rebecca."

"It's my pleasure. I'm happy to talk to you whenever. I'm only a phone call away."

"I'd like that. I'm beginning to realize I spend too much time alone."

"There were days, even weeks, when I didn't leave my house after my husband died. I just didn't want to go anywhere."

Richard bobbed his head.

Rebecca paused, making eye contact once again. "Could I give you a piece of unsolicited advice, widow to widower?"

Richard chuckled. "Go ahead."

"Whether you decide to remarry again or not, take it slow. Develop a friendship with the woman first. I've seen too many people jump into another relationship full speed ahead, only to have it end in disaster when they realize they truly aren't compatible."

"That's good advice. One of my old friends in Selinsgrove was trying to get me to sign up to a dating website. He told me that's how the young people do it."

"Young people." Rebecca huffed. "They live their entire lives online. They're always connected to a device. We should take dating advice from them? Pfffttt."

Richard grinned. "Good point."

"I don't want to go back to the old ways, either, when they used matchmakers or whatever. I can pick my own damn husband."

Now Richard was laughing. "I dare anyone to tell you otherwise."

"Damn straight." Rebecca laughed with him.

"But friendship is important, as you mentioned. Someone to talk to, to have dinner with. Yes, this is important." He turned to face her. "Rebecca, may I take you to dinner?"

She paused for just a moment. "Yes. Though I'll need to make arrangements with your children."

"I think they can get along without you for one evening."

"I have my doubts." She grinned.

The pair exchanged smiles and continued their walk.

Chapter Twenty-One

October 2012
Edinburgh, Scotland

Professor Emerson was impatient with mediocrity.

Julia was well aware of this. But it amused her to see the Professor wrestling with his adherence to excellence in all things while simultaneously transporting a six-week-old baby to Europe.

The University of Edinburgh, in keeping with their official travel policies, booked Professor Emerson a coach seat. The Professor impatiently upgraded his seat to first class and booked an adjacent seat for Julia, as well as a seat across from them for Rebecca.

The university arranged for a taxi to ferry Professor Emerson and his family to their hotel. The Professor dismissed the taxi (almost wrathfully) and hired a private driver and Range Rover to be at his beck and call during the duration of his visit.

The university arranged for a graciously appointed king bedroom at the Waldorf Astoria Caledonian hotel for the Emersons. The Professor promptly placed Rebecca in the king bedroom, and for himself and his family he booked the Alexander Graham Bell suite, which provided a view of Edinburgh Castle.

"They're going to think you're a diva," Julia whispered, as the bellhops delivered their luggage, stroller, and baby implements to their suite.

"Nonsense," Gabriel said primly. "I'm covering the additional expense. What's it to them?"

Julia bit her lip, wondering how to explain it. But when she saw the view of the castle through the enormous windows, she decided to let it go. Edinburgh was beautiful. The suite was beautiful. And she was very, very tired.

Gabriel surveyed the work of the bellhops approvingly and tipped them generously. Then he crossed to where Julia was standing by the window. "Go lie down." He stroked her cheek affectionately.

"I thought we were supposed to stay awake, to fight off jet lag." Julia yawned in spite of herself. "It's time to feed Clare."

"Feed her and then lie down. I'll take her out in the stroller for a walk."

"Really? I didn't think you slept at all on the plane."

"A walk will do me good, although I may take a nap this afternoon. We've been invited to dinner with the university council tonight. The gala and reception are tomorrow."

"Okay." Julia yawned again. She lifted Clare from her baby carrier and kissed her before settling them both in an armchair next to the fireplace. The bellhops had started a fire, which was sparking cheerfully. "What about Rebecca?"

"She's decided to explore the city." Gabriel's eyes twinkled. "I think she's gone in search of a Highlander."

"Godspeed, Rebecca." Julia crossed her fingers to wish her luck.

Chapter Twenty-Two

That evening, Julia entered the luxurious Jacobite Room in Edinburgh Castle. Through the windows on the far side, she could see the sparkling lights of the exquisite city, blurred a little by the raindrops that clung to the panes of glass.

The room itself had a vaulted ceiling that was lined with wood. Wooden beams supported the structure, which put Julia in mind of the hull of a ship.

They'd finished a sumptuous, multicourse dinner with dignitaries from the university in the Queen Anne Room and had now retired to this more intimate setting for after-dinner drinks.

On their arrival at the castle, the Emersons had been welcomed by a piper, under flaming torches. The university hosts were incredibly hospitable and had even arranged for Julia and Gabriel to view the Scottish Crown Jewels and the Coronation Stone before dinner.

After dinner, Julia had excused herself to the ladies' room and called Rebecca, in order to check on Clare. Relieved that all was well, she returned to the reception and saw her husband encircled by members of the university court and city officials.

His blue eyes caught hers and he smiled, a ray of sunshine just for her. She smoothed the skirt of her black velvet gown. They'd dressed to match one another. The Professor wore a tailored black suit and tie, his hair carefully combed, his dress shoes shiny. His gold pocket watch and fob threaded through the vest beneath his suit jacket. And he'd eschewed his beloved Scotch for coffee, in keeping with his commitment to sobriety.

He beckoned her with his eyes, unwilling to interrupt the well-dressed gentleman who was talking in his ear scarcely without drawing breath. But Julia felt uncomfortable breaking into the conversation. She inclined her head in the direction of the bar and made a beeline toward it, quietly ordering a cup of tea.

Gabriel gazed longingly at the tumblers of single malt ambrosia the other guests were drinking. He waited for a break in the conversation so he could join his wife at the bar. Surely he could find something better than coffee.

"Mrs. Emerson, I'm Graham Todd." A middle-aged man, equally well dressed but in a navy suit, approached Julia from the side.

He held out his hand and she shook it. "Pleased to meet you. Call me Julia."

Graham smiled kindly beneath his graying beard. He had reddish hair that was beginning to gray and strong eyebrows. His eyes were blue and rather keen. One got the impression by looking at him that he didn't miss much.

"I understand you study Dante, as well." Graham sipped Scotch from his crystal glass. He sounded English rather than Scottish, at least to Julia's ears.

"Yes, I'm studying with Cecilia Marinelli at Harvard."

"I recognized your name from Don Wodehouse's invitation list. Will you be participating in the workshop in April?"

"I will." Julia paused, unsure whether it would be presumptuous to ask Graham the same question.

"Don was my supervisor at Oxford. I'm the Dante specialist here at Edinburgh."

"It's good to meet you. Edinburgh is an incredible city, and Gabriel is really looking forward to being part of the university community."

"Will you be joining him?"

Julia hesitated. "I would like that. I need to work out a few things with Harvard, because I'm supposed to be in coursework next fall. Of course, I couldn't mention anything to them until after tomorrow, when the Sage Lecturer is announced."

Graham nodded his head. "Of course. We'd be delighted to have you in our department. While we haven't set our courses for next year as yet, I can certainly send the schedule to you as soon as it's finalized. What will you write your dissertation on?"

"Thank you. I'm still putting together a proposal for Cecilia, but I had thought of exploring Guido da Montefeltro's death scene in the *Inferno*, contrasting it with that of his son Bonconte in the *Purgatorio*."

"What do you find interesting about Guido?"

"Well, I was fascinated by his account of his own death, and how he claimed St. Francis of Assisi came for him when he died but was defeated by a demon."

"Ah," said Graham. "Fairly straightforward, isn't it?"

"Dante encounters Guido in the circle of the fraudulent. I'm not sure we can treat his testimony as truthful."

Graham tugged at his beard. "A good point. But where's the fraud?"

Julia leaned forward eagerly. "Dante tells us that Hell is structured according to the virtue of justice. So despite what Guido says, justice places him in the Inferno. If he is there justly, why should Francis appear?"

Graham lifted a shoulder. "Francis is unsuccessful in saving Guido, as I recall."

"If Francis is a saint, he would agree with Dante that justice structures Hell, which means he wouldn't be second-guessing God. So either Francis didn't appear at all, or he appeared for a different purpose. And Guido is lying in either case."

Professor Todd chuckled. "Ah, you must be the young lady who needled Don into taking a second look at Guido. He's become obsessed with him."

Julia reddened. "Oh, no, I didn't needle him. But he came to hear my Guido paper at a conference and he argued with me a little."

Graham's eyes grew knowing. "The last time I saw Wodehouse argue with a graduate student, the student abandoned his graduate program and became a shepherd."

"Oh, dear." Julia was horrified.

"I don't think you're in danger of quitting Harvard and becoming a shepherd?" Professor Todd gently teased.

"Um, no." Julia sipped her tea. "I'm just trying to finish my coursework so I can take my area examinations."

Graham looked at her thoughtfully. "Let me introduce you to some of the other faculty in Italian studies and especially to my department head. We may have some courses that would be appropriate."

He stretched out his arm, indicating that Julia should precede him.

With a grateful smile, she walked into the breach, catching Gabriel's eye as she moved.

When he saw her being welcomed by colleagues from the university, he beamed with pride.

Chapter Twenty-Three

I t was raining.

Professor Emerson had come to the conclusion that the residents of Edinburgh were greatly in need of an ark. It had done nothing but pour since he and Julianne arrived at the castle for dinner.

He turned up the collar of his Burberry raincoat and adjusted his tweed cap, switching his umbrella to his left hand. After he and Julia arrived back at their hotel, Julia had realized they'd run out of diaper cream. And, as she was quick to remind him, diaper cream was essential to the baby's health.

Gabriel went downstairs to the lobby in search of the concierge but was dismayed to discover she was not on duty.

"This would never happen at the Plaza," he'd grumbled to himself as he queried the front desk staff. Indeed, the Plaza Hotel in New York had never left him or Julianne wanting, no matter the hour.

The Professor was further dismayed to learn that there wasn't a twenty-four-hour pharmacy or supermarket close to the hotel. Even the Marks & Spencer at Waverley Station was closed. And that was how he'd found himself in the back of his hired car, being chauffeured through the rain to a large twenty-four-hour supermarket in Leith, some twenty minutes away.

Arriving at the supermarket was one thing; finding diaper cream was quite another, especially since the supermarket didn't seem to carry any of the brands they used back in America. Gabriel called Julianne three times as he walked the aisles trying in vain to discover the correct item. After being told in no uncertain terms by his wife that she was going to bed and that she would speak to him when she woke up for Clare's next feeding, he purchased four different products, hoping at least one of them would suffice.

When he finally returned to the Caledonian he was in a very bad humor. He scowled up at the brightly lit Edinburgh Castle as he exited the hired car. The doorman greeted him with an open umbrella and escorted him into the hotel.

It was at that moment Gabriel received an incoming text from Jack Mitchell.

He shook the rain from his coat and cap and walked straight to the Caley Bar so he could read the text privately. He ordered a double espresso from the bartender, grousing internally about his inability to order Scotch.

It's a crime against hospitality, he thought. *All that beautiful Scotch, just waiting for the right palate to appreciate it. With this rain, I'll probably catch pneumonia and die. All Sage Lecturers should be issued antibiotics on arrival. Perhaps as part of the welcoming fruit basket.*

As the bartender made his espresso, the Professor withdrew his cell phone from his pocket and read the text.

> Nothing on the Nissan.
> If you see it again, take a photo.
> Will check in on J's roommate and the senator's son.

The text was clear enough. Looking for a black Nissan without a license plate number in the Boston area was next to impossible. Still, Jack was nothing if not thorough. He was going to look into Natalie Lundy, Julia's former roommate, and Simon Talbot, her ex-boyfriend.

Gabriel's lip curled in distaste. If he ever saw that son of a bitch again . . .

He closed the text message window and placed his phone on top of the bar. A picture of Clare gazed up at him from the screen.

The rain stopped, the clouds parted, and Professor Gabriel Emerson smiled.

He removed his coat and cap, hastily putting them aside along with his umbrella and his shopping bag. He ran his hand through his unruly hair and quickly sat, scrolling through the photographs of Clare and Julianne.

A trip to the store after midnight isn't so bad; not when such angels wait for me upstairs.

The bartender served the espresso, along with a small plate of biscuits and a glass of ice water.

He sipped his coffee and was suddenly seized with a coughing fit.

It's already begun. I've contracted pneumonia.

"I won't have what he's having." A female voice sounded to his right. "I'll have a martini, please, up with an olive."

Two seats over stood a dark-haired woman who spoke with a smooth English lilt. She placed her leather briefcase on the floor next to her chair and sat, thanking the bartender as he poured her drink. He set a small platter of nuts in front of her, which she sampled immediately.

Gabriel sipped his coffee again, hoping it would soothe his cough. He was almost satisfied with the result.

"Bit cold out, isn't it?" She smiled conspiratorially.

"Glacial. Does it rain like this all the time?"

The woman shrugged. "I live in London. But the summers here are very nice. The sun doesn't set at night until past ten o'clock."

"Humph," said Gabriel.

"American?" she asked, after tasting her martini.

"Yes."

"What brings you to a rainy Edinburgh?"

"I'm a guest of the university."

"Me as well." The woman looked over her shoulder. "I was supposed to meet my crew here, but I think they've gone out without me. Bollocks."

Gabriel finished his espresso and ordered another. "What kind of crew?"

"Television." The woman moved her glasses from on top of her head so she could read the bar menu. "We've come up from London to cover something at the university.

"I can't believe they left me." She looked around the bar, which was almost empty. "Those bastards."

"You're a television presenter?" Gabriel asked politely.

"God, no. I'm the producer." She lifted her martini in his direction. "Cheers."

"Cheers." Gabriel lifted his cup in return.

"Right. So what are you doing for the university?"

Gabriel paused as the bartender served his second espresso and another plate of biscuits. "A series of meetings, knowledge transfer, that sort of thing."

The woman's mouth twitched. "Are you the one with the knowledge, or is it the other way round?"

"Mostly me."

"What kind of knowledge are you transferring? Gravitational waves? Theology? The price of cheese and international trade?"

"Dante Alighieri." Gabriel drank his espresso.

The woman put down her drink. "Really?"

Gabriel smothered a smile. "Yes, really."

"Dante is interesting but he spent an inordinate amount of time talking about Hell."

"And traveling through it."

The woman laughed. "Yes, but no one believes in Hell anymore. Isn't it difficult to interest people in Dante? To make him relevant?"

Gabriel turned in his chair. "Dante addresses love, sex, redemption, and loss. Those subjects are of ultimate concern to all human beings. If you skip *Inferno*, you miss the best parts."

"But it's all about sin, isn't it? Punishment. Torture. Very badly dressed people."

"Think of it as a redemptive exploration of human behavior. Each deadly sin represents a singular obsession, and Dante shows us their consequences. It's a cautionary tale, more than anything. Since he labels his work a comedy, he's telling us he thinks the story of humanity has a happy ending."

"Not sure the souls in Hell are happy, but I take your point." The woman removed her olive from her martini and ate it. "What are the deadly sins again?"

"Pride, envy, wrath, sloth, avarice, gluttony, and lust."

"Ah." The woman shivered. "Now my Catholic upbringing is coming back to me. Although you could say that in the news business, we tend to be acquainted with sin in all of its various forms. So you're presenting your lecture tomorrow?"

Gabriel froze. His status as Sage Lecturer was not to be known by the public until the announcement tomorrow. "I didn't say that."

"But you're a professor of literature?" The woman turned her head and gave Gabriel an expectant look.

Gabriel forced a smile. "Just a Dante enthusiast from America, happy to meet some of his Edinburgh colleagues."

At that moment, a rather rowdy group of men and women entered the bar and walked straight toward the woman. She cursed them, but with a smile on her face.

Gabriel abandoned his second espresso and quickly charged his refreshment to his suite.

The television crew ordered drinks, talking boisterously among themselves.

Gabriel retrieved his coat, hat, and umbrella. As he turned to go, the woman approached him.

She extended a business card. "Eleanor Michaels, BBC News. We'll be covering the Sage Lectures announcement tomorrow."

Gabriel adopted a stoic expression. It would be rude—and undoubtedly suspicious—to refuse the card.

"Nice to meet you, Miss Michaels." He accepted the card and shook her hand. "What are the Sage Lectures?"

"You tell me. And it's Eleanor." She leaned forward. "I know it's shrouded in secrecy, and no one is supposed to know anything before the announcement, but I hope you'll give us an interview tomorrow."

He lowered his chin patiently. "Enjoy your evening."

"See you tomorrow. Hope the rain ends." The woman smiled before returning to her colleagues.

Gabriel pocketed the card and went upstairs to the suite.

Stercus, he thought.

Chapter Twenty-Four

The following afternoon
Old College
The University of Edinburgh

This is very grand, Julia thought as she entered the Old College Quad on foot. The college itself was very regal and made of stone, rising in front of her with high arched windows and elegant pillars.

Since Gabriel had to arrive early, Graham had agreed to meet Julia in the quad. He greeted her with a friendly smile and walked her to the entrance, being careful to avoid the immaculately manicured grass.

Julia was grateful for her university escort, as finding the Playfair Library Hall wasn't easy. The hall was bright and had a large barrel ceiling. White pillars lined the space, along with a series of marble busts perched atop plinths.

Julia regarded the bookshelves and their contents with envy, wishing she had time to explore the collection.

Almost all of the two hundred fifty seats in the hall were taken. And there was a large media section gathered at the back of the room, behind the last row of chairs. Julia noticed that BBC News was present, along with several other press organizations.

Graham escorted Julia to the front row. She was careful as she walked in her high heels, determined not to stumble in front of the crowd of people.

Gabriel was nowhere to be found.

"I'll find you after." He'd kissed her in their suite more than an hour ago and lowered his voice to a whisper. "See me in my office after class."

Julia had trembled at his words, which brought her back to the command he'd given her on the very first class of his she'd attended.

He must be joking, she thought, as she walked toward the front. *He doesn't have an office. At least, not yet.*

But Gabriel never joked about sex. No, on the subject of the erotic arts he was always serious.

Which means that we . . .

Julia didn't finish the thought. Seated in the front row were two figures she recognized. She paused, confused.

"There she is." Katherine Picton rose and crossed over to Julia. The two women embraced.

"I didn't know you were coming," Julia faltered.

"I heard a rumor that this year's announcement of the Sage Lecturer would be worth attending." Katherine's eyes shone mischievously. "I'm not alone. I believe you two have met?"

Katherine stood back and gestured between Julia and an aged man who wore a tweed jacket and dark corduroy trousers.

"Don Wodehouse." The man removed his glasses and extended his hand to Julia.

"Professor Wodehouse, it's good to see you again." Julia's voice was faint, for she was in shock. She mustered a smile.

"Graham." Professor Wodehouse shook hands with his former student, although his greeting was remarkably cool.

Graham appeared unfazed by the professor's demeanor and smiled. "Julia has been telling me about her paper on Guido da Montefeltro."

Julia tensed.

"Yes, I'm familiar with that paper." Professor Wodehouse replaced his glasses on his nose. "I'm interested to hear what Mrs. Emerson has to say about Dante's treatment of Ulysses."

Julia felt almost light-headed. "I haven't focused on that text, but I'm looking forward to discussing it with everyone at the workshop you've organized in April."

Graham chuckled next to her.

"Yes, there will be plenty of time to discuss Ulysses." Katherine nudged Professor Wodehouse. "We need to sit down. I see the guest of honor has arrived."

At that moment, Gabriel entered the hall with a group of university officials, in full regalia. Julia found herself seated in between Graham and Katherine as Professor Wodehouse took a chair on the other side of Katherine.

Gabriel and the officials gathered on the raised platform. Julia recognized most of the dignitaries from the reception the evening before.

Having just survived a brief challenge from Professor Wodehouse, who by all accounts was intimidating, Julia's heart beat quickly. She was reminded of how, more than three years ago, she sat in Gabriel's seminar at the University of Toronto—a young, grass-green graduate student who'd hidden a secret love for her professor in her heart. How far they'd come.

She had survived Toronto and their separation. She had survived

Christa Peterson and Paulina Gruscheva. Despite her inherent shyness, she'd won a place at Harvard. All that remained was for her to complete her program and then she, like Gabriel, would have the academic freedom to study and write what she pleased.

Professor Emerson looked very handsome, dressed in his Harvard crimson over a gray suit. His pale blue shirt and darker blue tie made his sapphire eyes seem bluer.

She'd wanted to match his gray suit, but she'd succumbed to his last-minute plea to wear something brighter.

"I need to be able to find you," Gabriel had pleaded over breakfast. The sound of his voice was strangely vulnerable.

Julia could not refuse. Vulnerability was something he shunned like mediocrity. Yet he could be vulnerable with her, privately. She treasured and protected those moments.

So she eschewed the gray dress she'd wanted to wear and replaced it with a sleeveless kelly green dress. The dress was modest and fell to her knees, but the color was daring and the wide neck exposed her collarbones.

Gabriel had predicted that most of the audience would be clad in dark colors. He was correct. In a sea of black, navy, and dark tweed, her green dress made her highly visible, which was precisely what he'd wanted.

And she was wearing a pair of red-soled stiletto heels. Somehow her right leg had felt better that morning and so she thought she'd chance it. She hoped Gabriel would appreciate her choice.

When his eyes finally found hers, he stood very still. The principal of the university was speaking in his ear, but Gabriel's attention was fixed on his wife. His lips curved up into a half-smile and he gave her an intense, branding look before turning his attention back to the principal.

Now Julia could draw breath. Gabriel had arrived and he had found her. She'd never been more eager to be found.

Julia wondered how Clare was adjusting to an afternoon with Rebecca at the hotel. The past two days had been the Emersons' first excursions without the baby and Julia felt curiously bereft. In order to resist the urge to text Rebecca, she focused on her dress, noticing the way the material gave off a subtle sheen under the lights. Then she patted her hair. She'd worn it in a French twist, pinned at the back of her head.

"When Gabriel delivers the Sage Lectures, he'll be in McEwan Hall, which is much larger." Graham leaned closer from his seat.

She glanced around the room. "How much larger?"

"This room only seats two hundred fifty people. McEwan Hall seats a thousand."

Julia gulped. She hadn't really grasped the pomp surrounding the Sage Lectures, although she had been impressed by the warm and generous hospitality of the university. Graham had been very kind, as had his colleagues. It seemed to be a wonderful community.

The head of the School of Literatures, Languages, and Cultures made a few opening remarks and introduced the director of the Research Office, who spent a great deal of time highlighting the excellent research profile of the university before describing the importance of the Sage Lectures in the field of the humanities.

Julia noticed that Gabriel's body language never changed, even when the principal was introduced and he began cataloguing Gabriel's long list of accomplishments. Gabriel's piercing blue eyes moved in an unhurried fashion from the principal to Katherine Picton, with whom he exchanged a warm smile, and back again.

He caught Julia's eye and winked. Julia winked back, feeling warm all over.

She surveyed the audience, noting the presence of what looked like undergraduate and graduate students, as well as faculty members and other members of staff. That was when it struck her.

Gabriel didn't have graduate students. Yes, Boston University had hoped he'd be able to attract them, but since Italian studies didn't have a graduate program, students interested in studying Dante at the master's or doctoral level had to enroll in the Department of Religion, in which Gabriel was cross-appointed. But a doctorate in religion wasn't what a true Dante specialist needed, especially if he or she wished to teach in a department of Italian or Romance studies.

The University of Edinburgh has a doctoral program in Italian.

Indeed, she was sitting in front of several of the faculty members of that program, while Professor Todd sat next to her.

Julia's heart skipped a beat. Gabriel had taken the job at Boston University so he could be close to her while she studied at Harvard. But professionally, the job was not the best fit. And Katherine Picton had said as much, in the conversation in which she'd suggested Julia spend a semester in Scotland.

The University of Edinburgh recognized Gabriel's accomplishments. The Sage Lectures were drawing enormous attention, including the attention of the media. Other universities and research institutes would take notice. Perhaps Edinburgh would invite him to stay. . . .

The principal finished his introduction and Gabriel joined him at the lectern. The men shook hands.

Gabriel adjusted the microphone to accommodate his six-foot-two height and withdrew his black-rimmed eyeglasses from inside his suit jacket. A hush fell over the audience as he adjusted his notes on top of the lectern.

"Mr. Principal, members of the University Court, colleagues, ladies and gentlemen, you honor me with your attendance. I'd like to thank the University of Edinburgh for their generous invitation, which I gladly accept.

"Thanks are due also to my home institution of Boston University for its support of my research. I also want to thank my lovely wife, Julianne." Gabriel gestured to her. "Because of her support and the support of Boston University, I will be able to relocate to Edinburgh for the 2013–2014 academic year and deliver the Sage Lectures.

"I have been invited by the principal to say a few words about the series of lectures I intend to deliver next year, here at the incomparable University of Edinburgh. Allow me to begin."

He cleared his throat. "'*Voi non dovreste mai, se non per morte, la vostra donna, ch'è morta, obliare.*' So speaks Dante in *La Vita Nuova*, '*Except by death, we must not any way forget our lady who is gone from us.*'

"In this work, Dante gives us poetry from his heart, describing the constancy of his devotion to Beatrice." Gabriel made eye contact with Julia, looking at her over the rims of his glasses.

"Dante Alighieri was born in Florence, Italy, in 1265. He is known for his poetry and political writings, as well as for his activism in Florentine politics. But he is also known for his passionate and unconsummated love for Beatrice.

"Dante met Beatrice Portinari when they were both nine years old. '*Apparuit iam beatitudo vestra,*' he writes. '*Now your blessedness appears.*'

"Dante and Beatrice crossed paths again in 1283 and Beatrice's greeting was so moving, Dante writes that at that moment he saw the culmination of blessedness. This moment is immortalized in Henry Holiday's painting *Dante and Beatrice.*" Gabriel nodded toward the back of the room and a projection of the painting appeared on a screen behind him.

Julia held her breath. The painting was personal to her and Gabriel and for more than one reason. He'd purchased a copy of it years ago and had kept it with him ever since. And at the moment, it was hanging on the wall in their bedroom, back in Cambridge.

"Dante's life is shaken by this second meeting with the virtuous and beautiful Beatrice. He loves her. He worships her. He devotes much time and attention to praising her in thought and in poetry, but Beatrice marries Simone dei Bardi in 1287." At this Gabriel paused, making eye contact with the audience. "Dante is married, as well. But he doesn't write poetry in praise of his wife. Indeed, *La Vita Nuova* paints a picture of a lovestruck, single-minded man who adores another man's wife from afar.

"Is it love? Is it lust?" Gabriel paused. "It's certainly passionate. Although Dante and Beatrice have become a model of courtly love, the truth is we don't know what would have happened if she hadn't died, suddenly, at the age of twenty-four.

"Dante describes a conversation between himself and the adulterous lover Francesca da Rimini in *Inferno* canto five. Is this a nod to what might have happened, had Beatrice not died? Or is there a different subtext to Dante's conversation with Francesca? I'll explore my answers to those questions in the lectures."

Gabriel shifted the pages of his notes.

"*La Vita Nuova* is Dante's first-person account of his encounters with Beatrice and his love for her. He ends the poem with a solemn pledge to study and show himself worthy, so that he may write something in tribute to her. He hopes his soul will go to be with her in Paradise after he dies."

Gabriel nodded once again and a new image appeared on the screen behind him. "This is one of Sandro Botticelli's illustrations of Dante's *Divine Comedy*. In this image, we see Dante confessing to Beatrice and Beatrice revealing her face. The conversation is recorded in *Purgatorio* canto thirty-one."

Gabriel looked down at his notes. He adjusted his glasses.

"In *La Vita Nuova*, Dante provides us with an account of a man's obsessive devotion to his virtuous muse. Many of you know the rest of the story—how Dante mourned Beatrice's untimely death for the rest of his life and how he penned *The Divine Comedy* at least in part as a tribute to her. The *Inferno* begins with Dante's confession that at the midpoint of his life he'd lost the right path and strayed into shadows.

"The poet Virgil comes to Dante's aid and explains that he is there at Beatrice's request. In conversation with Virgil, Beatrice identifies Dante as her friend, and she declares she's worried he's beyond rescue. According to her, Dante has been turned aside by fear.

"But it's the blessed Virgin Mary who sees Dante's distress first. Mary tells St. Lucy, and it's St. Lucy who seeks out Beatrice, wondering why she hasn't helped the man who loved her so much that he left behind the vulgar crowd. At hearing that, and bestirred by her love for him, Beatrice makes haste to seek out Virgil.

"Skipping ahead to *Purgatorio* canto thirty-one, we have a very different account of Dante and his troubles. Beatrice accuses Dante of forsaking his devotion to her and being deceived by young women, whom she refers to as Sirens."

A murmur lifted from the audience. Next to Julia, Katherine and Professor Wodehouse exchanged a look.

"Dante responds to her charge with shame." Gabriel cleared this throat. "But then, a few lines later, the three theological virtues beg Beatrice to turn her holy eyes onto 'her faithful one,' Dante." Gabriel's eyes met Julia's and held them.

"What are we to make of the reversal in *Purgatorio*? Beatrice condemns Dante for faithlessness and he reacts in shame. Then the theological virtues—faith, hope, and charity—declare that Dante is, in fact, faithful to Beatrice.

"Did Dante keep his promise to Beatrice? Or did he fail? On the one hand, we have a written record of Dante's devotion to Beatrice, and that record includes *The Divine Comedy*. On the other hand, we have Beatrice's harsh words—words that Dante himself writes—and the subsequent purging of Dante's sins in Purgatory.

"In the Sage Lectures, I will juxtapose Dante's exchange with

Francesca with his conversation with Beatrice. I'll shed light on the literary puzzle of Beatrice's condemnation and Dante's pledge by examining the *Purgatorio* in light of both *La Vita Nuova* and *The Divine Comedy* as a whole.

"Dante is the author of the works in question, but he's also a character in the story. I will offer a metalevel reading of the texts that will contrast Dante the author with Dante the character." Gabriel grinned impishly, his blue eyes twinkling behind his glasses. "Perhaps Dante's true purgation consists in penning the *Purgatorio* itself."

The audience laughed.

"So I invite you, colleagues and friends, to join me on a journey of redemption. Our path will wend its way through Hell and Purgatory, and eventually arrive in Paradise. Along the way, we'll meet villains and cowards, as well as great men and women of renown.

"We will explore what Dante can teach us about human nature and humanity at its best and at its worst. And we will learn more about the extraordinary love story of Dante and Beatrice. Thank you."

The audience erupted in applause.

Gabriel acknowledged the audience with a nod, his gaze finding Julia. She smiled as she clapped and instantly, Gabriel's shoulders relaxed.

She hadn't realized the tension he'd been carrying, for he hid it well.

The director of the Research Office shook Gabriel's hand as he retreated to his seat. And then the director made a few closing remarks before inviting everyone to a reception in a neighboring hall.

Gabriel made a move in Julia's direction but was intercepted by the principal, who clapped him on the shoulder.

As the audience filed out and the principal continued to engage Gabriel, Julia joined Katherine, Graham, and Professor Wodehouse at the reception.

"Where are you in your graduate program?" Professor Wodehouse asked Julia, as they stood holding their wineglasses.

Julia tasted her wine hastily before she answered. "I've finished two years. Next fall, I take my final courses and then I take my examinations in the winter."

Professor Wodehouse frowned, which really was rather frightening. "You said next fall? What are you doing now?"

"I'm on maternity leave." Julia's cheeks reddened.

Wodehouse's frown deepened. "Good heavens." He peered around the room. "Where's the baby?"

"She's with a friend at the moment."

"And how old is your child?"

"Just six weeks."

"Good heavens!" he exclaimed, his eyebrows lifting to his hairline. He surveyed Julia quickly. "My wife wouldn't have traveled to London six weeks after giving birth, let alone gotten on an airplane and crossed the Atlantic. Now I understand what Katherine meant." He drank from his wineglass.

Julia glanced at Katherine, who was deep in conversation with Graham a few steps away from them. She was tempted to ask what, precisely, Katherine had said. And she found the temptation too great to resist. "Katherine?"

"Katherine said you were more tenacious than your husband. You know him, obviously, and so you can imagine my reaction to her pronouncement." Professor Wodehouse looked at Julia approvingly. "I'm beginning to think Katherine is right."

"Thank you." Julia's voice was a little weak, partially because she was trying to figure out if the professor was complimenting her or censuring her.

"So you're on leave this year and your husband is in Edinburgh next year. I take it you'll be commuting back and forth?"

"I don't know." Julia was carefully noncommittal. She wanted to mention her plan to take courses in Edinburgh and then return to Harvard to take her exams after the lectures were complete, but she remembered she hadn't spoken to Cecilia about it. Cecilia and Professor Wodehouse were friendly, which meant she couldn't mention her plan. At least, not yet.

"I'm sure you're tenacious enough to work it out." Professor Wodehouse's expression changed into what could have been a smile. It was difficult to tell.

"Tenacious enough to work what out?" Katherine's brisk voice interjected.

She and Graham moved closer to Julia to join the conversation.

"Commuting across the pond. Mrs. Emerson is at Harvard while her husband is at Edinburgh next year," Wodehouse explained.

Both Graham and Katherine looked at Julia.

Before she could answer, Gabriel appeared, having divested himself of his Harvard crimson. "Good afternoon, everyone. Thank you for coming."

He kissed Katherine on the cheek and shook hands with the others.

"Julianne," Gabriel murmured. His blue eyes radiated warmth and concern, relief and desire.

Julia wanted to embrace him, to hold him tightly and find safety in his arms. But there were too many peering eyes.

Gabriel moved, taking her hand in his and stroking his thumb across her knuckles.

He lifted her hand to his lips and pressed a lingering kiss against her skin, his eyes fixed on hers.

"*Soon,*" his lips whispered.

Julia felt her skin heat.

He released her hand and placed his own protectively at her lower back, then turned to Professor Wodehouse. They exchanged a few remarks before he and Graham excused themselves.

Julia took hold of Gabriel's elbow, eager to tell him what had just transpired, but they were interrupted by a group of faculty members.

Gabriel introduced Julia and Katherine and they exchanged pleasantries. As the reception wore on, Katherine fell into conversation with an old friend and Gabriel introduced Julia to more people than she could count.

Finally, they stood by themselves in a corner.

Gabriel leaned forward, his lips hovering near her ear. "Miss Mitchell?"

"Yes?"

Gabriel's breath whispered against her neck. "It's time for our meeting."

Chapter Twenty-Five

Gabriel opened the door to a small office, which was situated on a deserted corridor on the main floor of the college. He stood aside to let Julianne enter, and closed and locked the door behind them. "They gave me a key to this room so I could store my regalia."

The office boasted floor-to-ceiling bookshelves on two walls and a large window that looked out onto the quad. Gabriel crossed to the window and pulled a sheer curtain over it, shielding them from passersby.

His regalia was packed away in a garment bag that hung carefully on the back of the door. His briefcase sat forgotten on a leather chair, next to a floor lamp. Light shone in through the sheer curtains and so Gabriel didn't bother with the lamp. He strode toward Julianne, engulfing her in his arms.

"We don't have much time." His voice was a whisper, as if the very walls were listening. "I'm supposed to go back upstairs for interviews. I'm sorry."

"You did a great job. The audience reacted well to your talk. Katherine was very pleased." Julia was feeling off-balance in the wake of her conversation with Professor Wodehouse. She was a little worried her plans would get back to her supervisor before she had the chance to speak to her directly.

Gabriel tightened his embrace, burying his face in her exposed neck.

"I saw you holding your own with Don Wodehouse," he spoke against her skin. "I think you've acquired a fan."

"He scares me." She inhaled Gabriel's scent—Aramis and peppermint.

"I think he scares everyone." Gabriel kissed her neck. "But he's a man. Why wouldn't he want to talk to the prettiest girl at the reception?"

Gabriel's hands sought her face and he lifted it, looking down with warmth into her eyes. "You are so beautiful."

She smiled shyly. "Thank you. I was hoping you'd like the dress. I packed it thinking I'd wear it to one of the parties."

He moved back, surveying her appraisingly. "A goddess in green."

His lips met hers before she could reply, his kiss firm but reverent. For a moment, at least, he didn't move. His mouth simply pressed against hers.

Julia reached up to wind her arms around his neck.

Gabriel's lips whispered across hers, pecking the corners of her mouth. He kissed and retreated, kissed and retreated, almost as if he were tasting a fine wine and wished to savor it. Their bodies pressed together. "I'm glad you're here."

"Me, too." Julia resisted the urge to broach the subject of next year. She hadn't had a chance to describe her conversation with Professor Wodehouse.

"I suppose you're wondering why I asked you to my office." Gabriel traced a single finger down her neck.

She turned and kissed the edge of his hand.

"Take down your hair," he whispered.

Julia obliged, deconstructing her hairstyle. She withdrew pin after pin, placing them on his desk.

Gabriel grew impatient.

"Let me," he said gruffly. He brushed her hands aside and drew long, searching fingers through her waves of chestnut hair.

She closed her eyes.

It was an intimate thing, she thought, to have Gabriel touch her hair. She sighed contently.

"Were all these items really necessary?" Gabriel grumbled, holding up what he thought was the last pin.

"Yes." Julia patted her hair, finding a few stray pins he had missed. "They were."

"The effect was stunning." He combed her hair with his hands so it cascaded about her face. He touched her neck again. *"The door is locked."*

His eyes met hers as his hand dropped to the zipper of her dress. He eased it down her back, never breaking eye contact.

The green material gathered at her hips and she leaned forward, exposing her full cleavage, as she tugged the dress off.

"Allow me." Gabriel knelt, bringing her hand to his shoulder for balance. He helped her step out of the dress and placed it carefully on the edge of the large, heavy desk.

"You'll ruin your suit," Julia murmured, her hand still on his shoulder.

"Fuck the suit." Gabriel sat back on his heels and stared.

Julia wore an elegant black satin-and-lace basque, paired with gossamer underwear. Garters and black silk stockings encased her legs. On her feet she wore the high Christian Louboutin heels Gabriel almost worshipped.

A low oath escaped his lips. "I was not expecting this."

"Surprise." Julia felt conspicuous, although Gabriel's reaction was more than she had hoped. She withdrew her hand and placed it at her hip. "I was thinking we'd celebrate back at the hotel."

"I'm not waiting. Hang the interviews." Gabriel broke eye contact so his gaze could roam her body. Julia's breasts were very full and almost overflowing the top of the basque. But the garment flattened her stomach and accentuated her small waist. In high heels, her legs lengthened and she was a great deal taller.

Gabriel's hungry perusal made her feel powerful.

She preened, pushing her hair back from her face.

"I'm speechless." He touched the curve of her hip, stroking the skin just above her stocking. "You're a siren. Will you pose for me? So I can photograph you?"

"Not now." She leaned forward and grabbed his tie, pulling him toward her. Her lips hovered over his. "You know, it's been six weeks since Clare was born, and I was cleared by Dr. Rubio before we left. So . . ." She arched her eyebrows.

Immediately, Gabriel was on his feet and divesting himself of his suit jacket and tie, casting them aside. He crushed her to his chest, his mouth fused to hers, as his hands rested on her barely covered backside.

Gabriel brought his hips to hers and she moaned at the sensation, feeling him rise beneath his trousers.

"Someone is going to hear us." She traced her tongue across his lower lip before slipping inside.

"Then you'll have to be quiet." Gabriel kissed her deeply and lifted her onto the desk.

"I can't be quiet, not with you touching me like this."

Gabriel smirked and spread her legs, stepping in between them and pressing himself up against her.

Julia hugged his hips with her knees, her high heels grazing the backs of his thighs. "I'll stab you. Maybe I should take them off."

"No fucking way." Gabriel's voice was hoarse as he lifted his hands to cup her breasts. He touched and stroked, passing his thumbs over her nipples until they grew taut. He peeled back the covering from her left breast and bent his head, kissing and tasting the round, full flesh.

Julia ground herself against him, her heels spearing his trousers. She bit the inside of her mouth, in order to stay silent.

His mouth closed on her nipple, gently, but he did not draw.

Julia pulled his dress shirt free. She began unfastening his buttons.

Again, Gabriel grew impatient and pulled the shirt over his head, throwing it onto the chair.

He bared her other breast in preparation for his mouth, worshipping her other nipple.

Her hands coasted up and down his bare back, urging him on.

Without warning, his hand rummaged behind her and fastened on a letter opener.

"I'll buy new ones," he rasped, as he flicked the letter opener between her hip and the edge of her panties. The silk ripped cleanly. He repeated the motion on the other side, placing the letter opener in his teeth as he withdrew the silk from between her legs.

Her eyes darted to his as she sat on the edge of the desk, legs wrapped around his hips, breasts bared and now fully exposed.

He grew still, letter opener between his teeth.

He removed the letter opener and put it on the desk. "I didn't scratch you, did I?"

She shook her head.

He loosened her legs from his waist and knelt before her, his hands reaching back to cup her behind. He pulled her toward his mouth.

Julia rested her weight back on her hands as Gabriel kissed the insides of her thighs—light, unhurried kisses.

He drew the skin of her upper thigh into his mouth and pulled. She shuddered.

With his shoulders, he spread her legs still wider, and nuzzled her center. His mouth grazed her up and down and back and forth before he introduced his tongue.

Julia screwed her eyes shut as Gabriel began to feast.

He kept his own leisurely pace as he licked and nipped. Then finally, he stroked her with his tongue with quick, repetitive moments and she clenched, legs shuddering and insides fluttering.

He continued to taste her as her tremors receded and then he withdrew, looking up at her with a very pleased expression.

She sagged back on her arms, a wide smile on her face.

Gabriel wiped his face with a tissue and proceeded to unfasten his belt. He removed his trousers and black boxer briefs before standing in between her legs again.

"I don't have a condom." His hands rested on her knees.

"I came prepared." Julia leaned over to pick up her purse and quickly withdrew a condom. "But I started taking the pill a couple of weeks ago."

Gabriel took the condom from her and ripped it open with his teeth. "Just in case the pill isn't effective yet." He rolled the condom onto himself, swiftly and efficiently.

She widened her legs. An invitation.

Gabriel brought their bodies together, his strong arms winding around her back. He nudged between her legs, his mouth finding hers.

As he kissed her deeply, he slowly slid inside.

It was an exquisite fullness she'd missed. It had been so long since they'd been joined this way.

Gabriel cursed as he was fully seated inside her. "This may be quick." He sounded as if he were in pain.

She squeezed his hips with her legs. "I'm ready."

Gabriel didn't need any further encouragement. He stroked in and out, continuing to kiss her, his thrusts growing progressively rougher.

"Are—you—okay?" he managed to say, his lips dropping to her collarbone.

"Hurry." She tugged at his hair, urging him on.

Gabriel's movements quickened and he lifted his mouth to hers. She welcomed him and his tongue swept inside her mouth.

A few more thrusts and she felt her pleasure crest. Her grip on his shoulders tightened as she signaled her orgasm.

Gabriel continued moving inside her, anchoring her to his body with his arms. He came with an expletive, stilling.

She held him close as he released.

Gabriel's head slumped to her shoulder and he exhaled loudly. She pressed a kiss to his hair.

They were both quiet as their heart rates decreased and their breathing slowed. Julia nuzzled his ear with her nose.

"You'll catch cold," Gabriel whispered.

"Not if you continue holding me."

He chuckled and kissed her shoulder. "Sorry about the underwear."

"I can't bring myself to care."

"That's my girl." Gabriel pulled back and kissed her tenderly. "My beautiful, smart girl."

He disengaged from her body and swiftly disposed of the condom. Then he retrieved tissues, attending her first before seeing to himself. He retrieved his suit jacket and placed it around Julia's shoulders, while he redressed.

He gave her his naked back as he lifted his dress shirt.

"Gabriel!" She covered her mouth in horror.

He strained his neck, looking over his shoulder. "What?"

Julia pointed to the scratches and scrapes her heels had wrought above his backside and across his shoulder blades. She winced. "I'm sorry."

"I'm not." He flashed a grin that rivaled the sun. "I wear my love scars with pride."

She cringed, for she regretted marring his skin.

He lifted her chin with a single finger. "We wound one another, but we can also heal one another." He lowered his gaze. "The healing I received from you is perhaps the most important of my life."

"Gabriel," she whispered, grasping his arm at the wrist.

He kissed her. "I'm sorry I have to go. They'll be looking for me upstairs."

"I need to get back to the hotel to feed Clare. I only left two bottles with Rebecca." Julia hopped down from the desk but nearly fell over when her right heel hit the floor.

"Steady." He wrapped his arm around her waist as she tottered on her heels. "Are you all right?"

"I'm fine." She brushed her hair behind her ears and lowered her eyes, pulling up her basque to cover her breasts. The numbness in her right leg had returned and so she'd almost turned an ankle as she tried to stand. But she wasn't going to tell Gabriel about it—she didn't want to worry him, especially not at such a critical time for him as this.

"Are you sure?" He lowered his head so he could look into her eyes.

She flashed a quick smile. "Of course." She picked up her dress and he helped her step into it.

Gabriel zipped up her dress. "Our hosts are planning another dinner this evening. I'll call you when I know the details."

"I'm not sure I can make it. I may need a nap after what we just did."

Gabriel grinned wolfishly. "I'll call you anyway. And if you'd rather stay in, that's fine. I'll detach myself as soon as I can."

He began cleaning and tidying the desk, placing the letter opener in the center, almost as if it were a souvenir. He looped his tie over his neck but didn't bother tightening it. "Maybe you and I can visit the pool tonight. Or the spa."

"That would be nice."

At that moment, a knock sounded at the door. "Professor Emerson?"

Gabriel stilled. "Yes?"

"You're wanted upstairs, sir," the male voice called. "Eleanor Michaels from the BBC is looking for you."

"I'll be right there." Gabriel gave Julia a look of consternation.

She covered her mouth to smother a laugh.

"You go," she whispered. "I'll wait until the coast is clear, and then I'll lock the door behind me."

"Fine." He rolled his eyes heavenward and shook his head.

She groomed him quickly—straightening his tie, adjusting his suit jacket, and smoothing his hair. She took a tissue and wiped his face clean of lipstick.

He turned around in a circle, extending his arms wide. "Am I presentable?"

"Delectable." She sighed longingly. "The BBC will love you."

"I love only you." He kissed her firmly and retrieved his briefcase and garment bag. Then he slipped into the corridor, careful to only open the office door a crack.

Julia waited until the footsteps receded. And then she collapsed in a chair, fanning herself with both hands.

Chapter Twenty-Six

A few days later
Harvard University
Cambridge, Massachusetts

C ome in." Cecilia Marinelli's lightly accented voice responded to
Julia's knock.

Julia opened the door and stuck her head inside the office. "Hi,
Cecilia. Do you have a minute?"

On seeing Julia, Cecilia's expression shifted. She nodded stiffly
and gestured to Julia to enter.

Julia was puzzled by her reaction. She stood awkwardly, until
Cecilia finally invited her to sit down.

Cecilia was petite, with bright blue eyes and short dark hair. She
was from Italy, originally, and had arrived at Harvard the same year
as Julia.

"I thought you were on maternity leave." Cecilia removed her glasses and set them on her desk. She did not smile.

"I am. I was hoping I could talk to you for a minute." Julia clasped her hands in her lap, feeling nervous.

"I heard the news, of course. The administration is touting Gabriel as one of its most important alumni. Congratulations on the Sage Lectureship." Cecilia's tone didn't match her words.

"Thank you. He's very excited."

"I saw his topic for the lectures." The edges of Cecilia's mouth turned down. "It's interesting but too romantic. Also, metalevel readings of Dante are very common. I expected more, much more."

Julia was stunned. Cecilia and Gabriel had always been on friendly terms. Her criticism stung.

Oblivious to her student's reaction, Cecilia continued. "So you and Gabriel will be commuting next year while he's in Edinburgh."

"No," Julia almost stuttered. "Well, that's what I wanted to ask you about. I—"

"You can't take another leave of absence," Cecilia interrupted, switching to Italian. "Not after your maternity leave. You need to take courses next fall and put together your dissertation proposal."

Julia's gaze dropped to her boots, wondering what she had done to offend Cecilia. They'd had a warm exchange by telephone when Julia explained she was taking a maternity leave. And they'd traded equally amiable emails about Professor Wodehouse's workshop.

Julia's heart rate increased as she contemplated how she could smooth things over with her supervisor.

"I've already begun working through the reading list you gave me for my dissertation proposal," she volunteered.

"You should also work through the reading list for Don Wodehouse's workshop. I'll send it to you."

"Thank you." Julia brightened. "I saw Professor Wodehouse in Edinburgh. His student, Graham Todd, teaches there."

"I know Graham." Cecilia's frown relaxed. "And it's good for you to get to know Don. It's important you show everyone you're serious about your studies and that you aren't simply recycling Katherine Picton's ideas. Or your husband's."

Julia almost choked. "Cecilia, have I done something wrong?"

"Actually, you've done something right. You offered a new perspective on the case of Guido da Montefeltro at the Oxford conference last year, rather than relying on the work of Katherine or Gabriel. That's why Wodehouse noticed you. But sometimes, doing excellent work isn't enough." Cecilia sounded bitter.

"You have to be focused. You have to be disciplined. You're on a fellowship in this department, which we awarded to another student while you were on leave. Now you want another leave of absence so you can go to Edinburgh? I'm sorry, but I can't support that."

Julia began wringing her hands. "What if I don't take a leave of absence, but just enroll at Edinburgh for the fall semester? Graham Todd introduced me to some of the members of his department. I can find out what they're teaching and provide you with the course descriptions to assess if the credits can transfer."

Cecilia bristled. "Edinburgh is not the same as Harvard."

She pointed in the direction of the office of Greg Matthews, the chair of her department. "I doubt Greg would approve of you taking your final classes at Edinburgh."

Julia leaned forward. "Cecilia, please. Could I just find out what the courses are and show them to you?"

Cecilia measured her for a moment. "I make no promises.

"Did you know the dean called Greg at home on the day the Sage Lectures were announced, wondering why no one from this department has been a Sage Lecturer in the past fifteen years?"

Julia faltered. "I didn't know that. I'm sorry."

"So am I." Cecilia's lips twisted derisively. "Gabriel is an alumnus of this department and so the dean and the chair can claim him. Greg told me Gabriel applied for the endowed chair that Harvard gave me. Now the dean thinks Greg made a mistake.

"I earned this position." Cecilia's tone grew harsh. "I'm further along in my career than Gabriel and I have more publications. Now Greg is bringing Katherine into the department. Why?"

Julia took a deep breath. "I don't know."

"I earned my endowed chair. I left Oxford to come here. But that doesn't count for the dean. He insists his faculty must win every award. He says Boston University is embarrassing him."

Julia's eyes strayed to the office door, which was partially open. This conversation had not gone as planned. Not at all.

Cecilia dropped her voice. "You are on maternity leave and you must return in the fall. How do you think it will look if the top student, my student, left for Edinburgh? At the same time I am passed over for the Sage Lectures, at the same time Katherine is invited to join my department? No. You must finish your coursework here."

Julia felt something like despair settle in her stomach. She nodded, worried that if she opened her mouth, she'd burst into tears.

Cecilia put her glasses on again. "Katherine is in her seventies. She may choose to retire at any moment. And your life is entwined with hers enough, since she is godmother to your child. If I decide to drop you as a student . . ." Her voice trailed off.

Time seemed to slow. Julia's chest felt constricted as she tried to draw breath. She sat quietly, wondering if she'd heard what she thought she'd heard.

In the space of a few sentences, Cecilia had dropped the equivalent of a(n academic) hydrogen bomb. Although she wasn't stating for certain that she would drop Julia as a student, she was threatening to. Losing a graduate supervisor in the middle of a program would have devastating consequences for any student, especially if there were no assurances she could find another supervisor.

Cecilia stood. "So, you should continue reading in preparation for your dissertation proposal. And I will send you the reading list for Don Wodehouse's workshop."

Julia bobbed her head and meekly thanked her supervisor before escaping into the hall.

She walked swiftly in the direction of the nearest ladies' room and was able to make it into a stall without anyone seeing her tears.

Chapter Twenty-Seven

G abriel saw Julianne from a distance, walking across the Harvard campus.

He'd parked the car after dropping her off and had placed Clare in a baby carrier/over-the-shoulder contraption that had a fancy Swedish name.

He thought it made him look like a kangaroo. (Which was, perhaps, why he attracted so much female attention from passersby, many of whom stopped to say hello to the baby and to gaze somewhat dreamily at her attentive father.)

When Julia saw him, she sped up.

"Let's go." She grabbed his hand, greeted Clare, and then commenced dragging him along the footpath.

Gabriel planted his feet. "What's the matter?"

"We'll talk in the car." She tried in vain to move him along.

"The car is over there." He jerked his thumb in the opposite direction. "What's the matter? What's going on?"

"Please," Julia begged, eyes filling with tears.

Gabriel could not refuse. He put his arm over her shoulder and directed her toward the car. "Tell me what happened."

Julia looked around nervously. "Cecilia said *no*."

Gabriel's head swiveled in Julia's direction. "What?"

"Cecilia said that if I want to work with her, I need to be here next fall."

Again, Gabriel planted his feet. "She threatened you?"

Julia swiped under her eyes. "Not in so many words. She said she'd read the Edinburgh schedule, but that it would look bad for her to send her top student there, especially with Katherine coming into the department."

Gabriel cast a murderous look at the building in which Cecilia's office was located. His feet began moving. "I'll speak to her."

"No!" Julia tugged on his arm. "I don't want to make a scene. Let's talk in the car."

"I'll call Greg Matthews. That will put an end to it." Gabriel lifted his chin, his blue eyes sparking.

"If you do that, she'll drop me." Julia's voice was just above a whisper.

Gabriel regarded her. Then he looked at the building.

He cursed. "They can't do this. Students study abroad from that department all the time."

"Yes, in Italy. Not Scotland." Julia tugged on his arm and they continued walking.

"The issue is the coursework. If you can get the courses you need in Edinburgh, they should be able to transfer. You'd be below the maximum number of transfer credits, correct? You only need three courses."

"Yes, but not even Graham Todd knows what courses will be offered next year. They haven't set the schedule."

"Bullshit. Whatever they were lacking, Graham or one of his colleagues could offer you a directed research course."

"I hadn't thought of that." Julia was having difficulty keeping up with Gabriel's long strides, even ignoring the strange numbness in her leg.

He seemed to recognize her distress and slowed his pace. "I'm sorry. I didn't mean to rush you."

"I'm okay," Julia lied.

"I don't understand why Cecilia has turned on us. I thought we were friends." Gabriel muttered a few choice expletives.

"She mentioned something about the dean scolding Greg Matthews, since no one in his department has been asked to give the Sage Lectures in a long time."

"That's true. But the lectureship is international. And it covers all fields in the humanities, not just literature."

"Greg told Cecilia you were considered for the endowed chair they gave to her. The dean brought it up." Julia and Gabriel exchanged a look.

"Considered and rejected," Gabriel scoffed, sounding bitter. "I like Greg, but being awarded the Sage Lectures after being turned down by his department was a very satisfying middle finger to all of them."

"Now Cecilia is giving me the middle finger."

Gabriel stopped. He unlinked their connection and placed his hands on her shoulders. "She's giving *me* the middle finger. You're just a convenient target."

Julia ignored his remark and instead looked down at her child and took her tiny hand. "Hi, Clare."

The baby gurgled and smiled, kicking her feet out the sides of the baby carrier.

Julia returned Clare's smile. "We shouldn't talk about this in front of her. She'll pick up on the negative vibes."

"All right," Gabriel said stiffly.

They continued their walk to the car.

"But this is not over." He gave Julia an ominous look.

Chapter Twenty-Eight

"What do you want to do?" Gabriel sat facing Julianne in their bedroom.

Rebecca was giving Clare a bath and readying her for bed.

Julia picked at the material of her jeans. "Cecilia said she'd look at the Edinburgh courses. Once I get the schedule, I'll show them to her."

Gabriel sat back and crossed his arms. "Cecilia also told you she wouldn't approve a semester abroad."

"I have to try," Julia said quietly.

"We need to talk to Katherine."

"No."

"Why not?" Gabriel stood and began to pace. "She can offer advice."

"Katherine will confront Cecilia and then Cecilia will drop me."

"I'm beginning to think that's a good thing," Gabriel huffed.

"No, it isn't. If Cecilia drops me, word will get out. It will damage my reputation. And I won't have a dissertation director."

Gabriel stopped pacing. "Work with Katherine."

"I've already worked with Katherine. She supervised my MA thesis at Toronto, remember? How do you think it would look for me to work with her for both my thesis and my dissertation?"

"I think it will look fantastic. She's the top Dante specialist in the world."

"Cecilia said I'm too close to Katherine as it is."

"Bullshit." Gabriel continued pacing, like a caged lion. "Cecilia is not objective. Her assessments are clouded by envy."

"Katherine can't be my supervisor until she starts at Harvard, which is next year. Even then, she only has a visiting appointment."

"She's there to supervise graduate students. That was the deal."

"What will it look like if Cecilia, who is the endowed chair in Dante Studies, refuses to work with me?"

"It will look like she's a jealous bitch, that's what it will look like."

"What happens if something happens to Katherine? She's in her seventies. What if she decides to leave? Or what if she . . ." Julia covered her face with her hands.

"Katherine is healthier than all of us." Gabriel crouched in front of her, placing his hands on her knees.

"Some students take four to five years to complete their dissertation." Julia's voice was muffled. "Katherine will be in her eighties by then."

"It won't take you that long. Katherine understands the commitment involved." Gabriel squeezed Julia's knees.

"It isn't just the dissertation. Katherine is family."

Gabriel pressed his lips together. "Family is everything. That's why I'm not going to Scotland without you."

Julia lowered her hands. Their eyes met. "I don't want you to cancel the Sage Lectures. You have to go."

Gabriel patted her knee. "Then let me intervene."

"That will make it worse. Cecilia is angry. We need to give her time to calm down."

"I don't want to wait."

"I don't, either, Gabriel. But remember, I'm supposed to be going to Professor Wodehouse's workshop with Cecilia in April. If I create a rift with her now, that could jeopardize my invitation."

"Wodehouse is in charge."

"Please, Gabriel. I'm just asking for a little time."

He stood, frowning. "You give up too easily. People take advantage of you."

She stood toe to toe with him, her lower lip trembling with anger. "I'm not giving up! I'm simply not making a power move right now. I'm trying to be smart."

"It's smart to fight."

"It's smart to survive long enough to fight another day. Then you can regroup and confront your enemy with a reasoned strategy and greater support. Then perhaps you won't need to fight."

Gabriel stared. "You've been reading *The Art of War.*"

"No, I've been studying feminist literature."

Gabriel's mouth twitched and his anger melted away. "I know better than to fight that army. I surrender to you and your sisters." He pulled her into his arms.

She hugged him back.

"But only for now," he whispered.

Chapter Twenty-Nine

The following afternoon
Boston Fencing Club
Brighton, Massachusetts

Gabriel was frustrated. He'd received another text from Jack
Mitchell.

> Looked into the roommate and the senator's son.
> Nothing.

As always, Jack was the soul of brevity. Gabriel would have to call
him in order to find out the full import of his text.

At the thought, Gabriel thrust his saber, warming up before facing his opponent.

He hadn't told Julianne about the black Nissan or her uncle
Jack's latest mission. Since there was nothing to report, at least to

date, his decision was vindicated. But there were other, deeper concerns that weighed on him.

Julianne had been adamant he not intervene with Cecilia. Although he could have ignored Julianne's wishes, he wouldn't do so. Which meant he was feeling impotent in addition to being angry. Impotence was not a state he was familiar with, which was why he was at his fencing club, working out his multiple frustrations.

His coach and fencing partner was Michel, a quiet, older gentleman who hailed from Montreal. Michel was a former Olympian and a formidable opponent. Gabriel admired him.

Gabriel preferred the saber to the foil or épée, because it was the fastest of the three fencing events. It rewarded aggression through the right of way and used a heavier weapon. The slashing capability of the saber was enormously satisfying.

Gabriel longed to challenge Julianne's enemies to a duel, one by one. But he would have to be content to fence with his coach. The men put on their helmets and saluted one another.

One of the other members of the club, who was acting as referee, shouted, *"En garde. Prêts? Allez!"*

And the bout began.

Michel attacked immediately and Gabriel parried, continuing into a riposte. Michel quickly parried and made contact with Gabriel's right shoulder, scoring a point.

As the fencers retreated to the *en garde* lines, Gabriel adjusted his helmet.

The referee shouted and the bout resumed.

Both Gabriel and Michel wore conductive uniforms that were connected via long cables to an electronic box. The cables themselves were retractable, so as not to constrict movement. When a valid part of the body was hit, the box would record a point. However, it was the referee's job to determine the right of way; only fencers with right of way could score a point.

Gabriel knew he could have worked out his aggression by pounding the heavy bag at the gym. But fencing channeled his anger and dampened it. In order to fence, he had to force himself to remain calm and to concentrate.

Michel capitalized on any and all weaknesses and was especially gifted at circular parries and ripostes. Gabriel was younger and faster. He deflected an aggression and launched a counterattack, hitting Michel's helmet, which was a valid target.

The fencers battled, back and forth and back and forth, in short, controlled attacks. Michel's score began to climb and Gabriel struggled to catch up.

He was sweating beneath the uniform. Both fencers began removing their helmets to mop their faces in between points.

Finally, Michel reached fifteen points and the bout was over. Gabriel removed his helmet and shook hands with his coach, then shook hands with the acting referee.

"Your mind is elsewhere," Michel scolded Gabriel in French.

Gabriel pressed his lips together. There was no point in denying it.

"A short break, then again." Michel pointed to a nearby row of chairs and walked off to speak to another fencer.

Obediently, Gabriel sat and drank from his water bottle.

Julianne was his sun and his moon. Someone had treated her unfairly, driving her to tears.

He mopped his face with a towel and rested his arms on his knees. He did not want to go to Edinburgh alone.

Changing Cecilia's mind was going to be difficult, if not impossible, especially since she seemed to have taken his own recent success as an indictment of her career. Gabriel wanted Julianne to stand up to her—to call her bluff. But Julia wanted to wait and to regroup.

Gabriel was not a man given to waiting. He'd never been so, even after his experience in St. Francis's crypt. Gabriel was a fighter. He'd be damned if he'd spend one week away from his wife and child, let alone an entire year. And especially not because of some academic's hurt pride.

Michel appeared in front of him and kicked his foot. "Let's go. And this time, you need to focus. My grandmother could best you today. And she died thirty years ago."

Gabriel lifted his head and cast his coach a look that would have frozen water.

Michel appeared amused. "Good afternoon, Gabriel. I was waiting for you to show up."

With a laugh, Michel retrieved the referee.

Gabriel followed, exhaling fire.

Chapter Thirty

Halloween
October 31, 2012
Cambridge, Massachusetts

Julianne's cell phone vibrated with a text.

She and Gabriel were trick-or-treating with Clare, while Rebecca remained at the house to hand out candy. Clare, who was not yet two months old, was dressed as a pumpkin. She wore a footed sleeper underneath an orange vest that featured a jack-o'-lantern's eyes, nose, and mouth. And she wore an orange cap that had a stem attached to it.

Gabriel snapped an infinity of photographs of said pumpkin before they'd even left the house.

He'd balked at the notion of taking Clare trick-or-treating, given her tender age, but once Julia had dressed her in the costume, he changed his mind. The proud papa strutted with Clare in his arms, in-

troducing her to the neighbors, some of whom remarked on the flamboyance of flamingos that had appeared on the Emersons' lawn back
in September. And the single sunglasses-wearing flamingo that still sat
in the front yard, much to Gabriel's embarrassment and Julia's glee.

The text on Julia's phone read,

> Jules, where the hell are you?
> I called the landline and got the machine.
> Did you dress Clare for Halloween? I want to see!
> Luv, R.

"Who's that?" Gabriel peered nosily at Julia's screen.

"Your sister." Julia texted a response as they walked to the next
house.

> Hey, Rach.
> Sorry about that.
> We're trick-or-treating.
> Call me.
> Luv, J.

"I haven't heard from her since before we went to Scotland." Gabriel adjusted Clare's cap, for her stem had gone awry. She looked for
her mother over his shoulder.

"I texted her about what happened with Cecilia." At this Gabriel
glowered. "We've been playing phone tag."

A moment later, Julia's phone rang. She hung back on the sidewalk while Gabriel carried Clare to their neighbor Leslie's front door.

"Jules! What's Clare wearing?" Rachel's voice was exuberant, which
made Julia relax. The last time they'd seen one another, Rachel had
been very unhappy.

"She's dressed as a pumpkin. We took a lot of pictures. I'll email them to you." Julia watched as Leslie opened her door and reacted with delight at the sight of Gabriel and his baby. Julia placed Rachel on speakerphone so she could discreetly take photos of her family.

"Good," said Rachel. "Listen, I'm sorry I didn't call you when you told me what went down with your supervisor. How are you feeling?"

Julia calculated her words carefully. She explained about Gabriel's lectureship and their difference of opinion as to what to do about Cecilia.

Rachel was horrified. "I'm sorry, but I wouldn't let that woman dictate my future. Students study abroad all the time."

"Unfortunately, when you're a graduate student, you're under the patronage of your supervisor. If she drops me, and she can without having to justify her decision to anyone, then I'm stuck. I won't have a supervisor, and that will set me back months if not a year."

Rachel swore loudly. "What did Katherine say?"

"I haven't told her."

"You haven't told her?" Rachel practically shouted. "Are you nuts? Katherine is like Wonder Woman in an age-appropriate pantsuit. She can fix anything."

Julia stifled a laugh. "She's at Oxford this year. There's nothing she can do."

"I thought she was switching to Harvard."

"Not until next year."

"Then work with her, instead."

"It's not that simple. I can't work with her until after she arrives. And it will look bad if Cecilia refuses to be on my committee. Word will get out."

"But Katherine is Wonder Woman. Why would you want to work with Black Widow, when you can work with Wonder Woman?"

"I thought black widows were spiders."

"Stay current, Jules. Black Widow is an Avengers superhero. Do you want me to go talk to her?"

Julia made a strange gurgling sound in her throat. "Talk to Cecilia?"

"Yeah."

"No. Thank you, but no, I don't want you to talk to Cecilia." Julia watched as Gabriel walked toward her with Clare, carrying a bag of candy. "I'm hoping Cecilia will change her mind before next summer, which is when I have to set things up with Edinburgh, if I'm going."

"Academia is fucked up. Seriously. I thought Philadelphia mayoral politics were dysfunctional, but academia is a whole other level."

"You aren't wrong."

"Speaking of black widows, what's happening with Rebecca and my dad?" Rachel changed the subject.

Julia locked eyes with her husband, who had overheard Rachel's question.

Gabriel gave Julia a quizzical look. "Why is she asking that?"

"Nothing is happening," Julia replied. "Rebecca is here, with us. Richard is in Selinsgrove. Nothing has arrived from him in the mail."

"They're probably sexting."

"Rachel!" Gabriel exclaimed, looking a little green.

"Tell my brother I'm kidding. Dad doesn't even know how to text," Rachel said gloomily. "Hey, I know. Why don't we set Dad up with Katherine?"

Julia silently stared at her phone. "Do you know how old Katherine is?"

"No."

"Well, she's much older than Richard."

"Yeah, well, Wonder Woman was much older than Steve Trevor. It worked for them."

"Let me speak to her." Gabriel exchanged Clare for Julia's cell phone.

"It's me," he announced. "Why are you asking about Rebecca and Richard?"

"It was just a question," Rachel backpedaled meekly. "I was wondering if things were . . . progressing."

"They went to dinner."

"So they went on a date after Aaron and I left."

Gabriel lifted his face to the sky, as if seeking divine intervention. "Although neither of them informed me as to the correct adjective to describe their dinner, I can tell you it wasn't a date."

"How do you know?"

"Because I know Richard," Gabriel sounded impatient. "Which raises the question, why are you asking me and not your father?"

Rachel was silent for a moment. "He's your father, too."

"I repeat the question."

Julia tapped his arm and glared at him.

He shrugged and she gave him a scolding look in return.

Gabriel pursed his lips. "I don't mean to be—unsympathetic."

Julia widened her eyes.

"How are you feeling, Rachel?" He gave Julia a look as if to say *See? I can be sensitive.*

"I'm okay. I just don't want to be blindsided, you know? In case Dad decides to invite Rebecca home for Thanksgiving."

"That won't happen," Gabriel said firmly. "Rebecca has already booked her flight to Colorado to see her son. She's spending Thanksgiving and Christmas with her children and never even mentioned the possibility of visiting Selinsgrove."

"Okay." Rachel sounded relieved.

"You need to talk to Richard." Gabriel lowered his voice.

"All right. Aaron just got home. I have to go. Tell Jules and Clare I love them and send me pictures of her costume."

Gabriel's lips turned up. "I will. She looks great."

"Bye, Gabriel." Rachel ended the call.

Julia's gaze met Gabriel's. "What was that all about?"

"She's jumping to conclusions because she's too stubborn to speak to Richard directly." Gabriel handed Julia the bag of candy they'd been collecting and took Clare into his arms. "Come on, pumpkin. There are more neighbors to meet."

"If we're going to keep walking, then I need a chocolate bar." Julia perused the contents of the candy bag. She unwrapped some chocolate and took a large bite before feeding some to Gabriel. "I don't know what we're going to do with all this stuff. You know babies can't eat candy."

"Ah yes, I am aware of that." Gabriel angled for another bite.

Julia fed him, and he licked the melting chocolate from her fingers.

She stared from her fingers to his mouth.

He gave his lower lip a sensual lick. "I'm sure we'll find a use for it, Mrs. Emerson. Two more houses and then we can explore erotic uses of chocolate at home. Let's go." He began walking in the direction of the next house.

Julia gazed at her fingers and then hurried after him.

Chapter Thirty-One

Thanksgiving
November 2012
Selinsgrove, Pennsylvania

That's a good-looking turkey." Scott Clark, Gabriel and Rachel's brother, gazed admiringly across the living room. Scott was six foot three and broad-shouldered, with blond hair and gray eyes, and was married to Tammy. He had adopted Tammy's son, Quinn, when they married.

The turkey in question was Clare, who'd been dressed in a costume by her aunt Rachel. Quinn, who was three years old, was sitting next to the baby, who was lying on a blanket. He was trying to hand her toys, which elicited squeals of delight and laughter. Occasionally, he would pet her head.

"Thank you for noticing the costume." Rachel dropped down onto the floor to play with the children. She was happy to be home, if a little nostalgic. And although she hadn't mentioned it, she was relieved Rebecca was in Colorado for the holiday.

Her father hadn't seen her since his visit in September, or so Julia had said. Rachel felt a twinge of guilt for feeling jealous of her father's friendship with a woman his own age. It seemed her grief ran deeper than she realized.

She turned to gaze at the front windows. Julia had put battery-operated candles in each of them, a custom in Massachusetts. Rachel couldn't help but remember her mother doing the same thing, but with a single lit candle that hoped for Gabriel's return.

Gabriel entered the room carrying an enormous turkey on a platter and set it in the middle of the dining room table. "Dinner is served."

The family found their chairs. Scott put Quinn in a high chair between Tammy and himself. Rachel insisted on holding Clare while Julia ate, choosing to eat later. And as ever, Richard sat at the head of the table, smiling proudly at his children and their spouses.

"Let's pray," he announced. Everyone held hands.

"Our Father, we thank you for this day and for the many blessings you have given to us. Thank you for Grace and for our children. Thank you for their wives and husband and for their children. Thank you for the addition of little Clare, who is such a joy. May you keep us safe. May you show us your light. Bless this food and the hands that prepared it. Amen."

Rachel said *Amen*, but she hadn't closed her eyes. Still, in the midst of his prayer she felt a comforting presence. She wished the presence were that of her mother.

As Richard carved the turkey, he addressed Julia, who sat at his right. "When are Tom and his family coming over?"

"They were supposed to come tomorrow, but Tommy was running a fever this morning and so they're at the Children's Hospital in Philadelphia. Diane says Tommy will be fine, but they're admitting him for observation." Julia helped Richard serve the turkey and began passing serving dishes piled with vegetables.

"I'm sorry, Jules." Scott's voice was gentle. He gave her a sympathetic look.

"Tommy has already had two major heart operations, and he's supposed to have another soon. My dad and Diane send their best to everyone." Julia gave Scott a strained smile.

"What's wrong with your brother?" Tammy asked quietly.

"He was born with hypoplastic left heart syndrome, which means the left side of his heart was undeveloped," Julia explained. "But the Children's Hospital has treated a number of infants with the same condition. So he's in good hands."

"Where's Rebecca? Gabriel said she made the pies and the rolls." Scott began cramming one of said rolls into his mouth, absolutely ignoring the death glare he was getting from his sister.

"Her son lives in Colorado and she's spending the holiday with him." Julia glanced at Rachel out of the corner of her eye and busied herself with putting food on her plate.

"How do you feel about Rebecca, Dad?" Scott continued. "She's a nice lady. Hell of a cook."

Richard froze, suspending the carving knife and fork in midair.

"Seriously, Scott. Is there a land mine you haven't stepped on?" Rachel snapped. "Oh, wait. I've got one. Everyone has experienced a visitation from Mom, except me."

"What are you talking about?" asked Scott. "What visitation?"

Rachel stared at her brother for a beat. "Well, at least I'm not the only one."

"Not the only one what?" Scott's eyebrows shot up.

"*Rachel.*" Richard gave his daughter a pained look.

She turned her face away.

An uncomfortable silence filled the room.

"We have some news." Aaron changed the subject, putting his

arm around his wife. "I was offered a job with Microsoft New England. And I took it."

"What? Congratulations!" Scott reached across the table to shake Aaron's hand. "I thought you already worked for Microsoft."

"This is more research-oriented. I'll be working with a team of programmers, right in Cambridge." Aaron hugged Rachel's shoulders. "I start in January."

"You'll be closer to Gabriel and Julia." Richard smiled and continued carving the turkey as exuberant congratulations passed around the table.

Julia eyed Rachel cautiously.

"What about you, Rach?" Scott asked. "What about your job in the mayor's office in Philadelphia?"

Everyone looked at her expectantly. She bounced Clare on her lap. "I turned in my notice because I found another job. I've been hired to be a public relations supervisor at Dunkin' Donuts in Canton, just outside Boston. Dunkie's is in the same company as Baskin-Robbins, which means I'll get unlimited coffee, doughnuts, and ice cream." Rachel blew a raspberry against Clare's neck and the baby squealed.

"That's a dream job," Tammy observed. "I love Dunkie's."

"Exactly." Rachel sat up a little straighter. "They have incredible brand recognition, and everyone loves them. Corporate headquarters is casual; I'll be able to wear jeans to work. And they have lots of incentives and perks." She exchanged a look with Aaron, who grinned.

"I'm so happy for you." Julia hugged her friend. "You'll be closer to us and you'll be able to see more of Clare."

"We've put our condo up for sale. Hopefully, we'll close before we move. Now we're looking for somewhere to live." Rachel batted her eyelashes at her brother.

Gabriel exchanged a look with Julianne. "Where do you want to live? Canton? Back Bay?"

"We don't know," Aaron interjected. "We need to sell our place first and we need to consider Rachel's commute time."

"Driving out to Canton every day will get tiresome," Gabriel announced. "You may want to live out on the south shore and have Aaron commute to Cambridge."

"Who wants to live on the south shore? We want to be where the action is. And where the baby is." Rachel bounced Clare on her lap.

Julianne opened her mouth, but before she could invite Rachel and Aaron to stay in Cambridge, Gabriel grasped her hand under the table. And squeezed.

"Let's discuss it later," he whispered in her ear.

"But whatever happens," Rachel continued, "we will be around while you're in Edinburgh, Gabriel. Which means we can help Julia while you're gone."

Gabriel started. Although his eyes stared straight into Rachel's, his words were directed at his wife. "I'm not going without them."

Rachel appeared confused. "I thought Jules said her director was demanding she stay at Harvard?"

"That's what her director said." Gabriel took a drink of water. "I refuse to take *no* for an answer."

A long look passed between Julia and Gabriel. Her eyes darted to Rachel and back again. She lifted her eyebrows at her husband.

He pushed back his chair. "Let's toast to Aaron and Rachel. Congratulations on your accomplishments. And good luck with this new chapter of your life."

Everyone lifted their glass to toast the couple.

Richard finished carving and serving the turkey and finally sat down.

Julia sampled three or four bites of her dinner, and Clare began to cry.

"I'll walk with her." Rachel lifted the baby to her shoulder and stood.

But a few minutes later, when the baby didn't settle, Julia inter-vened. "She's probably hungry. I'll take her upstairs to feed her and be right back. Excuse me, everyone."

She kissed Clare on the cheek and climbed the stairs to the sec-ond floor.

❋

"Is dinner over?" Julia asked Gabriel as he entered the master bed-room.

He shook his head. "We are going to wait to serve dessert until after you have dinner. Is she finished?"

"Just finished." Julia handed him the baby and he put her over his shoulder.

After he'd burped and changed her, he picked up a stuffed rabbit toy and brought it close to her nose and then withdrew it. Clare grinned and waved her arms and legs. He repeated the movement. "Do you like the bunny, Clare? Do you like the bunny?"

He waggled the toy at Julia. "Did Rachel buy this?"

"No. Paul sent it."

Gabriel dropped the bunny on top of the changing table. "Angel-fucker."

"Language," Julia admonished him, trying to keep a straight face.

"We'll have to destroy it. It's clearly contaminated." Gabriel regarded the toy with distaste.

"Don't be ridiculous. About a week ago, Paul sent a very nice card, with the bunny and a copy of *The Velveteen Rabbit*. I thought it was kind."

Gabriel sniffed. "He always had a rabbit fetish. In fact, he used to call you Rabbit."

"He did." Julia could only laugh at Gabriel's indignation, which was rather amusing. "He doesn't anymore. So when we see him at Professor Wodehouse's workshop in April, you don't need to worry."

Gabriel growled. "So he's going?"

"He said so in his card."

"Which was addressed to you, I imagine?" Gabriel picked up the bunny with two fingers, examining it as if it held the secrets of the universe.

Clare tracked the movement and reacted by waving her arms enthusiastically.

"The package was addressed to Clare. But the card congratulated both of us." Julia crossed to where Gabriel was standing and hugged him around the waist. "It's time for you to let go of the past. You've held a grudge long enough."

"I was nice to Paul the last time we met. We even shook hands." Gabriel placed the bunny on Clare's chest to see what she would do. The toy slid off to the side and she squawked a little.

"You're still making him call you *Professor Emerson*."

Gabriel drew himself up to his full height. "I *am* Professor Emerson." He glanced over at the baby. His expression softened. "Since Clare has grown attached to the rabbit, I suppose she should keep it."

Julia hugged him again. "See? That didn't hurt at all."

She kissed his cheek and exited the bedroom, hurrying down the hall so she could finally enjoy her Thanksgiving dinner.

Gabriel lifted his daughter and gazed into her big blue eyes. "Daddy will buy you a better bunny."

Clare laughed.

Chapter Thirty-Two

"C ome take a walk with me," Gabriel whispered.

Julia was standing in the kitchen, holding Clare, having just finished clearing the table. She noticed that Gabriel was holding a familiar-looking blanket.

She looked out the kitchen windows over the back deck and toward the old orchard that stood behind the house. The orchard was one of Gabriel's favorite places on earth. And in its center was a clearing he revered like a cathedral.

They'd spent their first night together, chastely, in that orchard, years ago when she was a teenager. Gabriel had asked her to marry him in that same sacred place. And they'd made love there once or twice. Or more. She'd lost count.

Gabriel's eyes were solemn. Something lurked beneath their sapphire depths.

"I need to help clean up." Julia gestured at the pots and pans and dishes that were stacked all over the counters.

"We've got it." Rachel made a shooing motion with the dish towel she was holding. "Go."

"Go ahead." Richard nodded. "Most of the dishes will go in the dishwasher."

Julia bounced Clare in her arms, making eye contact with Gabriel.

"We'll help when we come back," he offered.

"And I can take the baby." Tammy held her arms out and Julia transferred Clare to her.

Tammy hugged the child close. "I've missed having a baby. I can't wait to have another one."

"What?" Scott came up behind her, touching Clare's head.

"I miss having a baby." Tammy's expression grew hopeful.

"You never said anything," Scott whispered, touching her face. He leaned forward and whispered something in her ear.

"So yeah, you guys can go for a walk." Rachel lifted her voice, trying to draw attention away from the private exchange between Scott and Tammy.

"Are you sure?" Julia asked.

"Go." Once again, Rachel waved her dish towel like a flag.

"I left my coat in the car," Julia said to Gabriel.

"One minute." He kissed her cheek and disappeared out the front door.

As he walked to the SUV that was parked in the driveway, he felt something eerie behind him. He turned his head slowly and saw a black Nissan idling three houses down, across the street.

Gabriel examined the car out of the corner of his eye. When he was satisfied it matched the car he'd seen in Cambridge, he calmly walked the length of the driveway to the old garage and opened the door.

No more than thirty seconds later, he emerged from the garage carrying an aluminum baseball bat.

He broke into a run as soon as his feet hit the sidewalk, sprinting toward the black Nissan.

The driver revved the engine and peeled out, leaving tire marks on the asphalt.

Gabriel switched the bat to his other hand and picked up a large rock. He threw it hard. The rock hit the car's rear window, shattering it on impact.

The car swerved as the glass spilled out over the trunk and onto the road.

Gabriel watched as the driver turned down a side street, speeding out of sight.

After taking a moment to calm down, Gabriel walked nonchalantly back to the house, not caring if any of Richard's neighbors had witnessed the altercation. He retrieved Julia's coat from the car, depositing the baseball bat in the back of the SUV, just in case.

Chapter Thirty-Three

I t's warmer than I expected." Julia unbuttoned her coat as they walked across the back lawn. The inky sky stretched above them, and the stars and moon shone down. But the temperature was unseasonably warm, especially given Gabriel's determined walking pace.

He shined a flashlight to illuminate the way, gripping Julia's hand tightly.

She kept pace with him despite the discomfort in her leg. The numbness hadn't gone away, although it varied in intensity. Still, she'd hidden it from Gabriel, and Dr. Rubio, and everyone else. Somehow she hoped it would simply disappear.

They entered the woods, picking their way over fallen branches and sticks to embark on a well-trodden path.

Julia wondered about her recent issues with memory. She was still sleep-deprived, despite dropping Clare's two-o'clock-in-the-morning feeding. Getting more sleep had aided Julia's memory, but she still struggled to assimilate new information. Ever since coming home from the hospital, she'd found she needed to read and reread academic books and articles, in a way she never had before. Novels were different. Late at night or early in the morning, Julia would read ebooks on her cell phone.

"Careful." Gabriel shined the flashlight over a large fallen branch. He stopped, grabbed Julia by the waist, and lifted her over it.

She laughed in surprise, although she appreciated his gallantry.

She'd been in these woods hundreds of times, most of them with Gabriel. She was fairly sure she could find her way back to the house, even under the cover of darkness. Although she remembered with horror the time she'd gotten lost. . . .

It occurred to her that perhaps the human memory was like the sea. It moved with regularity, carrying bits of things on a current. But when the tempest came, that which was long forgotten bubbled to the surface. Julia never thought about being lost in the woods, if she could help it. But the memory would bubble up unbidden or trouble her in dreams. She clasped Gabriel's arm, moving her body closer to his as the orchard swallowed them up.

"Not far now." His tone was comforting.

A few more steps and they stood at the edge of the clearing.

Gabriel sighed. "Paradise."

He led Julia to the center of the clearing and spread the blanket. Then he tugged her to recline atop it, switching off the flashlight. He held her hand as they gazed up at the stars and beyond. "Katherine emailed me."

"What did she say?"

"She asked if she could spend Christmas with us and Clare. I didn't respond. I wanted to ask you first."

"That's all right with me, if it's all right with Richard."

"I'll ask him." Gabriel paused. "You know that Katherine will find out about Cecilia."

"Not from us."

Gabriel's body tensed. "It's bound to come out."

"It's still my decision." Julia turned her head, examining what she could see of Gabriel's strong profile. She elected to change the subject. "What do you like about the orchard?"

He took his time answering her question. "It's peaceful. The woods are so thick, even in fall, you feel as if you're in your own private world. I can think here."

Julia lifted his hand to her mouth and kissed it. "I've been thinking about your lectureship."

Now he turned his head. "What have you been thinking?"

"Everything about it is so fancy. The dinner they threw us at the castle. The announcement and reception. The media interest." She gazed at him in admiration. "You could speak on any subject you want. And people would listen."

"They expect me to speak about Dante."

"Yes, because that's your area of specialization. But you could choose any subject. Anything at all."

Gabriel looked back at the stars. "I enjoy studying Dante. This is a chance for me to work something out."

"What?"

"About Dante and Beatrice. I feel as if Dante is hiding something in *The Divine Comedy*—that he isn't telling us the whole story."

"The whole story about what?"

"They marry other people. He's devastated when Beatrice dies and resolves to become a better man. He writes poems in tribute to her. But then he admits to having strayed from the right path at the middle of his life, and Beatrice tells Virgil Dante did so out of fear."

"So far, so good."

"Indeed. But there's the passage in *Purgatorio* where Beatrice scolds him about other women. He admits his guilt, bathes in the river of forgetfulness, and then the theological virtues declare him faithful to Beatrice."

Gabriel turned on his side to look at Julianne. "Faithless, faithful. He can't be both at the same time."

"No, he can't. That was the demon's point when he described Guido da Montefeltro's sin."

"So which is it, Beatrice?" Gabriel whispered. "Faithless or faithful?"

"Dante always writes with more than one meaning. I don't think Beatrice is just talking about Dante's devotion to her. She's talking about God."

"That's right."

"Dante admits his guilt—both at the beginning of the *Inferno* and when he feels shame in front of Beatrice."

"Yes."

"I don't understand how Beatrice can be so forgiving at the beginning of the *Inferno*, when she says Dante is trapped by fear and she begs Virgil to help him, and then so condemning in *Purgatorio*."

"I don't, either. But I'm hoping to figure it out."

"You'll have to do some detective work, but it sounds like fun. You have a year to prepare your lectures."

"Yes." With his other hand, Gabriel reached over to touch Julia's face. "You define love for me. And I believe Beatrice defined love for Dante, which is why I think we're missing part of their story."

"Grief clouds the mind," Julia said gently. "Look at my father. I don't think he would ever have gotten involved with someone like Deb Lundy if he hadn't been so messed up after my mother died."

"That's true."

"Your sister is having a hard time right now. Much as I think it's hilarious she believes Katherine is Wonder Woman, her pairing of Katherine with Richard is ridiculous."

"*Ridiculous* is a bit strong, don't you think?" Gabriel's tone was grave. "Wonder Woman can have her choice of partners at any age."

Julia struck Gabriel playfully in the chest. "It's the costume. It does things to people."

"It does indeed." Gabriel captured her wrist, his voice growing husky. "Which raises the question, why didn't you dress up for me for Halloween?"

"Buy me the costume, and help me get a good night's sleep, and I'll dress up for you anytime."

Gabriel moved closer to Julia on the blanket, wrapping his arm around her waist. "I'll hold you to that."

"Please."

Gabriel chuckled and his smile widened. "How fortunate I am to have married my Beatrice and to be lying by her side."

He kissed her reverently, pressing his lips to hers. When he lifted his head, he stared down into her eyes. "You can't fault me for wanting to do everything within my power to protect you. And to take you and Clare with me to Scotland."

"Of course I can't fault you." Julia reached up to twine her fingers in his hair. "We want the same thing. But my situation at Harvard is precarious."

Gabriel's eyes reflected understanding. "It's difficult for me to stand by and do nothing."

"You aren't doing nothing." Julia's whisper grew fierce. "You're supporting me."

"I just love you so desperately." Gabriel lowered his head and tugged on her lower lip. He spread his lips across hers, firmly and with intention.

His hands parted her coat and lifted her sweater, spanning her waist and stroking the bare skin with his thumbs.

Julia made a noise and they parted. "Here? Now?"

"I want you." Gabriel's eyes shone with desire. "Right here and right now."

Her hands lifted to his shoulder and she caressed his neck as their mouths joined once again. Their lower limbs tangled with one another.

Above them, the moon hid behind a cloud and darkness became emboldened. Gabriel seized that opportunity to flick open the button on Julia's jeans and rest his hand across her abdomen, avoiding her scar.

She fluttered beneath him.

His lips found her neck in the dark, trailing kisses up and down her throat. He worshipped the indentation at the base of her throat and ascended to the space behind her ear. "What do you want?"

"I want you to touch me." She covered his hand with hers and inched his farther down, retreating when he dipped below her underwear.

His fingers caressed her before passing between her legs.

He kissed the expanse of skin above her breasts before unbuttoning her shirt with one hand. With practiced ease he continued to embrace her with his lips, while his long fingers sought their prize.

He lowered her bra, exposing her breast to the night air. His mouth descended, kissing around the nipple while stroking her below.

"It's all right," she encouraged him, applying light pressure to the back of his head. "I'm not overly sensitive tonight."

He chuckled against her skin, for her eagerness pleased him. Experimentally, he licked her nipple. It constricted in the cool November air. Then his warm mouth engulfed her, licking and gently teasing.

Julia lifted her hips as a strangled moan escaped her chest. She was trying to be quiet.

"You can be loud," he encouraged her, taking her nipple into his mouth once again. "We have more privacy here than at the house."

She gave voice to her pleas, begging him to taste her other breast and lifting her hips as he stroked between her legs.

"Do you want to come?" he rasped, paying homage to her other nipple.

"I want to come with you inside me." The confession had scarcely left her mouth when he was tugging down her jeans and removing his own.

The voyeuristic moon shone, giving light to Gabriel's endeavors. He took one of her hands in his, resting it beside her head.

He cupped her opposite hip and separated her legs more widely. His hips nested with hers.

Gabriel's eyes measured hers as he pressed forward. Again, with the practiced ease born of lovers who'd coupled to infinity, he slid inside.

Julia moaned.

"I want you to move." Gabriel's speech was terse, clipped. He seemed overwhelmed, holding himself still over her.

Julia did as she was bidden, lifting her hips and gripping his backside to urge him deeper.

Gabriel watched. Then he captured her mouth, kissing her deeply. "You arouse and delight me."

"Good," she managed to say, lifting her hips once again.

Gabriel began to move, slowly at first, marking his pace by Julia's reactions. Then he began to speed up, thrusting more deeply.

Julia's hands slid up to his shoulders and she clung to him as he drove inside her.

She wanted to signal to him that she was close, poised just on the edge. But before she could whisper in his ear, she fell. Her hands gripped Gabriel's shoulders and she tightened, eyes wide open, as she climaxed.

Gabriel watched raptly, increasing his pace in order to chase after her. She'd already softened in his arms and almost hazarded a smile when his own pleasure overtook him.

His jaw hung slack and his hips jerked. A few more thrusts and then he, too, was still.

He exhaled against her lips. "Sweetheart?"

"I'm good."

Julia snuggled against her beloved under the blanket, while the stars in the canopy of Heaven winked down at them.

Chapter Thirty-Four

Tammy and Scott took Clare into the living room while Richard and Rachel attacked the dishes.

Richard picked up a crystal goblet and began drying it. "I can remember doing this with your mother. The crystal can't go in the dishwasher, she said, and so we'd have to wash it by hand."

"She was right." Rachel continued washing and rinsing crystal and placing it carefully on the drying rack.

"I'm proud of you." Richard's tone was low.

"For what?"

"For having the courage to embark on a new path. I know you enjoyed your job in the mayor's office, but I always envisioned you doing something more creative. Your new position sounds exciting."

"Yeah, I'm looking forward to it." She finished washing the crystal and drained the sink. Then she filled it with fresh, soapy water and began tackling the stack of pots and pans.

"Your mother would be proud of you."

Rachel fixated on scrubbing the inside of a pot.

"Talk to me, sweetheart." Richard leaned against the counter and focused his whole attention on his daughter.

Rachel paused. "Mom visits you and Gabriel but she hasn't visited me."

Richard's silver eyebrows lifted. "What do you mean?"

"You see Mom in your dreams. Gabriel told me she's appeared to him and spoken to him. But she hasn't appeared to me."

Richard folded his dish towel pensively. "It's true I dream about your mother. Not every night, but many nights. I find those dreams comforting. It's not certain she's appearing to me. It could be wish fulfillment on my part."

Rachel lifted her head. "You don't believe that."

Richard hesitated. "No, I don't. I think some of it is wish fulfillment, but there have been a couple of conversations we had that I believe to be genuine.

"I can't speak for Gabriel. Perhaps Mom had unfinished business with him."

"What about me?" Rachel dropped the pot into the water, causing suds to splash all over her clothes. "I'm her daughter. We were close. Why doesn't she have unfinished business with me?"

Richard put down his dish towel. "I don't know the answer to that question. What would you like to tell her, if she were here instead of me?"

Rachel peered out the window, over the back patio. "I'd tell her I love her. And that I wish we'd had more time."

"I wish the same. I never expected to lose your mother so early. I thought we'd grow old together. Travel the world. Annoy our children." He tousled Rachel's hair affectionately.

Rachel examined the pot and rinsed it out. She placed it on the drying rack.

Richard lifted the pot in order to dry it. "I knew your mother, perhaps better than anyone. She loved you without reservation. I know she's proud of you. I know she still loves you. And whether or not she is actually present here in the house, I feel her love and her comfort. And I am convinced she is always with us."

Rachel placed the roasting pan in the sink and began scrubbing. "That's because you believe in God and an afterlife."

Richard jerked. "Don't you?"

"Sometimes. Sometimes, I doubt."

"I wrestle with my own doubts, as well. Especially at night. But I have felt your mother's presence. And I have no doubt, no doubt at all, as to what I was feeling. That feeling has nothing to do with the other beliefs you just mentioned."

Rachel glanced at her father. His expression was concerned, and earnest, and honest. And she knew him well enough to know he did not lie.

Richard put the pot in one of the drawers and leaned against the counter. "I know I'm not your mother. I know I'm just—your dad. But I'm here. I'm here and I'm listening."

"Dad." Rachel shook the suds off her hands and wiped them on her apron. Then she hugged her father. "I'm glad you're here. Don't think you aren't important to me. I just miss Mom."

"So do I." Richard hugged her back. "I know you have concerns about Rebecca. We are friends and I hope we will remain friends. But I am not going to pursue a new relationship or remarry. My heart belongs to your mother. I'm going to do my best to live a life that honors her memory. I'm going to remain devoted to you and your brothers, and your families."

Rachel sniffled against his shoulder.

"Life can change in an instant." Richard's voice shook. "But we have to have hope and look forward. And not waste our time in conflict with those we love. So don't be angry at your mother because she hasn't appeared to you. And don't fight with Scott."

"I like fighting with Scott." Rachel's voice was muffled.

"Could you try to like it a little less?"

"That I could do. I love you."

"I love you, too."

Father and daughter hugged in the kitchen, while nearby, a candle flickered in the window.

Chapter Thirty-Five

*C*rack!

Gabriel sat up, his face pointed in the direction of the noise.

"What is it?" Julia asked, clutching the blanket to her naked chest.

Gabriel hushed her, straining his hearing while fumbling for his clothes.

Snap! Another branch broke, sounding closer.

Gabriel stood and yanked on his clothes. Julia did the same, slightly dazed.

As he scanned the tree line, Gabriel perceived what he thought was the beam of a flashlight. It was visible only for a second, and then it was gone.

"Someone is out there," he whispered, pulling on his coat. "I want you to run back to the house, quick as you can."

He felt around for the flashlight and began rolling up the blankets.

"We should stay together," Julia whispered back, thrusting her arms into her coat.

Gabriel helped her to her feet and handed her the flashlight. "No. It could just be a teenager, spying on us. Or it could be something else. I want you to go back to the house. Can you find the way?"

"What else could it be? A deer?"

"There isn't time," Gabriel hissed.

Julia noted his agitated tone and decided not to press him. She tucked the blankets under her arm. "Should I call the police?"

"Not yet." Gabriel kissed her on the forehead and pointed her toward the house. "Run."

Julia switched on the flashlight and hurried into the woods.

Chapter Thirty-Six

G abriel sprinted to the tree line. The moon favored him, pouring light above the trees, which dispersed to the ground below.

Noises came from just ahead. Gabriel gave chase, but the figure wasn't visible nor was any flashlight.

Gabriel knew the woods well. His long legs ate up the distance as he pulled closer and closer to the source of the sounds.

And then the noises stopped.

Gabriel slowed, turning his head in an effort to discern any possible clue. The moon chose that moment to hide and the woods were dark. He could barely see a short distance in front of him.

He stood next to a tree and waited, listening for any movement. A breath of wind whispered through the trees. His heart pounded in his chest.

Someone was out there. Someone had come across him and Julianne in the clearing. Someone who drove a black Nissan was stalking him.

Now he was standing in the woods effectively playing a game of chicken with an unseen intruder.

He inched forward, placing his feet carefully to avoid stepping on a branch. He circled around where he thought the trespasser might be, hoping to use the power of surprise.

But when he came to the center of the circle, there was no one to be found. Unless the intruder had dematerialized, Gabriel must have lost him. After thirty minutes of searching, he gave up.

He switched directions, walking quickly and quietly back to the clearing, and then skirted it, heading toward the house.

He was almost to the edge of the back lawn when he came across something he had not expected—Julianne's flashlight, still lit, lying on the ground.

Panicking, he cast around until he found her, lying a few feet away.

Chapter Thirty-Seven

O h my God!" Rachel flew from the sink to the back door, suds and soapy water dripping from her hands.

She ran out onto the back deck, just as Gabriel crossed the lawn, carrying Julia in his arms.

"What happened?" Rachel ran to her brother's side, noting that Julia was conscious, but her pale face was pinched in pain.

"I think she broke her ankle." Gabriel's words were clipped, as if he, too, were in pain. His hair was disheveled, his coat streaked with dirt, and mud was spattered across his jeans.

"What about you? Did you fall?"

Gabriel ignored Rachel's question and brushed past her and Richard, carrying Julia into the house.

Scott, Tammy, and Aaron were all gathered in the kitchen.

"I tripped over a branch." Julianne gave the group a sheepish look. "And then I couldn't get up. I would have called for help, but I left my cell phone upstairs."

"Can you put weight on it?" Aaron stepped forward, a concerned look on his face.

Julia shook her head.

"I'm taking her to the hospital," Gabriel announced. "But before we go, you should know that I think someone else was out there. I chased them but couldn't find them."

"Me and Scott can go outside and look around," Aaron said.

"Also, keep an eye out for a black Nissan with tinted windows. I saw the same car outside our house in Cambridge and down the street before we went for our walk."

"You never told me," Julia whispered. Her eyes met Gabriel's and he looked away.

"Let me get some ice." Richard opened the freezer and removed a tray of ice cubes. He placed the ice in a freezer bag, sealed it, and wrapped it in a towel.

Julia took the ice pack gratefully.

"Did you get a license plate?" Scott asked.

"No visible license plate."

"Should we call the police?" Rachel interjected.

"We seem to have cops here every Thanksgiving." Scott crossed his arms over his chest.

Gabriel stopped in front of him. "Julianne's ex-boyfriend attacked her in her own home three years ago. A strange car sat outside our house in Cambridge on two separate occasions and then miraculously shows up in this neighborhood, on Thanksgiving. What do you want to say to me, Scott?"

Scott uncrossed his arms. "Was it Simon?"

"I don't know." Gabriel clenched his jaw.

A long look passed between the two brothers. Scott gestured to the door. "I'll take a look around with Aaron. If we see anything, we'll call you."

"What about the baby?" Julia managed to say, wincing in pain.

Gabriel was still for a moment. "Rachel?"

Rachel pushed past Scott. "I'll get the diaper bag. Tammy, can you put Clare in her baby carrier? We don't know how long Julia will be at the hospital and the baby will need to be fed."

"Thank you." Gabriel turned and carried Julianne out to the car.

A few minutes later Richard followed, carrying Clare.

Chapter Thirty-Eight

Later that evening
Sunbury, Pennsylvania

Gabriel approached Richard, who was rocking Clare in her car seat in the waiting room of the hospital.

Richard stood, his gaze focusing on his son. "What did the doctor say?"

"She thinks Julianne's ankle is broken. They're sending her for X-rays. I was not allowed to accompany her." Gabriel sounded bitter.

Richard continued rocking the baby, who, on hearing her father's voice, turned her head in order to look at him. "Emergency room physicians have to investigate all options when it comes to a suspicious injury."

"Suspicious?" Gabriel's dark brows knitted together. "What are you talking about?"

"A new mother comes to the ER and claims to have fallen. She is accompanied by an agitated husband who doesn't want his wife to be alone with the physician on call."

"That's preposterous." Gabriel swore. "I simply wanted to help. Julia has a medical chart at this hospital, because she's been here before. We've all been to this hospital. Grace used to volunteer here."

"I know," Richard said softly, a faraway expression on his face. "This is where Grace found you."

Gabriel hid his reaction by removing Clare from her baby carrier and cuddling her against his shoulder.

"You and I were here with Julia once before. Think about the circumstances surrounding that visit." Richard gave Gabriel a meaningful look.

A flash of recognition passed across Gabriel's features.

Richard continued. "A good physician would review Julia's chart and see that the last time she was here, she was treated for injuries related to a physical assault. Now she appears with a baby, having fallen during a walk through the woods. At night. With her husband, who appears agitated. Wouldn't you be suspicious?"

Gabriel nodded.

"Let the doctors do their job." Richard rubbed his chin. "Did you speak with the police?"

"No, but Scott called. He and Aaron combed the woods with flashlights. They didn't see anything. But I think we're going to take another look in daylight." Gabriel kissed the side of Clare's head. "I called Jack Mitchell."

"And?"

"I gave Jack the description of the car and asked him to find it. Tonight is an escalation . . ." Gabriel shook his head.

"Tell me what you think is happening."

"It can't be a coincidence that the same car is driving by our house in Cambridge and then shows up in Selinsgrove. A casual acquaintance or student wouldn't know about your house. We have different names. Only someone connected with either me or Juli-anne or both would know we would be here. The only person in that category who would want to harm us is Simon Talbot, Julianne's ex-boyfriend."

"Has she heard from him?"

"No. I haven't asked anyone to keep tabs because I thought we were rid of him. Jack said he'd look into it."

"But you didn't tell her about the suspicious car while you were in Cambridge."

Gabriel stiffened. "No."

Richard touched his son's shoulder. "I know you need to relocate to Edinburgh for your lectureship, and that Julia may have to stay at Harvard. I will move to Cambridge to stay with your family while you're gone, if my presence would be helpful."

Gabriel's gaze slid to his adoptive father. "You'd give up your teaching at Susquehanna? You'd leave the house?"

"I'm emeritus. I can take a year off and go back the following year. I could try to get a visiting research appointment in Boston or Cambridge. And I'll tell Grace where I'm going so she can find me in your guest room." Richard's tone was light.

"Thank you."

Richard retrieved a toy rabbit from the baby carrier. Clare made a noise and reached for the rabbit.

"Of course, it sounds like your sister and Aaron would like to move in with you, at least until they find a house."

"I haven't had the chance to discuss that with Julianne. But I have no intention of leaving my family behind when I go to Scot-land." Gabriel's tone was firm.

Richard nodded, electing not to press his son on how, exactly, he was going to carry out his intention.

Chapter Thirty-Nine

What's taking so long?" Gabriel jostled a crying Clare but she would not be soothed. "We've been here for hours."

Richard stood. "I can ask at the front desk."

"No, I'll go." Gabriel brought Clare to the desk and explained that he needed to locate Julianne as soon as possible. A few minutes later, a nurse emerged from the hallway and ushered Gabriel and Clare to one of the examination rooms.

"The neurologist is just finishing." The nurse knocked on the door.

Before Gabriel could ask why Julianne was seeing a neurologist, the door swung inward. Julianne sat in a chair, her left ankle wrapped in a tensor bandage. A pair of crutches stood next to her chair.

A short doctor, who had dark hair and dark eyes, stood at the door. "Come in," he greeted Gabriel.

"Are you all right?" Gabriel stared at Julianne with concern.

She gestured for Clare and he placed her in Julia's arms. He put the diaper bag at her feet.

"I'm okay," Julia hedged. She reached into the diaper bag and removed a small, thin blanket, which she placed over her shoulder. Then she discreetly moved Clare beneath the blanket and began to feed her.

"I'm Dr. Khoury." The physician introduced himself, shaking hands with Gabriel. He indicated for Gabriel to sit down. "I'm the neurologist on call."

"Gabriel Emerson. Is the ankle broken?" Gabriel was unable to take his eyes off his wife.

Dr. Khoury turned his back politely on Julianne and the baby, but addressed her. "Is it all right if I share your diagnosis with your husband?"

"Yes," Julianne replied quickly.

The neurologist continued. "Your wife's ankle is sprained and she sustained some torn ligaments, but according to the X-rays the ankle isn't broken. However, based on her reports of numbness in her other leg I was called in for a consult. I performed a number of tests and believe she sustained some nerve damage, possibly as a result of the epidural she received back in September."

Gabriel's eyes swung to the neurologist. "Nerve damage?"

"She has feeling in her left leg, which is why she is experiencing pain. But she has diminished sensation in her right leg. She said the numbness began around the time she came home from the hospital after having the baby."

Gabriel stared at Julianne. The look of surprise on his face quickly morphed into an expression of hurt, then blankness.

Dr. Khoury lifted his hands in a calming gesture. "Numbness is a common side effect of epidurals and occasionally a patient will experience it in only one limb. Sometimes it can take several weeks for the numbness to abate. Sometimes the nerve damage is permanent. I recommend following up with a neurologist in Boston, after the Thanksgiving holiday."

Gabriel assessed the neurologist quickly and passed a hand over his face. "Thank you."

"No problem." The neurologist continued giving Julia his back, out of respect for her privacy for Clare's feeding. "Mrs. Emerson, elevate your ankle to combat the swelling, and ice it as much as possible. Use over-the-counter medication for pain. And follow up with a neurologist when you get back to Boston."

"Thank you." Julia's tone was subdued.

"You're welcome." Dr. Khoury shook hands with Gabriel and exited the examination room.

Gabriel was deathly silent. Julia could barely hear him breathe. She peeked over at him. "Darling?"

"Were you going to tell me?" His tone edged toward harshness.

"I thought the numbness would go away."

Gabriel swiveled his head in her direction. "You thought or you hoped?"

Julia bit the inside of her mouth.

Gabriel dropped his voice. "So you were going to tell me after it abated?"

She nodded.

Gabriel grew silent once again.

Clare finished feeding on one side and Julia burped her and transferred her to the other breast. And still Gabriel didn't say anything.

When she'd finished feeding and burping Clare, Gabriel took the baby and changed her efficiently. Then he handed Julia the crutches.

"Thank you," Julia said meekly. She waited for Gabriel to say something.

He didn't.

He carried the baby and the diaper bag, while keeping careful watch as Julianne limped slowly from the examination room to the waiting room.

And he didn't speak the entire ride home.

Chapter Forty

Julia woke up. Her ankle ached and so did her heart.

Her visit to the emergency room had been a revelation. Her ankle wasn't broken, but she was suffering a side effect from the epidural that might never go away. And Gabriel had been angry with her. So angry, he wouldn't even scold her. He drove her to the house, helped her and the baby through the front door, and then sat in the car making phone calls.

When he entered the house, he'd taken a long shower and disappeared into his study. Now he was joining her.

He placed his glasses and cell phone on the nightstand, as was his habit, and pulled back the blankets. Seeing she was awake, he stopped.

A few seconds later, he slipped between the sheets and rolled onto his back, closing his eyes. The distance between them seemed insurmountable.

She adjusted her injured ankle atop the cushion it was resting on and closed her eyes. She was reminded of that night so long ago when she'd sneaked into Gabriel's room after she'd been attacked by *him*. Gabriel had been kind to her then. He'd been understanding.

A strong arm lifted and pulled her toward a warm, naked chest.

"I'm sorry I didn't tell you," she whispered.

"We're even, Julianne. I should have told you about the strange car that was watching our house."

"I don't think it was Simon. He isn't going to waste his time hanging around Selinsgrove on Thanksgiving. And he's very vain about his car. There's no way he'd drive a Nissan."

"Your uncle Jack is looking into it. I threw a rock and broke the rear window of the car. That should make it easier to find."

Julia lifted her head from the pillow. "You broke the window?"

"Yes." Gabriel sounded a little too pleased with himself. "I played baseball in high school. Did you know that?"

"No."

"Julianne, you can't hide health problems from me, especially now. We have Clare to consider." Gabriel's voice was quiet and eerily calm.

"I was hoping it would go away."

"You let it go almost three months without telling anyone," he chided her. "Never do that to me again."

"I won't."

Gabriel touched her hair. "We need you. *I* need you."

A tear welled in her eye and fell to her cheek. "I need you, too. No more running out into the woods by yourself."

"I can concede that. But I want you to tell me, in detail, about any and all health-related issues you have at present or have had recently."

Julia half smiled at his professorial tone. "Yes, Dr. Emerson."

He growled.

"I mean, *Professor Emerson*."

"Go on."

"I'm in good health with the exception of the numbness in my leg and now this sprained ankle. Which hurts like a mother."

"I'll get you something for the pain." He threw back the bed-clothes.

"It's right here." She pointed at the nightstand.

Gabriel walked around the bed and retrieved a couple of pills from the bottle, handing them to her. Then he gave her a glass of water.

She swallowed the pills with the water.

"Anything else health-related?" he prompted, getting back into bed. He pulled her slowly so as not to disturb her ankle and helped her rest against his chest.

"I have fibroids, but Dr. Rubio said they shrank while I was pregnant. I had been taking an iron supplement but I don't think I need it anymore. I'm supposed to go back for a checkup next September. Dr. Rubio will probably order an ultrasound."

"Anything else?"

"No. You?"

"I'm in recovery for chemical dependency. I have anger management issues, concerns about the safety of my family, and one Italian endowed chair at Harvard whom I'd like to confront. There's a driver of a black Nissan I'd like to punch."

Julia winced. "Anything else?"

"I'll sleep better when I know who has been stalking us."

Julia buried her face against his shoulder. "Part of me doesn't want to know about stuff like that. But it's important you share this information so I don't do something that would put us in jeopardy. I took Clare out in the stroller without you a few times. What if the car had followed us?"

"You're right. It isn't fair for me to be cross with you for keeping secrets when I've been doing the same thing." He kissed her hair.

"So you aren't cross with me?"

"I'm furious. It scared the hell out of me when the nurse told me you were seeing a neurologist. All kinds of scenarios went through my head—cancer, stroke, multiple sclerosis." Gabriel cursed. "We are a family, you and I. Family is everything."

"Okay." Julia didn't sound okay. "I want to say something. I know you don't want to hear this, but I am hopeful that once Cecilia gets over her jealousy, she'll sign off on me spending the fall semester in Edinburgh."

"That's a risky decision. I'd rather we confront her immediately."

"Maybe when she's around Graham Todd at the workshop in Oxford, she'll change her mind."

"That's months away!" Gabriel sputtered. "If she doesn't relent by then, it will be too late."

"I want to try. I want you to let me try."

"Fine." Gabriel sounded exasperated. "If Cecilia refuses to help, I'm getting involved."

"Gabriel, you know—"

"I'm giving your method a chance, but I want the option of using my method."

"Your method is to intimidate her."

"Nonsense."

"You promise?"

"Absolutely."

"Good." Julia kissed him firmly and relaxed against his chest. Soon she fell asleep.

Gabriel lay awake for several hours, exploring scenarios that involved civil discourse and persuasion. But when his thoughts turned to the driver of the black Nissan, he contemplated radically different alternatives.

Chapter Forty-One

December 1, 2012
Cambridge, Massachusetts

"Nothing fits." Gabriel spoke into his cell phone. He was in the nursery with Clare and had just changed her. Now he was attempting to dress her for the day. A large pile of clothing was strewn around the changing table, all of it discarded.

He'd called Julianne on her cell phone because she was currently enjoying breakfast in bed and resting her ankle.

"Who is this?" Julia joked, suppressing laughter.

"I've tried everything—sleepers, dresses, et cetera. Everything is too small."

"I think there's some three-to-six-month-sized clothing in the top drawer of the dresser."

Gabriel opened the drawer and pawed through it. "These are

completely inadequate. They're summer clothes. She'll catch pneumonia."

He withdrew a pink dress that had some embroidery on it and a pair of white things that looked like pants but had feet built in. "I found something that may work temporarily. But she's going to need a sweater." He placed Julia on speaker and put his cell phone aside.

"We have tons of sweaters and hoodies hanging in her closet. Let me see her when you're done."

"Only for a minute." Gabriel heaved a deep breath as he placed one hand on the baby and with the other strained toward the closet. He grabbed a pink hoodie. "I'm taking her shopping."

"You want to take Clare shopping?"

"She must have had a growth spurt. I'm telling you, there are only a few things left that will fit and most of them aren't warm enough." Painstakingly, he pulled on the white things and buttoned the dress in the back.

"Are you going to take Richard with you?"

"No. Rebecca asked for the day off. She and Richard are going on a walking tour of Beacon Hill this morning and then they're going to a movie."

"Huh," said Julia.

Gabriel straightened, still speaking into the phone. "Maybe I shouldn't leave you by yourself."

"I'm fine. With the ankle brace, I can putter around. But I'll probably just read all day. The list of books and articles Cecilia gave me is very long."

"Okay." Gabriel grabbed a soft plastic giraffe that Clare had recently begun chewing, and lifted her to his shoulder. "Come on, Principessa. Let's go see Mommy, and then we're going to find you a new wardrobe."

He grabbed his cell phone and exited the nursery.

❀❀❀

Gabriel enjoyed shopping at Copley Place. Although he didn't enjoy the crowds, and shopping with an infant in a stroller was not ideal, he liked the array of shops and services that could all be found in a single location.

He made his way to Barneys and was quickly directed to the children's section, where he was set upon by no less than three sales associates who resolved to outfit Clare in everything she needed.

Gabriel sat comfortably on a couch, with Clare in his arms happily gumming the giraffe, and sipped an espresso. On his approval, the associates assisted him in outfitting Clare for the next six months. And they furnished him with a far better bunny than the one that was currently residing next to her baby carrier.

Shopping is easy, he thought, as one of the salespeople placed a pair of soft pink leather ballet slippers on Clare's feet.

"She will wear them home," Gabriel directed with a smile.

(It should be noted that he resisted the urge to dispose of the bunny Paul Norris had given Clare, purely because she seemed to prefer that toy to the expensive one from Barneys. Gabriel sighed the sigh of a martyr upon that realization.)

He'd already returned to his SUV and buckled Clare into her car seat when his cell phone rang. It was Jack Mitchell.

Gabriel sat in the driver's seat and locked the doors. "Jack."

"I found your black Nissan. Registered to Pam Landry in Philadelphia."

Gabriel paused, racking his brain. "I don't know anyone by that name."

"Figured you wouldn't. But her son, Alex, took her car to a buddy of his to have the rear window fixed."

"Interesting." Gabriel looked at Clare through the rearview mirror. She was grabbing Paul's rabbit and sticking one of its ears in her mouth.

Gabriel winced at the sight.

"No connection between Alex Landry and my niece that I could find," Jack announced. "But he was in the same fraternity as Simon Talbot at the University of Pennsylvania."

Gabriel swore.

"Alex is a fuckup," Jack continued. "Did a lot of drugs, flunked out of school. Bounced around doing different jobs. Came into some money recently. Been throwing around cash."

"Can you connect him to the asshole?"

"Working on it. Not sure how they are communicating or how the cash was transferred. I think you scared the kid with the rock through the window. He told his mechanic buddy he had a gig out of town but that it ended. Gave the car back to his mother and is driving his own ride now."

"And what ride is that?"

"Red Dodge Charger with black racing stripes and Pennsylvania plates. Hard to miss."

"I'll keep my eyes open."

"Don't think the kid will be bothering you. Sounds like a simple surveillance gig—look but don't touch. Kid fucked up, you made him, you broke his window. Kid takes care of his Charger. He won't want you messing up the custom paint."

"Right." Gabriel pinched the bridge of his nose.

"Do you want me to make contact?"

"Only if he makes a move in my direction. What about the woods? Was that him?"

"Can't say. Kid doesn't seem like the type to embrace nature."

Gabriel hummed. It was possible he'd heard an animal in the woods, but that didn't explain what he thought was the beam of a flashlight. And if the trespasser wasn't Landry . . .

"I asked a buddy to keep an eye on your house. His ride is a blue Toyota with Massachusetts plates. Don't fuck up his window."

"Noted." Gabriel checked on Clare again. "Cost?"

"He's doing me a favor. But I have one piece of good news for you."

"I'm listening."

"Simon Talbot is on a plane to Zurich. Word is he reconciled with his father, but the senator wants his son out of the U.S. Got him a job in finance. Kid fucks up, the senator cuts him off permanently. That kid won't be driving by your house anytime soon."

"Excellent." Gabriel's shoulders lowered.

"Might be worthwhile to keep an eye on the kid in Europe. Want me to send one of my guys?"

"No, but I'm concerned he may have hired someone else to bother us. If you could keep digging, I'd be grateful. What do I owe you?"

"Family discount. Kiss my niece and grandniece for me." Jack disconnected.

Gabriel put his phone on the center console and carefully backed out of the parking space. He used the drive to his house to contemplate what Jack had told him.

Although it would appear Simon was no longer a threat, Gabriel was still cautious. He needed more information about the asshole's activities in Switzerland, and he knew just who to call in order to find out.

Chapter Forty-Two

Later that afternoon

S now." Julia pointed to the delicate flakes that wafted featherlike
in front of the living room window.

Clare reached her hand out to the window and then grabbed a
lock of Julia's hair and pulled.

"Okay, okay. We aren't interested in snow." Julia laughed, trying
to free her hair.

She'd stopped using crutches the day before and tried putting
weight on her ankle today. She'd wrapped it firmly and placed it in
a soft-sided brace, which gave her more support. Still, she moved
slowly and wouldn't carry Clare up or down stairs out of an abun-
dance of caution. She didn't want to fall.

"It's snowing?" Gabriel flipped a switch and the gas fireplace
flared to life, creating a cozy glow.

"Just a few flakes." Julia directed Clare's attention to the window once again. "Look, Clare. Snow."

Clare turned her head toward her father and began babbling.

"Good girl." Gabriel touched her cheek. "Snow is appalling and I approve of your disinterest."

Julia shook her head. "Think about Richard and Rebecca walking Beacon Hill in this weather."

Gabriel consulted his watch. "They'd be at the movies now. Does Rachel know Richard came up for the weekend?"

"Yes. I spoke to her this morning and she said Richard told her last week."

Gabriel's blue eyes grew peering. "And Rachel is fine with it?"

"She said she and Richard worked things out and that she wouldn't begrudge him a friend." Julia grinned. "But she's really happy Wonder Woman is coming to Selinsgrove to spend Christmas with everyone."

"Ah," said Gabriel. "Katherine would be horrified if she knew Rachel was comparing her to a comic book character."

"I think Katherine would be flattered. She has a good sense of humor."

"Hmmm." Gabriel glanced over Julia's shoulder, out the window, and became momentarily distracted. A blue Toyota was driving by their house at a snail's pace. It reached the end of the cul-de-sac, turned around, and drove by their house again.

Gabriel surmised the driver was Jack Mitchell's contact and watched as the car disappeared around the corner. He felt heartened knowing that someone else was keeping an eye on the house.

"Hello? Gabriel?" Julia snapped her fingers, trying to get his attention.

He forced a smile. "Sorry, darling. Entranced by the snow. What do you think of Clare's new wardrobe?" Gabriel extended his arms toward the array of items that had been carefully displayed on every available piece of furniture or flat surface in the living room.

"They're all very nice. But a bit extravagant, don't you think?"

Gabriel looked offended. "She's my daughter. I want her to have the best."

"But the best doesn't have to be the most expensive. Target makes nice baby clothes."

Gabriel wrinkled his nose.

Julia persisted. "I like nice things. You've bought me beautiful dresses and more shoes than I can wear."

"Shoes are works of art," Gabriel interrupted. "Think of them as an art collection."

"Yes, Professor. But think about the privilege Clare has. And think about where we live and all the privilege that surrounds us. I want to teach her that character counts—that being kind and generous make one beautiful."

"She's only three months old."

"Exactly. And has already received gifts from Tiffany, a valuable Renaissance manuscript from her godmother, and a designer wardrobe from Barneys."

"I can't refuse the gifts that Kelly or Katherine give her."

"No, you can't," Julia admitted, pushing her hair behind her ear. "I know it's the prerogative of aunts and godmothers and grandparents to spoil children. But we don't have to spoil her."

"Of course I want to teach her what true beauty is, and I say this looking at the most beautiful woman I've ever seen, both inside and out."

Julia flushed at his compliment.

He took a step closer and brushed his thumb across her cheek. "Why can't I buy my little princess nice clothes? She will only be a baby a short while. Next thing we know she'll be slamming doors, listening to appalling music, and ripping holes in her jeans."

"I hope not." Julia kissed the side of his hand. "Barneys is too extravagant for children, and I don't want her to grow up like some of the people I have to deal with at Harvard."

Gabriel thought of Cecilia. Then he thought of the snobbish scions of wealthy families he'd encountered during his undergraduate years at Princeton, and later, at Oxford and Harvard.

He placed a hand on Clare's head and she reached her arms out to him. He took her and instantly, she rested her head on his shoulder. "I don't want that, either. And I say that knowing that I, myself, have an attachment to luxury."

"An attachment?" Julia teased.

"You're the kindest person I know." Gabriel's eyes were solemn. "You are everything that is loving and gentle. With you as a role model, she won't be lacking in kindness, despite the faults of her father."

"Your faults are greatly exaggerated. From you she will learn bravery and strength and hard work. My kindness grew out of cruelty. I saw how my mother acted and determined to do the opposite."

"But that's why I want to spoil you. I wanted to bring you home a new pair of shoes today, but I thought that would be insensitive, given the state of your ankle." Gabriel pointed to a box. "So I bought you slippers, instead. Very warm. Very soft. And they should fit over your ankle brace."

"You bought me a present?"

"Yes, and I picked it out myself. Without any help." Gabriel preened.

Julia crossed over to open the box. She retrieved a pair of cranberry-colored shearling slippers, with a skidproof leather sole. She sat down and tried them on.

"They fit perfectly. Thank you." Her dark eyes shone as she looked up at her husband. "But I meant what I said; we can't spoil

Clare. I don't want her to think she has to look or dress a certain way in order to be valued."

Gabriel gazed over the baby clothes with a look of consternation. "You want me to take them back?"

"No." Julia stood in her new slippers and walked over to him. She hooked her hand around his neck and drew him down for a kiss. "I'm talking about your next outing."

"I sat on a couch and they brought everything to me," he confessed, swaying with Clare against his shoulder. "Does Target do that?"

"No." She lifted her injured ankle. "As soon as I'm better, I'll introduce you to the magic of Target. We can browse the aisles with a large red cart, sip a Starbucks coffee, and do everything ourselves."

"You and I have different understandings of the term *magic*," said Gabriel imperiously. His expression grew concerned. "How is your other leg?"

She averted her eyes. "Today the numbness was a little worse. But it's fine."

"We can consult another doctor."

Julia sat in a chair next to the fire. "I've already seen two neurologists. Neither of them has a treatment other than time."

Gabriel didn't look convinced.

He changed the subject by lifting Clare's foot. "You can hardly object to her footwear. The ballet slippers were essential."

Julia took a moment to admire the sight of Gabriel, bursting with pride about his little princess, and the baby herself, who was resting comfortably against his shoulder, sucking her fist. "Yes, I'll concede that the ballet slippers were essential."

"By the way, the BBC producer I met in Edinburgh contacted me."

"What did she say?"

"She asked me to come to London to be interviewed for a documentary about the Renaissance."

"Congratulations. When would you go?"

"We would go," Gabriel corrected. "They're setting things up for March or April. We could schedule the interviews around your workshop at Oxford and take Rebecca with us, or give her holidays and just go ourselves."

"I'd like that."

"We could go to the British Museum and explore its dark corners." Gabriel lifted his eyebrows suggestively.

"And get arrested." Julia laughed. "It will be spring then, which means we can take the stroller for Clare and walk around London."

"Good. I'll email Eleanor and talk about dates. Now, what does Mommy want for dinner?"

"Spring rolls?"

"Not takeaway. The princess and I are going to cook and listen to opera." Gabriel danced in a circle with the baby.

"Pasta?" Julia suggested, getting to her feet.

"An excellent suggestion. You can relax by the fire, darling. Leave the cooking to us."

"Oh no." Julia grinned. "This I want to see."

She followed Gabriel and Clare into the kitchen as the strains of Pavarotti performing Puccini's "Nessun dorma" emanated from the stereo system.

⁂

After attending Mass with his family the following morning, Gabriel closeted himself in his home office in order to make a phone call.

"Cassirer." The lightly accented voice answered Gabriel's call.

"Nicholas, it's Gabriel Emerson calling from America. How are you?"

"Gabriel, good to hear from you. I'm well, thank you."

"And your parents? How are they?"

Nicholas paused. "They are managing. They spend most of their time abroad."

"I'm so sorry." Gabriel's voice was sympathetic.

"How is your family?"

"Julianne is well. Our daughter was born in September. We named her Clare."

"Congratulations. That's excellent news. I'll pass it on to my parents."

"Please do." Gabriel cleared this throat. "I'm afraid my family is why I'm calling you."

Gabriel quickly explained the background of his interactions with Simon Talbot and his latest move to Zurich. "I need the name of someone trustworthy I can hire for surveillance."

"Surveillance?" Nicholas repeated casually—all too casually.

"Just someone to keep tabs. I'm hoping he'll lose interest in us with this recent move. But I want to be sure."

"Let me make a few calls."

"Thank you. Money isn't a concern and I'd be happy to reimburse you for the introduction."

"That isn't necessary. Do you need someone in America, as well?"

"I'm covered, but thank you. If there's anything I can do in return, please let me know."

"Not at all. This is for your family, with my compliments. I'll be in touch."

"Thank you." Gabriel disconnected the call and placed his phone on his desk.

On paper, Nicholas Cassirer was a wealthy Swiss businessman who was an avid art collector and a generous philanthropist. Gabriel had no reason to suspect the man of having ties to the underworld, apart from his ubiquitous black suits.

But Gabriel was not naïve. The Cassirers had sustained a robbery a number of years ago and the items had never been recovered. Nicholas had taken the theft very, very personally and his family had hired professional security that rivaled that of most heads of state.

Gabriel felt his neck. There was a chance he'd just incurred a debt he would later be called on to pay. But given the potential danger to his family, he was more than willing to pay the price, no matter how steep.

Chapter Forty-Three

December 12, 2012

Julia was awake.

She'd rolled over to face Gabriel a few minutes ago and he'd stretched out an arm and covered her waist. He was sound asleep, judging by his breathing. Funny how he reached for her instinctually, as if their souls were so in tune with one another, he could sense her presence even while sleeping.

She touched Gabriel's face—the face of the man she loved. She traced his aristocratic cheekbones and the slight dimple of his chin. Her fingers caught on the stubble.

She kissed his cheek and brushed her mouth across his. He murmured a response, but didn't move.

A wave of love and want washed over her. She wanted to drown in it.

She caressed his chest and floated her hand over his original tattoo and the new piece that was still healing. It was an image from one of Botticelli's illustrations of *Paradiso*; Dante swoons at the base of Jacob's ladder and Beatrice embraces him.

The tattoo artist who had marked Gabriel's right pectoral with the image had been the same artist who gave him the dragon and heart. Woven into Botticelli's image were the names *Julianne* and *Clare*, in an elegant minuscule script.

Julia's hand hovered over the image. It had been a surprise. Gabriel had been inked two days after his shopping spree with Clare.

I need to have you immortalized on my skin. And under my skin. And over my heart, he'd whispered, when he bared the image to her eyes.

She reached over and kissed his chest, just over his heart.

Gabriel shifted, but didn't awaken.

His body was a feast for her senses. So she explored him, her fingers dancing over his strong pectorals, his shoulders, his muscled arms.

She touched his ribs and dipped into his navel. Then she traced the ridges of his abdominal muscles. She reached the band of his underwear and stopped.

A sharp inhalation drew her attention.

Gabriel's eyes were open, their stark blueness standing out against the dark hair that swept his brow.

"I'm sorry. I didn't mean to wake you."

"Never apologize for touching me," he rasped. "If my soul is yours, my body is also."

He adjusted the pillow behind his head so he could see her better.

She sat back, carefully moving her ankle. "I need you."

"Then take what you need." Gabriel's eager, curious look was encouraging.

Julia returned her hand to his body, caressing and touching him, before cupping him through his underwear. He made a strangled noise.

She removed the underwear, tugging it determinedly down his legs before dropping it to the floor. Then she knelt next to him and placed his hand at the hem of her nightgown. Hastily, he tore off her nightgown and panties.

Without words, she straddled his waist, adjusting her position so no weight was placed on her ankle. She brought his large hands to her breasts and leaned into his touch.

Gabriel passed his thumbs over her nipples.

She reacted by arching against him, curving her spine.

He thumbed her nipples and replaced them with his mouth, fastening his lips over a rosy bud. He licked her.

Julia reveled in his ministrations until her want could not be contained. She moved back and wrapped her hand around him.

He gasped against her breast and she stroked up and down, her pace slow but sure.

Gabriel was already aroused. She touched him to please him, as his lips found her other breast.

Then she positioned him carefully and sank down, inch by inch.

Gabriel bit out a curse at the feel of her around him.

She rocked back and forth as his thumbs found her nipples again. And then she lifted herself up and brought herself down, experimenting with rhythm and depth of penetration.

She pulled his hands to her hips, one at a time, encouraging him to help her set the pace. But Gabriel was only too eager to let her lead and to watch her, eyes half-closed in pleasure.

Her palm found his chest, careful not to touch the tattoo that was healing. The face of Dante, leaning against Beatrice, gazed up at her. As if she were a promise ready to be fulfilled.

She closed her eyes. The feelings were too intense. One more ascent and she was falling, falling. Gabriel lifted his hips, increasing the pace, chasing after her.

He pulled her down as he thrust up and she felt him jerk inside her. She opened her eyes to see his gaze meet hers. His chest tensed beneath her palm.

She relaxed atop him and his body slowly softened.

A lazy smile passed over his face. "I'd like to be awakened like that every morning. Look at you—a beautiful, fierce goddess of love, who never takes except she gives tenfold more. Let me be your servant in love and desire."

"Gabriel." She touched his face.

"And you did all of that with an injured ankle." He grinned wickedly.

Before she could answer she was pinned beneath him and he was settling between her hips. He lifted her arms above her head.

"Now it's my turn, goddess. Let's see what you can do without any hands."

She laughed until he took her mouth.

"*My Beatrice*," he whispered.

Chapter Forty-Four

December 21, 2012

Julia was dreaming.

In itself, this was not an unusual occurrence. She had dreamed vividly throughout her pregnancy but found her sleep deep and dreamless after she brought Clare home from the hospital.

In the wee hours of the morning, while Clare slept soundly in the nursery, Julia dreamed she was back at St. Joseph's University, walking down the hall to the room she shared with Natalie, a fellow undergraduate.

It was Julia's birthday. She was supposed to celebrate it with her boyfriend but forgot her camera. Walking down the hall, she felt happy and excited.

In her dream, Julia knew what was about to happen. She knew what lay behind the closed door to her room. Still, she pulled out her keys and unlocked the door.

Thud.

The sound of the door hitting the wall was unusually loud. Julia stared at the door, wondering why it had made such an odd sound.

Crash.

Julia's eyes snapped open.

She was no longer in Philadelphia; she was in her bedroom in Cambridge. The night light plugged into the wall cast a gentle glow over the room.

But something wasn't right.

Julia lifted her head and saw a man standing a few feet away, holding the reproduction of Henry Holiday's painting in his gloved hands.

He stared straight at Julia.

The man was a behemoth—well over six feet, six inches and formed like a linebacker. His dark eyes were flat, emotionless.

He took a step in her direction.

Julia screamed.

Chapter Forty-Five

Gabriel awoke immediately, confused. He'd fallen asleep at his desk in his study.

He stumbled to his feet, not bothering to figure out why he wasn't in bed with his wife. Tearing open the door, he saw a large, dark figure moving down the hall. Gabriel stood between him and the nursery, where Clare was sleeping in her crib.

The figure didn't hesitate. He rushed toward Gabriel and threw a punch, directed at his jaw.

Gabriel ducked and drove his fist into the larger man's midsection.

The man was unfazed by the blow. He grabbed Gabriel by the shirt and threw him down, slamming him into the wall.

The man headed to the staircase but, as he passed, Gabriel grabbed his foot and twisted, bringing the man to his knees.

The man cursed in Italian and lashed out, striking Gabriel in the sternum.

Gabriel's heart was caught midbeat. It shuddered and paused before beating irregularly. Gabriel fell back, clutching his chest.

The man stood and lumbered like a large bear down the hall.

Gabriel found he couldn't move. He lay on his back, frozen, gazing up at the ceiling. He tried to draw breath.

"Gabriel?" Julia dashed from the bedroom, just in time to see the man disappear down the stairs.

"Clare," Gabriel managed to rasp.

"Where is she? Did he take her?" Before Gabriel could answer, Julia ran to the nursery door and opened it.

From the doorway, Julia could see that Clare was still in her crib. Julia rushed toward her and touched the baby's face. She stirred but didn't wake.

"Thank God," she breathed.

She ran back to her bedroom, picked up the cell phone, and dialed 911.

Chapter Forty-Six

Julia was glad Rebecca hadn't been there to surprise the intruder. She was a light sleeper and awoke early some mornings. Thankfully, she'd left for Colorado the day before in order to spend the Christmas holiday with her children.

Julia was seated on the couch in the living room, holding a sleeping baby. She hadn't wanted Clare out of her sight.

The Cambridge police were combing the house and the backyard. Gabriel was pacing nearby, having been checked and cleared by the paramedics. He'd been on his phone for the past hour.

Julia buried her face against Clare's hair. She'd thought Gabriel was having a heart attack. He'd been pale and short of breath when she found him in the hallway. The color had returned to his face and now he was pacing like a caged lion, angry and frustrated. As if he'd roar at any moment.

Julia whispered a prayer of thanks that she still had a family and hugged Clare more tightly. She wasn't sure how long she sat there before a pair of bare feet stood in front of her. (Parenthetically, it should be noted that even Gabriel's feet were attractive.)

He hadn't bothered to put on shoes and he was still wearing a pair of tartan flannel pajamas. He crouched next to her and placed a gentle hand on her neck. "Darling?"

He pushed her hair back from her face. "The company that installed the security system is sending someone immediately. According to them, the system is still armed. The intruder must have bypassed the alarm."

"How is that possible?"

Gabriel's face grew grim. "I don't know."

Julia rocked the baby, back and forth. "He didn't take any jewelry. He didn't even open the box."

"Cash, passports, electronics, artwork—everything is still here. The police are dusting for fingerprints."

"He was wearing gloves."

Gabriel froze. "Did he touch you?"

"No," Julia whispered. "When I woke up, I saw him holding the Holiday painting. I saw the gloves."

"When I went upstairs, the painting was on the floor. The glass shattered."

"He dropped it when I screamed."

"But you're all right?" Gabriel croaked. He reached a hand out to caress Clare's head. "Clare is all right?"

"I don't think he went into the nursery. The door was still closed and I hadn't heard anything on the baby monitor."

Gabriel passed a hand over his mouth. Things could have ended very, very differently.

"I'm sorry about the painting."

Gabriel squeezed her knee. "Better the painting than you!"

Julia took his hand and tugged him to sit next to her. She leaned into his side, shaking.

He wrapped both arms around her shoulders. "You're going to be fine. You're going to be fine and Clare is going to be fine."

"I thought he'd taken her." A tear streaked down Julia's face. "I thought you'd had a heart attack."

"I was just winded. But I could use a shot of Laphroaig right now."

"Me, too."

"I'll get you one." He spoke against her skin.

"I don't think nursing mothers are supposed to drink Laphroaig. But if I weren't nursing, hell yeah I'd be drinking your campfire Scotch."

It was not appropriate to laugh and Gabriel knew it. He held her close and restrained his laughter. "I don't have any Laphroaig. But if you want a drink, I'll get you one."

"Maybe later." The baby stirred against Julia's shoulder.

"Do you want me to take her? She must be getting heavy."

Julia shook her head. "I need to hold her."

"Mr. Emerson?" A plainclothes detective approached him. "Can I see you for a minute?"

"Of course." Gabriel kissed his wife and followed the detective into the kitchen.

Julia continued to rock back and forth, praying everything would be over soon. It was three o'clock in the morning and she wanted to go back to sleep. But not here, not with a disabled security system and the painting of Dante and Beatrice broken upstairs.

A few minutes later, Gabriel returned. "It looks like the intruder came in through the garden. He hopped the fence and crossed the yard to the back door, leaving footprints in the snow."

Gabriel noted Julia's rocking motion. "Why don't you lie down? I'll take Clare."

"I don't want to stay here another minute." She swayed to her feet.

"Okay." Gabriel scratched the stubble on his face. "We'll go to a hotel. Do you want to pack a bag?"

"I don't want to go upstairs by myself." Julia's voice was very small. It almost broke Gabriel's heart.

"I'll go with you. Let me tell the detective." Gabriel returned to the kitchen for a moment and then walked back to Julia. He took Clare into his arms. "I'll carry her up the stairs. I'm sorry I fell asleep at my desk. I should have come to bed."

"I'm okay," Julia's voice grew steely. "But I have to get out of here."

"I'll call the Lenox as soon as we get upstairs. Pack whatever you will need for a day or two. I'll call the security company and let them know we're leaving."

Julia nodded. At that moment, all she cared about was getting herself and her child out of the house. The security company was doing too little, too late.

Gabriel ascended the staircase with Julia close behind.

❈❈

While Julianne stood in the closet, packing for herself and Clare, Gabriel put the baby in her playpen. She was still asleep.

Gabriel crossed himself and said a silent prayer of thanks.

He walked over to his nightstand and was about to pick up his phone charger when he stepped on something.

"Son of a . . ." Gabriel lifted his foot in order to see what he'd stepped on.

"Are you okay?" Julia stuck her head out of the closet.

"I'm fine. It's nothing."

Julia returned to her packing.

Crouching down, Gabriel saw that he'd stepped on what looked like a small sculpture. He retrieved a tissue from the nightstand and picked up the object.

The sculpture was grotesque—a small, two-headed bust with a skull on one side and a face on the other. Gabriel turned the object over, careful to keep it covered by tissue. Letters had been carved into it: *O Mors quam amara est memoria tua.*

Gabriel knew without doubt the object wasn't his. It didn't belong to Julianne, either. Such objects had been popular in the Middle Ages and the Renaissance, as a kind of reminder of one's mortality: *O Death, how bitter is your memory. Remember you must die.*

The piece he'd stepped on was finely crafted and old. To his untrained eye, at least, it seemed to be of museum quality. Since it was unlikely the Cambridge police kept such mementoes in their pockets, only one other person could have dropped it.

"I'm almost done," Julianne called. She entered the bathroom and closed the door.

Gabriel covered the carving with more tissue and placed it in his briefcase with his laptop. Although it was possible the intruder had dropped the piece accidentally, it was equally possible it had been left on Gabriel's nightstand, mere inches from his pillow, as a warning.

As such, and given the medium of the message, Gabriel elected not to share his finding with Cambridge's finest. Instead, he was going to share the discovery with someone else.

Chapter Forty-Seven

What about your family? Are they all right?" Nicholas Cassirer sounded horrified.

"Julianne is shaken, but they're fine." Gabriel carefully closed the door of the bathroom in their hotel suite, so as not to disturb them.

Clare was now sleeping in her playpen and Julianne had collapsed on the king-sized bed. It was after five o'clock in the morning in Boston, and just before noon in Zurich, Nicholas's home.

Gabriel continued. "I've already spoken with the man you recommended for surveillance. He's in the Alps, watching the Talbot family ski. There haven't been any clandestine meetings or suspicious behavior."

"What was Kurt's assessment?"

"He thinks the home invasion has nothing to do with Simon Talbot. But he offered to make contact."

"I'd trust his instincts. It may be a good idea for him to have a word. He can be very persuasive."

"I'll follow up with Kurt today."

"What you've described sounds like the work of a professional art thief."

"Yes, but what professional breaks into a house that's occupied?" Gabriel's words left his mouth too late. He closed his eyes. "My friend, I'm sorry. I wasn't thinking."

Nicholas changed the subject. "The intruder handled every piece of art in your house, but ignored jewelry and cash. So he isn't an opportunist. I'm puzzled he didn't take anything. Perhaps he's planning to return."

"That's what I'm afraid of."

"Or he didn't find what he was looking for."

That gave Gabriel pause. "The most valuable pieces I own are in the Uffizi, as we speak."

"Yes, I know," said Nicholas. "The exhibition, with your name attached, has drawn international attention. Someone may have been inspired to visit your home and inspect your personal collection.

"Professional art thieves usually target specific works, for specific buyers. The thief knows you own the Botticelli illustrations, and he surmises you have other valuable pieces in your possession. He takes an inventory so he can approach a collector."

"You think he will return?"

"If he found something he can sell. He may be from Italy, or speaking the language may have been a calculated move to point you toward Italy. But it doesn't matter. When it comes to artwork, the black market is international."

Gabriel rubbed his forehead. "What's your recommendation?"

"Would you be willing to share your inventory? I may be able to discern what the thief is interested in."

"Certainly."

"I think you and Julianne should work with an artist to produce a drawing of the intruder. I have a contact at Interpol. They may recognize him."

"We'll take care of that." Gabriel opened his laptop bag and withdrew a ball of tissue. "There is one other thing. I believe the thief left a calling card."

"What kind of calling card?"

"It looks like a Renaissance memento mori. It's a small carving of a skull on one side and a face on the other. It may be genuine, I don't know."

"Can you send a photo?"

"Of course." Gabriel quickly snapped a picture with his phone and texted it to Nicholas. "I found it in my bedroom, after the break-in."

Nicholas hummed as he examined the photo. "Why didn't you give it to the police?"

"Because I didn't want it tagged, bagged, and placed in an evidence room. It's more useful if it can be authenticated and traced."

"I can recommend someone from my family's museum in Cologny. But you'd be better off approaching *Dottor* Vitali at the Uffizi. He may be able to trace the provenance for you."

"Italy, once again," Gabriel muttered.

"I have to say, the calling card changes my assessment."

"In what way?"

"It makes the invasion appear personal. If the memento mori was left intentionally, it could be a warning. A death threat. Is there anyone, besides the ex-boyfriend, who would want to harm you?"

"No," Gabriel answered quickly. "No one."

"You haven't offended someone with powerful connections? Someone in the art world?"

"No. I'm a professor. I live the life of an academic. The only people I offend are those who are ignorant of Dante."

"But that has to be a small group and, as you know, academics rarely if ever hire professionals to break into houses and examine artwork. My advice is to upgrade your security system. I will call the team that worked on my parents' house and ask them to visit you in America, as a personal favor."

Whatever his suspicions about Nicholas Cassirer's connections, Gabriel wasn't about to turn down such a generous offer.

"Thank you." Gabriel accepted quickly. "It's close to Christmas. When do you think they will be available?"

"I'll have them on a plane tonight."

"I appreciate it." Gabriel found his voice unusually gruff. "If there's anything I can do, just ask."

"I'm sorry this happened. I'll call my contact at the security company now. He'll be in touch."

"Thank you."

"And, Gabriel? I'd recommend sending your memento mori to the Uffizi as soon as possible. It may be the clue you're looking for."

"I will. Thank you." Gabriel disconnected and exited the bathroom.

He sat in an armchair and tapped his cell phone against his chin, thinking.

Nicholas had given him much to ponder, particularly the possibility that there was a connection between the break-in and the exhibit at the Uffizi.

Again, Gabriel was puzzled that the intruder hadn't taken anything. Almost all the artwork was on the ground floor, which meant the thief could have broken in, retrieved several pieces, and departed without alerting anyone of his presence.

The thief must have been looking for something—either something specific or making an inventory of the household. If it was something specific, he probably hadn't found it, or else he would have taken it. If he was taking an inventory, he intended to return.

If the intruder had broken into the house simply to terrorize them, he'd have done so. As it was, he'd used little violence, no weapons beyond his fists, and had left Julianne and Clare untouched. However, the memento mori could be interpreted as a threat. And it was a threat directed at him, since the piece was left on his side of the bed.

Gabriel wondered whether the intruder's rules of engagement were self-imposed, or imposed by someone who had sent him.

The Professor didn't have answers to these questions, but his gifted intellect continued to examine everything over and over again, until he finally tumbled into bed after sunrise, exhausted.

Chapter Forty-Eight

December 22, 2012
Zermatt, Switzerland

Simon Talbot exited his chalet at the CERVO resort, slipping on his gloves. He was meeting friends and family for drinks in the lounge *après*-ski.

He'd taken no more than two steps outside the door when something hit him, hard. He went flying backward into the snow.

"My God!" someone cried in German. "I'm sorry. Let me help you." A large man, dressed in ski clothes, reached out his hand. He hefted a dazed Simon to his feet, chattering his apologies.

"I'm okay," said Simon in English, trying to remove his hand from the man's iron grip.

Instead of releasing him, the man pulled him closer. "Forget the name of Julianne Emerson, or the next time I see you, you won't be able to get up."

Simon gaped. He was still in shock after being bodychecked and knocked over. But to hear the man switch to English and mention her name . . .

After a few seconds of stunned silence, Simon's face hardened. "Tell that asshole husband of hers I haven't done anything. She's nothing to me."

The man pulled Simon closer, bringing them nose to nose. "I don't work for him. And my employer does not accept failure. You've been warned."

Smoothly, the man drove his fist into Simon's abdomen, doubling him over. Without a backward glance, the man walked past the chalet and disappeared around the corner.

Chapter Forty-Nine

The Lenox Hotel
Boston, Massachusetts

The security company?" Julia prompted, sitting near the fireplace in the hotel suite. It was her habit to curl up in comfy oversized chairs, like a cat. But she found that her right leg bothered her in such a position, and so her feet were propped up on an ottoman.

Her ankle still troubled her, on occasion, and so she still wore a brace when she walked. With the terror and worry that accompanied the break-in, she'd barely noticed her ankle and the intermittent numbness in her leg. She was still in shock, she thought, and had refused to leave the hotel. Gabriel had arranged for a sketch artist who worked with the local police to meet with them in their suite and draw a likeness of the intruder, which Gabriel had sent to Nicholas and Interpol.

Gabriel had barely been able to coax Julia downstairs to the restaurant for dinner.

After dinner, the hotel staff had built a roaring fire in their suite.

Julia found the scent and warmth of the flames comforting. She'd even troubled the concierge to send out for graham crackers, marshmallows, and bars of chocolate, and had made s'mores, much to Gabriel's amusement.

He was indulging each and every whim, however, and had been doing so since they left their home. He had no idea how she was going to react to what he was about to tell her. So he waited until after Julia had made and consumed far more s'mores than was healthy, and fed several to him, as well, in an effort to create as relaxed an environment as possible.

He had a small bottle of Scotch from the minibar at the ready.

Now he was stretched out on the floor next to Clare, who was safely out of reach of the fire's heat. She was resting on her back on a special mat for babies, which was decorated with a jungle scene. A fabric-covered arch curved above her, from which were suspended lights, a mirror, and some toys.

But Clare only had eyes for her father, and her little head was turned toward him.

"Why hello, Clare." Gabriel spoke in his equivalent of baby talk. (Which is to say he spoke normally.)

Clare moved her arms and legs and smiled back.

"That's my girl." Gabriel smiled even more widely, chattering at the baby. Clare moved her chubby fists and gurgled.

Julia took great joy in Gabriel's excitement. "She's very particular about who she shares her smiles with."

"Of course she is. You save your smiles for Daddy." He took Clare's hand and she latched on to one of his fingers, squeezing. "Rachel called earlier. She said you aren't answering your cell."

Julia adjusted her bathrobe. "I switched it off. I didn't want to talk to anyone."

"I explained to her what happened and I called Richard, who was understandably concerned. Rachel was calling to let us know they found an apartment in Charlestown."

"Charlestown?" Julia repeated, surprised.

"They're in a brand-new apartment building on an up-and-coming street. It's just temporary, while they look for a condo."

"I'll call Rachel tomorrow. You were going to tell me about your meeting with the security company."

"Nicholas Cassirer arranged for the man who designed his family's security system in Switzerland to take a look at our house. I met him and his associate this afternoon."

"And?" Julia prompted. Gabriel was rehearsing information she already knew, which meant he was stalling.

"I'm sorry about what happened last night," he observed mournfully. "I've already taken the Holiday painting to be reframed. I worry that lending our illustrations to the Uffizi has drawn far more attention to us than I realized."

Julia shifted by the fire. She was the one who had wanted to share the illustrations with the world. But she hadn't expected someone to break into their home because of it.

"Nicholas's family were robbed several years go. The intruders took a few priceless pieces, including a Renoir."

Julia frowned. "It was in the news. Someone was killed."

"Yes." Gabriel covered his eyes for a moment. "The security consultant was very thorough. He looked at our existing system, walked around the property, and surveyed the perimeter. He went through the entire house."

"And what did he say?"

"He wondered why the intruder didn't take anything, since all the valuable artwork is on the ground floor."

"Maybe he was going to take something but wanted to check upstairs first." Julia shivered. Her gaze moved to Clare.

"It's possible. If you were him, what would you take?"

"I don't know." Julia paused, going through the house in her mind. "There's the statue of Venus. It's valuable, but it's small. There's the Greek and Roman pottery. I'd probably take Tom Thomson's *Sketch for 'The Jack Pine.'* The finished version is in the National Gallery of Canada. Our house is easier to break into than that."

"The intruder moved Cézanne's *The Barque of Dante.* I found it leaning against the wall. He must have taken it down to examine the back and the frame."

"That's probably the most valuable piece. Why didn't he steal it?"

"I don't know."

"The original by Delacroix is eight times larger and it's in the Louvre. Again, our house is easier to break into."

"And Cézanne's version could be hidden under a coat."

"Maybe he left it against the wall and intended to come back for it. But we surprised him."

"Maybe." Gabriel didn't sound convinced. "I sent an inventory to Nicholas. He hasn't gotten back to me, but I expect he'll flag that piece as the most desirable."

"Right. So what did the security specialist say?" Julia wrapped her arms around her waist, steeling herself for the answer.

"He was very thorough," Gabriel said slowly. "But he pointed out that we are exposed on Foster Place. We have a fence at the back but not the front. Our side door is steps from the street, so anyone can walk up. He can upgrade our security system to something state-of-the-art, but we're vulnerable in that location."

The color of Julia's face lightened several shades. "What did he suggest?"

"He suggested we move."

It took a moment for Julia to process the suggestion. "Move? Sell the house and move? Are you joking?"

"No, he suggested we move to a house with a proper wall in a gated community."

"Where?"

"Newton. Chestnut Hill." Gabriel observed Julia's face.

"Those properties are millions of dollars," she whispered.

Gabriel shrugged, in true Gabrielite fashion.

"Living in a compound would be like living in a cage. I want to live in a neighborhood, where we know our neighbors and I can take Clare for walks down the street."

Gabriel moved so he could roll onto his side and still keep an eye on Clare. "You won't be taking walks for some time. It isn't safe."

"That's assuming someone is trying to hurt me and Clare. The robber was only interested in artwork."

Gabriel pressed his lips together.

Julia's gaze focused on his eyes. "Uncle Jack said Simon was living it up in Switzerland and his old fraternity buddy gave up stalking us. What aren't you telling me?"

"There is one thing," Gabriel hedged. He retrieved his cell phone from the coffee table and scrolled through the photos to the last one. "Here."

Julia took the phone and glanced at the screen. "What am I looking at?"

"I think it's a memento mori object. I had the concierge overnight it to *Dottor* Vitali at the Uffizi."

Julia examined the image more closely. "Why?"

"I found it in the house, on the floor in our room."

Julia handed the phone back to Gabriel. "The robber must have dropped it. Maybe it was a piece he stole from someone else."

"Perhaps. Once I hear from Vitali, I'll ask Nicholas to put me in touch with his contact at Interpol. I sent them the image from the sketch artist, as well."

"You withheld evidence."

Gabriel scowled. "I'm not *withholding* anything. I simply wanted to find out if we could trace the piece to an owner."

"Or a theft."

Gabriel put the cell phone back on the coffee table. "That's why I want to know more about the piece itself and its history.

"Simon is still in Switzerland and he's being watched. Jack's friend has been keeping an eye on us but isn't watching the house twenty-four hours a day. However, Jack told me the man has taken this situation personally and is now conducting his own investigation.

"I'm inclined to agree with Nicholas that the thief was a professional and might be from Europe. He cursed me in Italian."

"The entire North End of Boston can curse you in Italian."

Gabriel lifted his eyebrows.

"Well, maybe not the entire North End," she relented. "But quite a few of its inhabitants."

Gabriel returned to sit by Clare and picked up the toy bunny he'd bought at Barneys. Clare grinned and waved her arms and legs.

"What happened to Paul's bunny?" Julia asked.

Gabriel wrinkled his nose. "It's around."

"You didn't throw it out, did you?"

"No." Gabriel sighed. "The baby likes it."

"Do you want to move?"

Gabriel turned his head to look at Julia. "No. I liked the house when we bought it and I love it now that we've renovated it and made it our home.

"My priority is to keep you and Clare safe. If there is a chance of another break-in, I'd prefer you and Clare were somewhere else. That means we need to move, at least in the short term."

Julia looked away.

Gabriel had touched a nerve with his last remarks. She was afraid to return to the house, although she didn't want to say so aloud. She wondered if she'd be able to fall asleep in her own room again. Certainly, she couldn't imagine placing Clare in the nursery. Clare would have to sleep in their room with them.

"Do we have to decide tonight?" Julia stared into the flames.

Gabriel gave Clare the bunny. "No. We don't have to decide anything tonight."

"What about the security specialist?"

"He's at our service. I think we'd be wise to have him upgrade the security system whether we move or not."

Julia met Gabriel's gaze. "We were supposed to leave for Selinsgrove tomorrow. We were supposed to pick Katherine up at the airport."

"Rachel and Aaron are picking up Katherine. I promise we'll be in Selinsgrove on Christmas Eve."

"It's Clare's first Christmas."

"It will be a good one, I promise."

Julia looked back at the fire.

"If the house is empty for a couple of weeks, perhaps the intruder will make his move," Gabriel pointed out.

"With a new security system? If he's a professional, he'll notice the upgrade."

"Hopefully, it will deter him." Gabriel's tone grew harsh. "And if it doesn't, he will get caught. If it were just me, I'd go after the thief myself. But I'm not leaving you and I'm not putting you or the baby at risk."

"You'd go after him?"

"Yes."

Julia began massaging her temples with her fingers. "I can't deal with this right now."

Gabriel got to his feet and carefully maneuvered her so he was sitting in the chair and she was nestled in his lap.

She buried her face in his neck. "I'm not sure I'll be able to sleep tonight."

Gabriel held her tightly. "I'm sorry I failed you."

"You didn't fail me. You did what you could and fought off the intruder, and in your pajamas, no less."

Gabriel's expression remained grave. "I'll tell the security specialist to start upgrading the system tomorrow. Then we can focus on Christmas. I haven't finished my shopping."

"I thought you finished it weeks ago."

"Maybe." He stroked the arches of her eyebrows and gently caressed her cheeks.

Clare began to cry and Julia quickly picked her up.

"Sssshhhh," Julia hushed. "Everything will be okay."

Gabriel observed his wife and child and prayed she was right.

Chapter Fifty

Christmas Eve
Selinsgrove, Pennsylvania

Gabriel sat in an armchair in the master bedroom, holding his laptop. The screen of the computer glowed blue in the darkened room. In the opposite corner, a whimsical night light projected pink stars on the ceiling, above Clare's playpen.

The two people he loved most in the world were sleeping. Exhaustion had taken its toll on Julianne, and she slept soundly now, too. Only Gabriel had difficulty sleeping.

Kurt, Nicholas's contact, had delivered a warning to Simon. Reportedly, the warning was clear, concise, and persuasive. Kurt doubted Simon would approach the Emersons again, either directly or indirectly, but he continued his surveillance, just in case.

Nicholas had surveyed the inventory Gabriel had sent him and agreed that the Cézanne and the Thomson were the two works most likely to attract interest from collectors. Nicholas seemed to think that art heists, even in private homes, were more common than one thought.

He'd discussed the memento mori with his contact at Interpol and shared both the photograph of the object and the sketch artist's image of the perpetrator. Unfortunately, the object didn't appear in Interpol's database of stolen art.

Using facial recognition software, the sketch was compared with images in Interpol's criminal database. There wasn't a match.

Thus, Gabriel was dealing with a professional art thief who had yet to capture the attention of Interpol and who had left behind what might be a museum-quality sculpted object that hadn't been reported stolen. It was all very puzzling, even for Professor Emerson. And the more he puzzled over the invasion of his home, the more distracted he became.

He hadn't expected to work on his Sage Lectures during the Christmas holidays, but he'd been reading Dante and his commentators on a daily basis. Since the break-in, Gabriel had found it difficult to concentrate.

The words on his computer screen taunted him,

"Nel ciel che più de la sua luce prende
fu' io, e vidi cose che ridire
é sa né può chi di là sù discende;

"perché appressando sé al suo disire,
nostro intelletto si profonda tanto,
che dietro la memoria non può ire.

"Within that heaven which most his light receives
Was I, and things beheld which to repeat
Nor knows, nor can, who from above descends;

"Because in drawing near to its desire
Our intellect ingulphs itself so far,
That after it the memory cannot go."

So Dante wrote in the first canto of *Paradiso*, imagining Beatrice at his side. So Gabriel, in attempting to pen a lecture fit for a world audience, was struggling.

When Dante was scolded by Beatrice near the end of *Purgatorio*, the narrative shifted. Theology structured the entire *Divine Comedy* but it became, perhaps, far more confrontational when presenting the purpose of humankind and the nature of God and his governance.

In *Purgatorio*, Beatrice told Dante that his desire for her was supposed to direct him to the highest good, which was God. So what was at one point a story of romantic, courtly love became a story of the love one should have for God. And as the relationship between Dante and God was transformed, so the relationship between Dante and Beatrice was transformed. Or so Gabriel thought.

Gabriel knew his interpretation could be textually and historically supported. But he wondered how the audience in Scotland would respond. Despite his cross-appointment in the Department of Religion at Boston University, Gabriel was not a theologian. And unlike Dante, he was hesitant to venture into such subjects.

But here he was, awake on Christmas Eve, pondering the vagaries of love, devotion, and salvation, all while those he loved most lay fast asleep.

Whatever promises Dante had made to Beatrice, he'd fallen short of those commitments after her death. Gabriel, too, had made promises; first, to his wife, and second, to his child.

How could he leave them in Massachusetts while he moved to Scotland? Someone had invaded their home, touched their things, and potentially left behind a threat. He could no more leave his wife and child unprotected than he could willingly tear out his heart.

In a flash, his fingers flew across the keyboard,

Dear University Council Members of the University of Edinburgh,

   While I am grateful for your generous invitation for me to deliver the Sage Lectures in 2014, I regret I must decline. If there would be a possibility to reschedule the lectures to a later date, I would be most grateful.

   I apologize for declining at this juncture and under these circumstances. However, I find my home and my family under threat and so I cannot in good conscience relocate to Scotland for the 2013–2014 academic year.

   With much regret,
   Professor Gabriel O. Emerson, PhD
   Department of Romance Studies
   Department of Religion
   Boston University

Gabriel sat back in his chair and reread the email. Then he closed his computer.

Chapter Fifty-One

Christmas morning
Selinsgrove, Pennsylvania

G abriel had been busy.

In true, Santa-like fashion, he'd stuffed the stockings that were hung with care from the mantel and placed carefully wrapped gifts under the Christmas tree.

(No, he hadn't wrapped the gifts himself. He'd done what every self-respecting husband did at Christmas; he'd had the associates at the various stores wrap gifts for him.)

Now he was lighting a fire in the fireplace.

"I thought Father Christmas wore red."

Gabriel cursed, his hand clutching his heart.

A warmhearted chuckle emanated from the armchair near the window. A wrinkled hand reached out and switched on a nearby lamp. "Happy Christmas."

"Happy Christmas, Katherine." Gabriel drew a deep breath as his heart began beating normally. She'd given him quite a shock and ever since the break-in, he'd found himself jumpier than usual.

He gazed down at the pajamas that Julianne had gifted him the night before—green tartan flannel with images of moose imposed on them. "Father Christmas is an environmentalist this year and paying tribute to the moose population."

"I didn't mean to startle you. I'm still on Oxford time and have been awake for hours. I took the liberty of assembling an English baked omelet for everyone. I hope you don't mind."

"Not at all."

"I left out the tomatoes because some people don't like them." She refilled her china teacup from the teapot next to her. "I'm grateful you allowed me to invite myself for Christmas. I've grown tired of my extended family and their shenanigans. Did you know my cousin rang me back in November to say they were having a vegan Christmas dinner? I tend toward vegetarianism but even for me, that was a bridge too far. I knew you'd have the good sense to serve something other than Tofurkey."

"Ah, yes. Julianne and Rachel are cooking a genuine turkey."

"Excellent." Katherine pursed her lips. "I had an interesting conversation with your sister on the way from the airport."

"Oh?" Gabriel sat near the fire and leaned forward, resting his forearms over his knees.

"Yes, *oh*. What's this about your house being robbed?" Katherine's blue-gray eyes pierced Gabriel's.

"An intruder disabled our house alarm and broke in. He didn't take anything, but we surprised him and chased him from the house."

"It's a wonder you weren't hurt! Thank goodness. And Julia and Clare are all right?"

"Yes. We're having the security system upgraded and decided not to return to the house for a while, in case the thief comes back."

Katherine clucked her tongue. "That's terrible."

"Yes." Gabriel rubbed the back of his neck.

"Your sister also told me that Julia isn't going to Scotland with you."

Gabriel avoided Katherine's peering eyes. "Julianne met with Cecilia after we returned from Edinburgh and asked if she would approve a semester abroad. Cecilia refused."

Katherine frowned. "What was her reason?"

"She said Harvard was better than Edinburgh. She said she would look weak if she sent Julianne abroad and that the administration was already complaining about her, wondering why she hadn't been asked to deliver the Sage Lectures."

"Ah." Katherine placed her china teacup and saucer on her lap. "I'm sure my recruitment to Harvard pricks pride as well. But what Cecilia doesn't know is that Greg Matthews has been recruiting me for years. I think I surprised him when I said yes. Have you spoken with Cecilia?"

"No. Julianne didn't want me to interfere." Gabriel tugged at his hair in exasperation. "She's hoping Cecilia will change her mind. She wants to broach the subject during the workshop in April."

"Graham Todd is a first-rate scholar, so Cecilia can't object to him on scholarly grounds. Although she could argue that the Edinburgh courses aren't a good fit with Julia's program."

"She can't argue that at the moment because Edinburgh's fall schedule hasn't come out yet. Graham was going to send it to Julianne."

"Indeed." Katherine finished her tea, staring off into space.

"What would you recommend?"

Katherine smothered a smile. "Your sister seems to think I'm Wonder Woman. I find the comparison rather amusing.

"As tempting as it may be for me to interfere, that wouldn't be prudent. I imagine Cecilia now thinks of you, me, and Julia as a confederacy of sorts. She won't take kindly to me sticking my nose into things."

"Right." Gabriel's body deflated. "I had thought the same."

"Greg made it perfectly clear I was being hired to supervise graduate students, which means if Cecilia drops Julianne, I'll gladly take her on. But I can't do so until my appointment begins."

"Thank you." Gabriel ran his fingers through his hair distractedly. "I know Julianne will appreciate it."

"This should be her decision. She should decide who her supervisor is and she should decide whether she takes a semester abroad. Cecilia shouldn't force her hand."

Katherine paused, leaning forward in her chair. "Don Wodehouse is impressed with Julia's mind. If she wanted to transfer to Oxford, Don would take her."

"Oh." Gabriel tugged at his hair. A move to Oxford might be good for Julianne, but it wouldn't be good for their marriage. He didn't want to commute across an ocean. He didn't want to live apart from Clare.

"But there's no reason for Julia to leave Harvard. Not while I'm alive and kicking."

It was almost imperceptible, but Gabriel flinched.

Katherine waved her hand in his direction. "Go ahead. Out with it."

"Of course Julianne would be eager to work with you. But she's concerned about the optics if Cecilia drops her and . . ." Gabriel trailed off, looking very uncomfortable.

"And she's terrified I'll die in the middle of her dissertation."

"Katherine, losing you would be a great personal loss." Gabriel gritted his teeth. "Damn the dissertation."

"I have no intention of dying."

"Good, because I forbid you to die."

Katherine's eyes widened. "Would that it were that easy—Gabriel

Emerson forbids one to die and one is therefore immortal. I don't think the universe operates that way, although I appreciate the gesture. I had thyroid cancer. I was diagnosed and treated back in Toronto and didn't tell anyone but Jeremy Martin. I didn't think it was anyone's business." Katherine's tone was matter-of-fact. "That was several years ago. I'm in excellent health and looking forward to moving to Harvard. I won't last forever, but I should live long enough to supervise Julia's dissertation."

"I didn't know you had cancer, Katherine. I'm so sorry."

"I'm fine. I'm just rounder than I used to be. Obviously my weight isn't a barrier to being Wonder Woman, so I can't find it in me to care."

Gabriel lowered his head and chuckled.

"Yes, it's possible Cecilia could make noises about Julia and her abilities and it will look odd if Cecilia refuses to be a reader on the dissertation. But Julia is already making a name for herself based on hard work. So a semester abroad will be a good opportunity for her, even if Cecilia decides to be petulant. I will do my best to neutralize the gossip, and if Julia continues to impress Don Wodehouse, he will as well." Katherine straightened in her chair. "And we are not to be trifled with.

"Now, since we've spoken of academic policies, cancer, and death, I'm going to invoke the privilege of an old woman and I'm going to tell you something." Katherine placed her teacup aside, her expression growing serious. "Gabriel, you must be careful not to sabotage your career."

He began to protest but Katherine interrupted by lifting a single finger.

"Look back at your life with an objective eye, and you'll see that I'm right. You got yourself into a predicament in Toronto, which ended all right but could have derailed your career. Now you find yourself in a potential conflict with Cecilia, and I know you must be thinking how you can get out of the Sage Lectures so you can keep your family together."

Gabriel shut his mouth firmly.

Katherine wagged her finger at him. "I knew it. Cecilia is threatening Julianne. You've had your house broken into and you're worried it will happen again. Now you're regretting your acceptance of the Sage Lectureship and thinking you'll fall on your sword in order to protect everyone.

"You made a promise, and you have to keep it, no matter what happens with Julia and Harvard. Backing out of the Sage Lectures, except in the case of death, will derail your career. As much as you and Julia are equally scholars and equally important, the truth of the matter is she is a student. She can find a new supervisor, she can transfer to a different graduate program, but you can't regain the respect of the academic community if you insult the University of Edinburgh. So before you do something that can't be undone, I want you to listen to what I'm saying.

"Julia has agency and she needs to make her own decision about who her supervisor will be. I can't speak about the security of your house but knowing you, you'll install a security system that will rival that of Buckingham Palace and no one will dare trouble you again. But you are going to Scotland next year, and that's that." Katherine brushed her hands together, as if she were ridding them of dust.

Gabriel was silent.

"It's far too early to be so morose." Katherine went over to him. "I've overstepped, I'm sure. But I care for you. In many ways, you and Julianne are my children—my academic children. Any legacy I have, academic or financial, will be passed to you and to my goddaughter."

Gabriel swallowed against the lump that formed in his throat. "I don't know what to say."

"You don't need to say anything. You have forbidden me to die, and I have forbidden you to turn down the Sage Lectures. Provided we each keep our end of the bargain, all will be well."

She patted him on the shoulder. "Cecilia will likely get over her fit of pique by April. And if she doesn't, Julia can study with me and I'll gladly send her to Scotland. When I have a chance to speak with her privately, I'll tell her. And I'll stress my good health."

"Thank you." Gabriel's tone was carefully polite.

Katherine squeezed his shoulder. "Now, Wonder Woman is going to make breakfast, wearing as your sister puts it, *an age-appropriate pantsuit.*"

She chuckled to herself and continued to the kitchen, leaving Gabriel to mull over her words.

Chapter Fifty-Two

H o, ho, ho. Merry Christmas." Old St. Nicholas himself (formerly known as Richard) entered the living room.

He wore a full white beard and a white wig beneath a red hat. His Santa suit was red velvet and trimmed with white. He carried a set of sleigh bells, which he jingled heartily.

He greeted Aaron and Rachel, who was taking pictures, and Katherine and Gabriel. Scott and Tammy were spending Christmas with Tammy's parents in Philadelphia and would travel to Selinsgrove a few days later.

As Father Christmas approached Julia and Clare, the baby burst into tears.

Richard stood back, stunned.

"Oh, dear," said Julia, holding her crying daughter. "I didn't expect this."

"I did," said Rachel. "Clare has no idea who he is. He could be an ax murderer."

"Really?" Gabriel gave his sister a censorious look. "An ax murderer?"

Richard moved the sleigh bells somewhat anemically. "Merry Christmas."

Clare continued to wail and turned her face into her mother's chest.

Richard lowered his arms. "I'm sorry."

"I'm not." Katherine stepped forward. "You're a very good Father Christmas. Authentic costume, hearty laugh. Well done, sir."

"Thank you." Richard didn't sound convinced.

"Rachel, play some music," Katherine commanded. "Something peppy."

"Um . . ." Rachel pulled out her cell phone and scrolled through the songs. She swiped across the screen and music began to play: "Rockin' Around the Christmas Tree" performed by Brenda Lee.

The music distracted the baby, who paused crying long enough to see Katherine put her hand on Father Christmas's shoulder and draw him into a dance.

After Richard overcame his initial shock, he tossed his sleigh bells aside and placed his hand at Katherine's waist, and the two seniors began to swing dance.

Gabriel stood by the fireplace, staring.

Rachel increased the volume of her cell phone and grinned at Julia, putting her fingers together to form the letter *W*.

Wonder Woman, she mouthed, before whistling at the dancers.

Clare forgot her crying and watched as Santa Claus and a prominent Dante specialist from All Souls College, Oxford, rocked around the Christmas tree.

It was, as Julia would tell Gabriel later, the best Christmas present ever.

※❀※

"Ah, here you are." Katherine breezed into the kitchen later that afternoon, after Gabriel had put Clare down for a nap.

Rachel had gone with Aaron to his parents' house for lunch and to open Christmas presents. Julia was starting on the turkey.

"Can I help?" Katherine peered around the kitchen.

"I was just going to peel the potatoes." Julia pointed to a large bowl in the sink. "They're washed and scrubbed. I'm making mashed potatoes."

Katherine pulled up a stool to the large island in the center of the kitchen and held out her hand. "Give me a peeler."

Julia obliged and the two women sat side-by-side, peeling potatoes and transferring them from one large stainless steel bowl to another.

Katherine held her potato peeler aloft. "Richard is very nice. He's handsome and a true gentleman, and certainly the man can dance. But as much as I appreciate younger men, I'm not getting involved with him."

Julia's mouth dropped open.

"So please tell Rachel." Katherine circled her potato peeler in the air. "She's a good girl, but remarkably persistent."

Julia almost choked. "Uh, I'll mention it to her."

"Now, I want to talk to you about Cecilia Marinelli."

Scheisse, Julia thought but did not say.

Katherine continued peeling her potato and lowered her voice. "Tell me what happened."

Julia stared into the bowl of potatoes and gathered her thoughts. When she was ready, she recounted the conversation that had occurred in Cecilia's office.

"Codswallop," said Katherine. "So how were things left?"

"I didn't want to argue with her. I told Gabriel I'd like to speak to her again when I have the list of courses from Edinburgh. Maybe Cecilia will be more receptive then."

Katherine efficiently finished her potato and began working on the next one. "You have to decide what you're going to do, of course. I will take you on as a doctoral student, if you wish."

"Thank you," Julia said quickly. "I'd hoped to have you and Cecilia on my dissertation committee."

"That may not be possible, if Cecilia is stubborn. But, Julia, Gabriel can't turn down the Sage Lectures." Katherine fixed her gaze on Julia.

"Of course not." Julia reacted in horror. "He isn't going to."

Katherine lowered her potato. "Are you certain?"

"He hasn't said anything."

"That's what I thought. It isn't my business to psychoanalyze him. He's a grown man and a friend. But there is something in him that's self-destructive. And I fear even now he's contemplating throwing the invitation to Edinburgh away, just so he can stay in Boston with you."

Julia looked stricken. "He can't do that. It would be a scandal and he knows it."

"He had a scandal in Toronto and as much as I've forgiven both of you for keeping me in the dark, I'm still put out." Katherine's expression was one of irritation.

"Katherine, I am so sorry. We never meant to—"

Professor Picton interrupted her. "You are going to have to work out this situation with Cecilia. Otherwise, your husband is going to find himself all alone in a dark wood, having strayed from the sure path."

The Dante reference was not lost on Julia. She nodded quickly.

Katherine lifted her potato peeler and held it like a scepter. "Cecilia is a friend but that doesn't make her infallible. She's punishing you and Gabriel because she's jealous, and that is a poor look for anyone. You need to take control of the situation and not be manipulated like a marionette."

"I will." Julia's tone was resolute.

"Good. And for the record, I am in good health and have no plans to expire." Katherine recommended potato peeling with new vigor, leaving Julia's potato-peeling skills far behind.

❀✻❀

"Come upstairs," Gabriel whispered to Julia, after dinner. His blue eyes sparked with promise.

"What about our family?" she whispered back.

"Everyone is fine." Gabriel gestured to the living room.

Diane, Julia's stepmother, was chatting with Rachel, who was playing with Tommy.

Tom, Julia's father, was doting on Clare and sitting with her on the floor.

Katherine, Aaron, and Richard were sipping sherry that Katherine had brought from Europe.

"Okay, but only for a few minutes." Julia relented. "Otherwise, they'll notice."

Gabriel took her hand in his and escorted her upstairs. When they entered the master bedroom, he locked the door.

Julia stood expectantly, waiting for him to kiss her.

But he didn't.

Instead, he entered the walk-in closet, switched on the lights, and emerged shortly thereafter, holding a tacky plastic pink flamingo that looked startlingly familiar.

Julia laughed. "Did you go back to the house and dig that out of the snow?"

"I removed it the day I met with the security company. And yes, I washed it." He handed it to her, his lips twitching.

"What am I supposed to do with it?" She took the flamingo dubiously.

"Open it." Gabriel pointed to an envelope that was strung artfully around the flamingo's neck.

Julia placed the lawn ornament on the floor and removed the envelope. "What is it?"

"It's your Christmas present."

"You already gave me my Christmas present." Julia gestured to the boxes and tissue that were strewn across the bed. Gabriel had insisted she open her gifts privately, and she was glad he had. He'd bought her underthings of various sorts, ranging from the elegant to the erotic.

She had gifted him with a new set of Montblanc fountain pens. And she'd had a very large black-and-white photograph of him and a newborn Clare printed and framed. The picture was so beautiful it made Julia's heart ache.

"Open it." Gabriel repeated.

She slipped her finger under the envelope's flap and stuck her hand inside. She retrieved a paper palm tree.

"Paper dolls?" she asked.

"No." Gabriel chuckled and turned the palm tree around so she could see what was printed on the other side.

Miami.

"I'm taking you and Clare on a holiday. We're staying in South Beach, overlooking the ocean. Merry Christmas." He appeared very pleased with himself.

Julia looked down at the palm tree. "I've never been to Miami."

"It's warm, there isn't any snow, and the food is exceptional. We'll be able to take Clare for walks in the sunshine and dig our toes into the sand. A true vacation."

She hugged him around the waist. "I'm shocked. I had no idea you were planning a trip."

"My first choice was Hawaii, but I thought that might be too long a flight for Clare. I've had it with winter, Julianne. If I don't see the sun soon, I'm going to lose it."

Julia resisted the urge to laugh. "We've had snow less than a month."

"I want to put some distance between us and Cambridge. I booked flights for January second from Philadelphia. We'll be gone two weeks."

"What about Rebecca? What about the house?"

"I invited Rebecca to join us, but she decided to extend her visit with her children. She'll meet us back in Massachusetts."

"And the house?"

"Still waiting to see if the intruder makes his move. The security company is monitoring everything; they've installed cameras, motion detectors, and a double-relay system, so the alarm can't be bypassed outside. I also spoke with Leslie. She's been keeping an eye on things for us and will continue to do so."

Julia met Gabriel's gaze. "When we get back, will we return to the house?"

Gabriel's expression shifted. "Let's talk about it in Miami. Jack's friend is still pounding the pavement, trying to find the thief. And Leslie is very attentive. She may be the best security system we have."

"I don't have any summer clothes with me. And I don't have summer clothes for Clare."

"You can buy bikinis and shorts in Miami."

"Bikinis? Gabriel, I just had a baby. And I had a c-section."

"Four months ago." His gaze dropped to her chest and lower down. "You look great."

"You are such a man." She shook her head.

"I apologize for nothing. I'm only irritated we have a house full of family and the walls aren't soundproofed."

"I bet the closet is soundproofed." Julia looked over his shoulder.

Gabriel turned the flamingo so it was facing the opposite direction of the closet. Then he lifted Julia into his arms and fairly ran into the closet, closing the door behind them.

"Let's find out, shall we?" His mouth descended to hers.

Chapter Fifty-Three

January 7, 2013
South Beach, Florida

Just as the Emersons were preparing to leave their hotel suite for the pool, Gabriel's cell phone rang.

He glanced at the screen. "It's a FaceTime call from Vitali. I'd better take it."

"We'll be at the Center Pool." Julia kissed her husband and pushed Clare in the stroller toward the door.

"Why not use our private pool, on the balcony?"

"Because there will be other mothers and children at the Center Pool. Clare might make a friend."

"Right. I'll find you shortly."

Gabriel moved to the desk in their suite and answered the call. "Massimo, hello."

"Good afternoon," *Dottor* Vitali responded in Italian. He gestured to the dark-haired woman who sat next to him, wearing a very smart red suit.

"Professor Gabriel Emerson, I want to introduce you to *Dottoressa* Judith Alpenburg. She recently joined us from Stockholm and she is the expert on religious objects at Palazzo Pitti."

"Pleased to meet you, *Dottoressa*." Gabriel nodded, reaching for his glasses.

"And you. Please call me Judith," she answered, her Italian lightly accented with Swedish. "I examined the memento mori you sent to us. It's an exciting find."

"Thank you, Judith." Gabriel put on his glasses and quickly retrieved a notepad and his fountain pen. "Can you tell me more about it?"

"Certainly." She put on a pair of white gloves and presented the small sculpture against a black velvet background. "This piece is very interesting. We tested the material, taking care not to damage the object, and discovered it is carved from elephant ivory. I would place the date of the object at about 1530. I will come back to the date in a moment."

She turned the object over. "As you can see, along the collarbone of the head, we have an inscription in Latin, *O Mors quam amara est memoria tua*, which I would translate as *O Death, how bitter is your memory*. Do you recognize the quotation?"

"I don't."

"The quotation is from Scripture. This is the first line of Ecclesiasticus forty-one, which in the Vulgate begins, '*O Mors quam amara est memoria tua.*'"

"Interesting." Gabriel resolved to look up the passage later.

"Similar items are on display in various museums, including the Museum of Fine Arts in Boston. And the Victoria and Albert Museum in London has several excellent examples.

"In my opinion, your carving is of high quality. There are a lot of details, as you can see. Worms and toads are figured over the head.

The face has an open mouth with exposed teeth, and there are folds of fabric covering the head. Leaves have been carved into the lower part of the object and it sits on a small circular pedestal. There is some damage to the piece—a crack in the head. But it is still a valuable and rare item. Certainly, one we would be proud to display."

"Can you tell me anything about the provenance?"

Judith smiled eagerly. "Yes, this is very exciting. The object, which I believe to be a bead, has been pierced vertically, so it could be suspended from a chaplet—rosaries or prayer beads are more common terms for this. There is a maker's mark on the bottom of the bead, which you can see." She lifted the figure and revealed the bottom. "When I saw the mark, I realized I had seen it before. So I went through the items we have at Palazzo Pitti, but I didn't find the same mark. However, when I went to Palazzo Medici Riccardi, I found something interesting."

Judith placed a large photograph next to the bead. "In the Palazzo Riccardi museum, there is this chaplet that belonged to Alessandro de' Medici, who was Duke of Florence from 1532 to 1537. Alessandro was thought to be of African heritage, which means that he was the first African head of state in the modern West. The chaplet was in his possession when he died and it eventually became part of the museum's collection.

"However." Judith's blue eyes lit up with excitement. "As you can see from the photograph, the chaplet is missing a bead. In fact, it's missing the largest bead at the end. I spoke with the archivist at the museum and he was unable to find a record of a missing bead. The chaplet came to the museum without it.

"But he pointed me to a letter written by Taddea Malaspina, Alessandro's mistress, and she mentions the bead going missing. It was lost, until you sent it to us."

Both Judith and Massimo smiled giddily through the screen.

"How do you know the bead I sent is the missing one?" Gabriel leaned closer to his cell phone, trying to get a better look at the photograph of the chaplet.

"The maker's mark matches the mark on the opposite end of the chaplet. The carvings and designs on the chaplet are identical to those on your bead. There's a repeated pattern." Judith took her finger and moved from the bead to the photograph, carefully pointing out the similarities.

Gabriel frowned. "Wasn't Alessandro murdered?"

"Yes," *Dottor* Vitali interjected. "He was assassinated by his cousin Lorenzino. Of course, now that we know your bead matches the chaplet at Palazzo Riccardi, I'm sure the director will contact you." *Dottor* Vitali smiled hopefully.

"Yes, of course." Gabriel was distracted, still trying to process what had just been revealed. "Massimo, why was Alessandro assassinated?"

"There are several theories. In my opinion, Lorenzino assassinated his cousin for revenge."

"Revenge?" Gabriel's eyebrows instantly shot up.

"Lorenzino was a friend of Filippo Strozzi. Alessandro tried to assassinate Strozzi and failed. Strozzi persuaded Lorenzino to kill Alessandro in revenge. But this is my opinion. There are other explanations."

"Did you discover anything about the more recent provenance of the object?"

"No." Judith glanced over at Massimo. "We were hoping you could help with that."

"I'm afraid I can't. The bead was found on my property in Cambridge. I contacted Interpol, through a friend, but the bead wasn't listed in their database of stolen artwork."

Dottor Vitali tapped his fingers on the table in front of him. "We can make discreet inquiries."

"I'd appreciate that, my friend. Since I'm not sure who the rightful owner is, I'd be grateful for any assistance in locating him or her."

Judith appeared disappointed, but she didn't comment.

"Certainly, we can help." Massimo's tone was reassuring.

"Thank you. Judith, it was a pleasure meeting you. Thank you for your research. I'm very grateful."

Judith inclined her head respectfully. "Thank you, Professor Emerson. It's a wonderful piece and I hope, if I may, that the piece can be reunited with the chaplet someday."

"Give my best to Julianne." Massimo artfully redirected the conversation.

"I will. Speak to you again soon. Good-bye." Gabriel signed off FaceTime quickly.

He pulled out his laptop, entered his password, and quickly pulled up an online edition of the Latin Vulgate. He scrolled through the book of Ecclesiasticus, commonly known as the book of Sirach, and found the verse from which the inscription on the memento mori had been taken.

"O death, how bitter it is to remember you for someone peacefully living with his possessions, for someone with no worries and everything going well and who can still enjoy his food!"

Gabriel scrubbed at his face. The purpose of a memento mori was to call to mind one's mortality. But the Scripture contrasted the bitterness of mortality with the peaceful life of a prosperous man.

Something about the Scripture reminded him of a reference in Dante. It took a few minutes of searching for Gabriel to find it, but in the first canto of *Inferno* he read,

"Tant' è amara che poco è più morte;
ma per trattar del ben ch'i' vi trovai,
dirò de l'altre cose ch'i' v'ho scorte.

So bitter is it, death is little more;
But of the good to treat, which there I found,
Speak will I of the other things I saw there."

Gabriel leaned back in his chair, removed his glasses, and closed his eyes.

Dante was referring to the dark wood he'd entered midway through his life. The memory of the wood was itself bitter, just like the bitterness of the memory of death.

But the Scripture was a caution to those living in prosperity. And Gabriel knew that he was among them.

Coupled with the symbolism of the Scripture, there was the provenance of the object itself. It had belonged to a man killed for revenge.

Is the object a message? he wondered. *And if I'm being warned or targeted for revenge, why?*

Chapter Fifty-Four

Julia was in love with Miami.

Hotel Estrella in South Beach had several pools. Families favored the Center Pool, which boasted an ocean view, daybeds, and cabanas.

Julia made herself at home on a double chaise longue underneath an umbrella and brought Clare to the side of the pool. They both wore hats and sunglasses. Julia dunked Clare's feet in the water and she kicked happily.

Julia had just ordered a frozen drink from an obliging waiter when Gabriel came striding down the deck.

He was wearing sunglasses and a black Adidas jacket, along with black swim trunks. Julia noticed that several heads turned as he walked toward her.

"Hi." He crouched next to them and gently tugged Clare's sunhat. "Do you like the water?"

Clare reached for him and he pretended to bite her fingers, making a growling noise. Clare shrieked and giggled, putting her hand out so he would do it again.

"Do you mind if I take a quick jog on the beach?" Gabriel asked Julia. "I need to clear my head."

"Are you okay?" Julia lowered her sunglasses.

Gabriel kept his eyes shielded. "Yes. Massimo had an update about the sculpture we found at the house. Nothing urgent. I'll update you when I come back."

"I ordered a virgin margarita. Do I need to change my order?"

The edges of Gabriel's lips turned up. "No. I'll be back soon." He deposited his jacket and his sandals with Julia before tugging Clare's hat again.

He waved just before he descended the staircase that led to the beach, leaving Julia to ponder what had left him so disquieted.

***

Gabriel ran.

He kept close to the waterline, enjoying the sounds and rhythm of the surf, his mind thousands of miles away in Florence, Italy.

The memento mori came from the Medici. In itself, it was a wondrous find. But how did the piece come to be in the possession of a thief? And why had he left it in Gabriel's house?

Professional art thieves sold their goods to collectors; they rarely kept them. A bead from a chaplet was a strange piece for a thief to have in his pocket, unless it was resting there for a purpose.

Revenge.

Gabriel quickly rejected the notion that he was being targeted for revenge. Yes, he'd offended his share of people over time, including disgruntled students and jealous colleagues. And no doubt his face had been plastered on more than one woman's dartboard, although he had been discreet with his liaisons and had tried to restrict them to women who understood the temporary nature of their connection.

There was Professor Singer, for example. But she was in Toronto and he doubted she'd hired a professional thief from Italy and asked him to leave a death threat in his house. That wasn't her style. Professor Singer would deliver any and all threats personally.

And there was Paulina. But she was happily married and living in Minnesota. They'd made peace and he believed she wished him well. Again, she had no cause for revenge, at least not now.

As for the thief's possible connection to Italy and perhaps to Florence, Gabriel couldn't imagine what he'd done to attract the ire of a Florentine. He'd been a lover of Italian history, literature, and culture for years and had supported the museums of Florence with generous donations.

Nicholas Cassirer's parents had sold him the Botticelli illustrations. But they were reproductions of Botticelli's originals, likely done by one of his students. Perhaps there had been other interested parties who would know now that Gabriel was the successful buyer. But to come after him now, after so many years, seemed unthinkable.

A piece of the puzzle was missing. Without it, he couldn't see the whole picture. Without it, he couldn't be sure of the thief's motives for anything. All Gabriel had were theories and hypotheses, several of which might fit.

He turned around and jogged back toward the hotel.

The best possible outcome was that the thief was scoping out Gabriel's collection and that the sculpture had been dropped accidentally. If the motive were revenge, and if Gabriel truly was the target, the thief could have killed him inside the house and Julianne wouldn't have been able to stop him. As it was, the thief had used only enough force to get away. He'd seemed entirely uninterested in Julianne and Clare, and for that Gabriel thanked God and would continue to do so.

What if he returns?

This was the question that plagued Gabriel—and in addition to it, the possibility that the thief would return while Julianne and Clare were in the house and Gabriel was in Scotland. That possibility was the stuff of night terrors.

Julianne's nemesis had a name and a face. Thanks to Nicholas Cassirer, Gabriel had a man following and reporting Simon Talbot's every move.

Gabriel's new nemesis was nameless, unidentifiable, and amorphous. His motives were indecipherable, his actions confusing, which made him far more threatening.

The new nemesis provided one more reason why Julianne should demand to go to Scotland in the fall. Gabriel still had the email he'd drafted to the University of Edinburgh. In less than a minute, he could decline the invitation and ensure that he and his family remained safe and together.

As he ascended the staircase to the hotel pool, Gabriel recalled Katherine's warning.

Although he valued his career and would be sorry to throw it away, it was better to risk a career than the safety of his wife and child. He'd already lost one daughter, long ago. He wasn't about to lose another.

Chapter Fifty-Five

"D id you ever read *Treasure Island*?" Julia was sitting on the edge of the pool, her legs suspended in the water.

"Years ago. Why?" Gabriel stood in the shallow end, swirling Clare in circles and dipping her in and out of the water. She seemed to enjoy it.

"Someone gives Billy Bones the black spot. It's a pirate death threat."

Gabriel wrinkled his nose. "Yes, I remember."

"Do you think the memento mori is a black spot?"

Gabriel looked over his shoulders, as if he were worried someone was eavesdropping. He walked over to Julia. "No. If the thief meant to kill me, he could have. I'm inclined to believe he dropped the carving accidentally."

"Accidentally?" Julia lifted her eyebrows behind her sunglasses. "Why would he be carrying a museum piece in his pocket?"

Gabriel spun Clare around quickly and she giggled. "Perhaps it was a token he took from another robbery. Perhaps he thinks of it as a good-luck charm, like a rabbit's foot."

"Perhaps he's a fan of the Grateful Dead. He's a Deadhead." Julia tried to keep a straight face, and failed.

Gabriel gave her a withering look. "Very funny. Why would he issue a death threat and leave, when he could have finished the job?"

Julia shivered and took a large drink of her virgin margarita. "I don't know."

"If it were an assassination, he would have done the job and left. There's no reason to leave threats. I think Nicholas is correct; the thief wanted to know what we had in the house, so he could report the contents to potential buyers."

"Right." Julia adjusted her large, floppy sunhat. "Should I put more sunscreen on Clare?"

"In a minute." Gabriel continued moving Clare in and out of the water. She banged her fists on Gabriel's chest, almost as if she were demanding he move faster.

"What about you, Professor?" Julia admired his fit upper body and lean, muscled arms. And the tattoos on his chest. Dante and Beatrice were emblazoned on his skin for the world to see, as were the dragon and Maia's name.

"I put some on before. After we see to Clare, perhaps you could help with my back." Gabriel stared at Julia's legs as they moved underwater. "How is your ankle?"

"Perfectly fine. But I'm worried about reinjuring it."

"And your other leg?" Gabriel had lowered his voice.

She lifted her right leg out of the water. "It bothered me on the airplane. But since we've been here, it's felt better. I hadn't even noticed it until you mentioned it."

"Hmmm," said Gabriel. "Do you think it's improving?"

"It's better than it was at Thanksgiving." She lowered her leg below the water. "What about the carving you sent to Vitali? Are we going to give it to the Cambridge police?"

"No. So far it hasn't shown up on Interpol's list of missing works of art, but that doesn't mean it isn't stolen. I've asked Vitali to make inquiries and see if he can find out who owns it."

"Whoever owns it will want it back."

"Then let him go and get it." Gabriel gave her a challenging look.

Julia lifted her hands, still holding her margarita. "Won't we get in trouble with the police for withholding it?"

"If the thief was the true owner, he'd implicate himself when reporting it stolen. If the true owner was robbed, hopefully *Dottor* Vitali will find him or her."

"You're screwing with the thief."

"A little," Gabriel admitted. He stopped moving. "Do you think I should give the sculpture to the police?"

"I think it's better for humanity as a whole for it to be in a museum. It belongs with the original chaplet. They may not accept it given how we found it."

Gabriel brought Clare over to her mother. "They have no proof of prior ownership. It disappeared after Alessandro's assassination. It could have changed hands dozens of times after that."

Julia tasted the salt on the rim of her margarita glass. "We might have been thinking about this the wrong way."

"What do you mean?"

"The thief may not know we have it. If it was dropped by accident, he can't be sure where it landed. It could be in the yard or on the street. He could have lost it in his car. He may come back to look for it, or he may decide it's too risky to return."

Gabriel sat next to her, holding Clare securely on his lap. "You and I are both eyewitnesses. We have a sketch of him. That, by itself, may give him pause."

"True." Julia finished her drink. "If we keep the sculpture's discovery a secret, he can't be sure we have it. Since we've upgraded the security system and we are both eyewitnesses, he may decide to target someone else. I think you should ask for the carving back and we should bind *Dottor* Vitali to secrecy, at least for a while. Let the thief search for the object elsewhere."

"That's a good idea." Gabriel reached over to take her lips. His gaze dropped to her indigo bathing suit. "You look beautiful, by the way."

Julia patted her abdomen self-consciously. "You don't think the bikini is too much?"

"I picked it out. I love it."

A warm glow suffused over her face, for his admiration pleased her.

"Enough talk of unhappy things," he whispered. "We're in a beautiful city, enjoying beautiful weather. I have plans for you tonight."

Julia leaned her head on his shoulder. "What kind of plans?"

"Adult plans."

He took her lips again and all thought of black spots and memento mori flew out of her head.

※※

"This is lovely." Julia gazed in wonder at the elegant dining room on the main floor of the SLS Hotel.

Gabriel had brought her to José Andrés's new restaurant, The Bazaar, which was located inside the hotel. The décor was airy and fresh, the staff numerous, and the music Latin inspired and sultry.

Clare sat in her baby carrier next to Julia on a love seat, dozing after a day outside. Gabriel sat across from the pair, his attention entirely fixated on his wife.

"I really like Miami. My entire mood has changed." Julia admired the golden cast to her skin that she'd earned over multiple mornings at the pool.

The sun had kissed her hair, lightening some strands of chestnut to golden brown and honey. She'd been letting her hair grow out and now it hung in sexy waves to her shoulders. On this evening, she wore a tangerine sundress that fell to her knees and bronze-colored sandals that laced up her lower legs.

Gabriel bought her a glass of champagne, which she sipped slowly, savoring the tiny bubbles. Despite all that was unknown and ominous in their lives, at that moment, Julia felt light.

Miami seemed to agree with Gabriel, as well. His tanned skin contrasted with the white shirt he wore unbuttoned at his neck. His hair was wavy from the Florida heat and his smiles were easy.

Julia fairly glowed as she drank her champagne and spoke enthusiastically with the waiter, who told her the history of the chef and his passion for food.

"We need to spend more time here." Julia gazed at the array of Spanish and Cuban tapas that were spread across the table.

"We can. We don't have anywhere to be until April." Gabriel served Julia some octopus cooked *à la plancha*.

"You can't be serious."

He served himself and chewed reflectively. "Why not? I'd need someone to courier some of my books and files, so I could work on my lectures. I'm sure Rachel wouldn't mind."

"It's tempting." Julia sampled the octopus and rolled her eyes heavenward. It was perfectly cooked and seasoned. Delicious. "It would be expensive to stay so long at the hotel."

Gabriel shrugged. "We're comfortable. I suppose if we decide to stay into February, we should rent a place."

"So you're still working on your lectures?" Julia posed her question nonchalantly.

"Yes." Gabriel's eyebrows knitted together. "Did you think I wasn't?"

"Oh no, not that. You know Katherine is worried you'll decline."

Gabriel rearranged the napkin on his lap. "Yes, she mentioned something of the sort.

"What about you? You'd need your books."

"I should be working through Wodehouse's reading list. It's been slow going."

"Bring your books to the pool. Or pull up the articles on the iPad." Gabriel lifted the chef's homage to a Cuban sandwich and took a bite. He paused, his eyes darting to Julia's. Without speaking, he passed the plate to her and gestured for her to take a bite. "It's incredible."

Julia sampled the sandwich and quickly agreed. "This reminds me, I want you to take me to Little Havana. I want to eat at the Versailles restaurant."

"Done. We'll go tomorrow."

"When would we go back to Massachusetts?"

Gabriel wiped his mouth with his napkin. He sipped his sparkling water and helped himself to some of the endive salad.

"Darling?" She waited.

"Let's give it a month for now. After that, I think the possibility that the thief will return becomes even more remote. If he's keeping an eye on the house, he'll see it's empty." Gabriel reached across the table to take her hand. "Besides, our anniversary is January twenty-first. Why don't we celebrate here?"

"When we go home, we'll return to our house?"

"If it's safe."

"I miss the house," Julia blurted. "I miss sleeping in my own bed. I miss the nursery and all of Clare's things."

Gabriel stroked the back of her hand with his thumb. "I miss the house, too."

"But I'm nervous about going back."

Gabriel dipped his chin, which was the closest to an admission of anxiety Julianne was likely to get.

"Even if we wait a month, there's no guarantee the thief won't come after that." Julia gestured with her champagne. "If he's truly hunting artwork and he's decided he wants our Thomson or the Cézanne, he'll come back eventually."

Gabriel's expression grew thunderous. "That is why I don't want you, Clare, and Rebecca in the house alone."

Julianne put down her champagne to give him her full attention. "What are you saying?"

Gabriel's sapphire eyes gleamed. "You know what I'm saying."

She leaned across the table. "Didn't you listen to what Katherine said? You can't break your promise to the University of Edinburgh."

"What about my promises to you? And to Clare?"

Julia sat back, shaking her head. "You have other options."

"Yes, you and Clare could join me in Edinburgh."

"I'm trying," Julia whispered through clenched teeth. "I probably shouldn't have approached Cecilia as soon as your lectures were announced. I caught her at a bad time."

Gabriel lifted his arms at his sides. "Months have passed. She hasn't changed her mind."

"April. Let me ask her when we're in Oxford. Graham Todd will be there. Maybe he will talk to her, too."

Gabriel rested his hands palms-down on the tablecloth. "I can give you until April, but only because the lectures are scheduled in the winter term of 2014. But if Cecilia refuses and you still choose to work with her, then I'm going to solve the problem myself. I won't have you on one side of the ocean, unprotected, while I'm stuck in Scotland. And that's that."

Julia's face fell. She lifted her fork and started picking at the food on her plate, then gave up and put the utensil down.

"Here." Gabriel stood, placing his napkin on the table. He came around to her side and nudged her over, sitting next to her on the love seat.

Julia was caught between a sleeping baby on one side and an obviously intent Gabriel on the other. She had nowhere to go. "What are you doing?"

"I'm touching you." He placed his arm along the back of the love seat and drew her into his side.

Julia trembled.

His mouth grazed the shell of her ear. "I've dimmed your light. Now all the brightness has gone out of the room."

When she didn't answer, he swept her hair behind her shoulders and grazed his fingers down her neck. "What can I do to bring back the smiling, happy Julianne of a few minutes ago?"

She turned toward him. "Promise me you won't give up the Sage Lectures."

Now it was Gabriel's turn to be silent.

Julia's mouth found his ear. "I won't let you sacrifice yourself for me. Never again."

Gabriel clenched his jaw. "We make sacrifices for each other. That's the point."

"This sacrifice is too big. And it isn't necessary, because there are other ways around it."

"I won't do anything without speaking to you first," he conceded.

Julia placed her hand on his knee. "I will be fighting just as hard to protect you, as you are fighting to protect me and Clare."

Gabriel's face softened, as did his voice. "It's the mother in the species that's truly dangerous."

"Exactly. Don't get between a mama bear and her family. Now, are you going to stay here or are you going back to your chair?"

"It's lonely over there." Gabriel flashed a rakish smile. "And you're gorgeous."

"You are infuriatingly charming."

"I have no idea what you're talking about." He nudged the strap of her sundress aside in order to press a light kiss to her shoulder. "But I'd do anything to make you happy again. Forgive me. I'm trying my best."

She gave him a half-smile. "I want another glass of champagne. But I know I'm not supposed to drink while I'm breastfeeding. When we get back to our hotel, I demand satisfaction." She gave him a knowing look.

Gabriel immediately beckoned to their waiter.

Chapter Fifty-Six

After they returned to their hotel, Julia fed and changed Clare and put her to bed.

Gabriel stood in the living room of their suite, gazing out at the ocean. He'd opened the sliding doors that led to the balcony. A soft, warm breeze brushed across the curtains, causing them to sway.

"Is she down?" he asked, hopefully.

"Yes."

He extended his hand and Julia went to him.

He'd turned out all the lights, except for the ones that glowed blue inside their private pool. The sun had slipped below the horizon and the stars were sailing above them.

He escorted her to the balcony, where he'd covered the daybed with cushions and soft blankets. And he'd lit candles, as was his custom, placing them artfully around the bed, with a few scattered near the pool. Soft Latin guitar music wafted from the stereo in the living room.

He lifted her hand and spun her in a circle, causing the full skirt of her orange dress to billow about her. Then he caught her in his arms. "We haven't danced in a while."

"I know." She made a contented sound and pressed her cheek against his chest, over his tattoo.

Gabriel was unhurried, moving lazily back and forth, his chin resting atop her head. "I'm sorry I ruined dinner."

Julia squeezed his waist. "It wasn't ruined. We just have a lot of things to worry about."

"I wish you'd let me worry for you."

She lifted her head. "Marriage doesn't work like that."

Gabriel sighed his agreement and pressed her close to his heart. His hands moved from her back to her waist and lower down. He cupped her backside firmly. "Incredible."

She reached up and pulled his mouth to hers.

A brush of lips, a hint of contact. They'd been lovers for some time and yet, after even a short absence, they took their time becoming reacquainted.

Gabriel kissed the corners of her mouth. He pecked the center. He drew her lower lip into his mouth and groaned.

Julia wrapped her arms around his neck and pressed her breasts against him.

He nudged at the seam of her lips with his tongue and she opened. She accepted him eagerly, her tongue twisting with his.

"I will never stop wanting you," she whispered, kissing him deeply again.

"Bless you for that." He spoke against her mouth before stroking inside.

A few minutes later, Julia pulled away. "Can anyone see us?"

"No. There's no one above us and I doubt anyone could see us over the glass of the balcony." His lips widened. "So long as we're lying down."

A gentle breath of wind whispered over them, causing her skin to pebble. "Did you have something else in mind?"

"Not tonight. Tonight, I am reminded of loving you on the balcony in Florence, when we were very new. I want to recapture that evening."

He lifted her hand and kissed it, his blue eyes finding hers. He brought her hand to his chest and pressed it over his heart. "See how it beats faster, knowing you're near."

She drew their connection to her own heart and pressed. "It's the same for me."

She released his hand, but he kept it where it was, his thumb caressing the tops of her breasts.

"Your eyes are shining," he observed. "Glittering like dark pools."

"I know what's in store for me."

"Come, then." He kissed her again, his fingers winding through the waves of her hair. They slid down her back and gripped her waist.

He eased her onto the daybed and stretched beside her, his kisses slowing to gentle pressure, lips against lips.

"What do you want?" he murmured, easing the straps of her dress down her shoulders.

"I want to see you."

Gabriel's eyes sparked. "Undress me."

Julia unbuttoned his shirt and swiftly pushed it over his shoulders. His hands moved to her bra and unfastened it with one hand. Now they were both naked to the waist.

Gabriel's skin was warm as he covered her, her nipples brushing against his chest hair.

He kissed the arch of her throat and descended the valley between her breasts, moving to cover one with his hand. The other he explored with lips and the merest edge of teeth. His tongue darted to taste her nipple.

He was careful to kiss and lick but not to draw on her. Still, she clasped his head urgently, pressing him closer to her breast.

When her grip lessened, he transferred his affections to the other breast. His hand dipped to the skirt of her dress and slid beneath it, ascending her thigh.

He lifted his head. "No underwear?"

Julia nodded, a subtle lift to her mouth.

"Surely you aren't forgoing underwear after I gifted you with enough for days?" His long fingers drifted below her hip bone into the crease between her hip and her inner thigh.

"It made me feel sexy. When you said you were going to touch me, at the restaurant, I wondered if you'd discover my secret right there."

Gabriel cursed. "If I'd known, I would have."

"We'd have been arrested."

"Not arrested." Gabriel smiled against her lips. "Merely asked to leave." He coaxed her legs apart, beneath her dress.

Her hand moved to his belt, which she unfastened. She touched him over his trousers before tugging the zipper down. Her fingers found the band of his underwear and slid beneath. She found him already hard and eager.

"Not so fast," he warned.

She explored him deftly until he grew impatient and moved her to a seated position.

"Off," he commanded, tugging at her dress.

She lifted her arms and he pulled the fabric over her head, dropping it to the floor. But Julianne would not suffer being the only one naked. She tugged at his trousers and boxer briefs until he lifted his hips and kicked them away.

It was darker now. The blue glow still lifted from the pool, while the pale starlight shone above.

The shadows cast by the candles danced over their naked forms as Gabriel covered her with his body.

With his hand he parted her, touching lightly. Julia tugged his hand away. She grabbed his backside and opened her legs, and his hips fell against hers.

"Are you in a hurry?" He smiled down at her.

"Clare might wake up." Julia's hands smoothed over his backside and she gripped him.

"She wouldn't dare." Gabriel kissed her nose.

"She has before." Julia's eyes met her husband's.

"Point taken." Gabriel covered her mouth with his even as their lower bodies slid against one another.

Julia groaned and urged him on with her hands.

He responded, surging forward and gaining entrance with one smooth thrust.

Julia put her head back, lifting her hips.

Her breasts rose tantalizingly below his face and he plied them with kisses, using the edge of his teeth against the round, full flesh.

She urged him forward and he began to move, her hands dropping away as he found a satisfying, slow rhythm.

"Look at me," he whispered, arching above her.

She gazed up into his eyes. There was possession, and protectiveness, and want. Anxiety, perhaps, and hope and love.

He watched her to decipher her reactions, to see what made her head loll back and her hands grip tighter. To read eagerness in the rise and fall of her breasts. To see urgency when she found herself on edge.

Self-control was not one of Gabriel's virtues, but his pride in being a good lover motivated its development. In the case of Julianne, making love to her inspired him to temperance.

He wished for their coupling to last as long as possible and to raise her to the heights of pleasure and keep her there until her body rebelled and she came. Only then would he chase his own completion.

"I'm close," she panted.

He increased his pace incrementally, drawing out her climb.

Her hands clamped on his backside like a vise and she pulled and pulled, bringing him deeper inside her.

She held her breath and her body tightened. He could feel her losing control.

He moved more quickly, dropping his head to kiss her breast.

She clutched him to her chest as her head rolled back. He felt as well as heard her pleasure overtake her.

Now he could chase.

His pace increased, faster and faster, his hand grabbing hold of her hip. A flaring of nerves and an exquisite quickening, and he was releasing inside her. His entire body contracted.

By the time he opened his eyes, she was already kissing him. Embracing his forehead, his chin, his mouth.

"It was so beautiful," she said, a touch of wonder in her voice. "It is always so beautiful with you."

"You're beautiful and you deserve all good things." He nuzzled her neck before gazing into her eyes. "Always."

He kissed her softly and moved to her side, breaking their connection. They lay entwined in one another's arms until the night breeze drove them indoors.

Chapter Fifty-Seven

January 15, 2013

T his is interesting." Julia handed her cell phone to Gabriel.

They were sitting side by side in the shade of a cabana, steps from the ocean. Clare was situated in a small children's cabana, resting atop a towel and surrounded by toys. Although she'd been placed on her back, she'd rolled onto her stomach. When she complained about being on her stomach, Julia moved her to her back. The process was repeated from time to time.

"Who is this from?" Gabriel removed his sunglasses to put on his reading glasses. He squinted at the screen.

"Professor Wodehouse."

"He's inviting you to give a paper?"

"Yes, my paper on Guido da Montefeltro. He wants me to deliver it on the first day of the workshop."

Gabriel scanned the email and returned the phone. "That's quite an honor."

"Do you think I should do it? I'll be making myself conspicuous very quickly."

Gabriel put his reading glasses away. "Of course you should do it. Wodehouse has already heard the paper and it has been published. He probably wants you to provoke the attendees."

"He'll be giving a paper on Ulysses." She scrolled through her email. "I don't know. Giving a paper, and then being followed by Wodehouse and his paper? I'll look terrible."

"Nonsense." Gabriel swung his legs over the side of the chaise and leaned over to retrieve Clare.

"Cecilia will be there."

"She's the one who first read that paper. She endorsed it."

"She may have changed her mind."

"Then Wodehouse will have her for breakfast. He's the one inviting you; it's his workshop and his reputation." Gabriel reached into the children's cabana and retrieved Clare, along with a book, *The Runaway Bunny*.

Clare reached for the book eagerly and began chattering.

"I also have an email from Graham Todd," Julia volunteered.

Gabriel sat Clare on his lap and opened the book to the first page. "What is he saying?"

"He doesn't have the schedule yet for the fall, but he's teaching a graduate course on angels and demons in *The Divine Comedy*."

Gabriel looked over with interest. "That sounds fun."

"Yes. He's also teaching a Renaissance poetry course for undergraduates, and he's asking if I'd like to be his teaching assistant. He said the workload wouldn't be onerous. He can't promise a stipend, although he thinks he could offer me an honorarium. But he says he's offering the position to give me experience." Julia put down her phone. "Edinburgh is rolling out the red carpet for both of us."

"I think someone has been talking." Gabriel sounded grim.

"Who?"

"A certain English person who happens to have the initials *KP*."

"Oh, you mean Wonder Woman?"

Gabriel shook his head. "Rachel is mad. Do you know she bought Katherine a Wonder Woman T-shirt?"

"Katherine will never wear it."

"No, but I'd lay money she frames it and puts it on a wall somewhere."

"The children in Florence thought you were Superman."

"They did." Gabriel smiled broadly at the memory. "And you were my Lois Lane."

"I'd like to go to Florence this summer. I'd like us to spend time with Maria."

Gabriel turned his head. Julia gazed at him hopefully.

"Of course. You know, she may be adopted at any time."

"I know."

He reached out to grab Julia's hand. "But we should spend some time in Florence and introduce Clare to the city and our friends. We can visit Umbria, as well."

"I'd like that."

"We've agreed to lend the house in Umbria to Rachel and Aaron for the last two weeks in April. So we'd have to go after that."

"That's fine."

"I'm still waiting for the BBC producer to set the dates for my trip to London. It may be while you're in Oxford."

"As long as Rebecca comes with me, I'll be okay. Professor Wodehouse has been very welcoming, but I doubt he'll allow Clare to register for the workshop."

Gabriel and Julia exchanged a look. He squeezed her hand and released it.

He lifted the children's book and began to read to Clare. He read slowly, positioning the pictures in front of her, and pointed to them. He asked Clare questions and waited, as if she would answer.

Clare leaned against his chest and stared in rapt attention at the pages of the book. When he was finished, he read her another.

Julia snapped pictures with her phone.

❀❀

The following morning, Julianne was being pampered at the hotel spa, on Gabriel's insistence, while he sat with Clare on the floor, playing with blocks. His cell phone chose that inopportune moment to ring.

Clare complained about the noise.

He fastened her securely in a high chair and placed a few toys in front of her, then answered the FaceTime call.

"Gabriel, good morning." *Dottor* Vitali's face appeared on the screen.

"Hello, Massimo. How are you?"

"Good, thank you." Vitali shuffled some papers on his desk. "I made some telephone calls about the memento mori. I didn't use your name. But I'm sorry to say, I haven't been able to discover anything. Museum directors around the world contact one another, from time to time, when artifacts appear. I've been approached on numerous occasions by people trying to sell valuable pieces. Sometimes the ownership is legitimate, sometimes not. I reached out to a few people to ask if they'd ever seen your carving. They haven't."

"I see," said Gabriel slowly. "Thank you for trying."

"Of course, of course. It's possible the piece has been in a private collection and handed down over time. Sometimes a family doesn't know what they have. They may think the object is a fake or that it is modern or something like that. But I can tell you no one is looking for that piece, at least at the moment. It isn't showing up on lists of stolen artwork and no one has approached any among my circle in order to sell it."

"Right. In view of that, Massimo, I think I'll have to ask you to return it. I'm uneasy lending it until I know more about how it came to be on my property."

Dottor Vitali's face fell. "I understand. We need to be clear on the provenance of an object before we accept it. In this case, provenance is a mystery."

"The mysteries in my life are legion at the moment." Gabriel frowned. "But I'm grateful for your assistance and for Judith's help as well."

"Certainly. I hope you and your family will come to Florence soon?"

"Yes, Julianne and I were just discussing that. Probably in May."

Dottor Vitali rubbed his hands together. "Excellent. We will see you then. I will arrange to have the carving returned to you."

"Thank you, my friend."

"Good-bye." Massimo ended the call.

Another dead end, Gabriel thought.

He shook off his disappointment and retrieved Clare from her high chair. "Let's go for a walk, while Mommy's out."

Clare responded by grabbing Gabriel's chin.

Chapter Fifty-Eight

The day of her second wedding anniversary, Julia was awakened by pain. She grabbed her lower abdomen, waiting for the pain to pass, but it didn't.

Quietly, she crept past a sleeping Clare in her crib and entered the bathroom, closing the door behind her before switching on the light.

She was not a medical doctor, but she knew her body well enough to know she was not suffering from indigestion or an upset stomach. When she went to the bathroom, she discovered her instincts were correct; she was having her period.

Her monthly cycle had taken time to return with regularity, even after she'd resumed oral contraceptives. Julia's brain was fuzzy in the early morning, as she had been kept up late enjoying the attentions of her amorous and devoted husband. But as she counted on her fingers, she realized her body was right on time.

She was concerned, however, at the unusual degree of pain she was experiencing, since birth control had in the past ameliorated it. And she was equally concerned with the amount of bleeding she was experiencing, which was far more than normal.

It occurred to her she should contact Dr. Rubio when she returned to Cambridge, since bleeding and discomfort were both side effects of fibroids. Although her fibroids had shrunk during her pregnancy, she knew it was possible they were growing even now.

Julia shut her eyes. She was squeamish at the best of times. And now was not the best of times.

She switched on the shower and adjusted the temperature. When she entered the shower, she positioned the hot spray on her lower back, hoping it would provide some relief. She refused to look at the water that fell at her feet and disappeared down the drain. It would not do for her to pass out, alone, while Gabriel was fast asleep.

Later, having attended to her needs and having wrapped herself in the soft, plush robe provided by the hotel, she called the front desk and requested a hot water bottle. Even though they didn't have one in stock, they quickly sourced one and delivered it.

Julia crept outside to watch the sunrise from their balcony, swathed in a blanket and with a hot water bottle resting over her womb.

I can't believe this happened on my anniversary, she thought.

All her plans and the special lingerie she'd hoped to wear would be for naught.

Sometimes being a woman sucks.

❁❁

"This is not how I planned our anniversary." Julia bemoaned the fact as she walked next to Gabriel and the stroller on the Lincoln Road promenade.

It was a beautiful, sunny day in Miami. Julia was clad in a bright, breezy blouse and black shorts, sporting her favorite sandals.

Gabriel, too, was wearing shorts, his eyes hidden behind his sunglasses. And Clare was clad in a sunsuit, wearing a sunhat to protect her face and eyes. She was fascinated by all the people and especially the many leashed dogs as they walked past her.

"I told the front desk we were staying for another week." Gabriel glanced at her out of the corner of his eye. "Happy anniversary."

She leaned against him. "Really?"

"I have plans for you and our private pool." Gabriel's tone was matter-of-fact. "When you're feeling better."

Julia found the thought tantalizing.

"How are you feeling?" Gabriel lowered his voice to protect her privacy.

He was tender with her, it was true. But the concern with which he treated her most pedestrian of female experiences was truly touching.

"Better. I took something for the pain, and being outside where it's warm helps."

Gabriel gave her a sympathetic look.

By accident, Clare dropped her favorite toy bunny (which was not from her father) over the side of the stroller. And then she leaned over to look at it.

Her father had a short learning curve. After almost losing the bunny on a walk the previous day, he'd fashioned a kind of short leash for the bunny and Velcroed it around the toy's middle. Which meant that should the toy fall, Gabriel could retrieve it by pulling on the leash. It really was ingenious. (Although Gabriel had contemplated leaving the bunny behind on more than one occasion, simply because of its origins.)

"I had another email from Graham." Julia sipped the ice coffee she'd just purchased. "I'd told him I couldn't commit to Edinburgh until my supervisor signed off on the courses. He offered to speak to Cecilia directly."

"Let him. Maybe he can talk some sense into her."

"I don't think that's a good idea. I told him this morning that I'd speak to her when I saw the list of courses. But I also said I was interested in the teaching assistantship."

"Good. It will be a great experience. I wonder if we could arrange to have you teach an undergraduate class over at Boston University." The wheels were already turning in Gabriel's mind.

Julia stopped. "You'd do that? You'd suggest that to your chair?"

"Why not? They hire adjuncts. I can't guarantee the chair will hire you, but we should ask."

"I'd like that." Julia resumed walking.

"We should look into it the fall after we come back from Scotland." Julia nodded.

"Julianne." Gabriel lowered his voice. "I've spoken with both Nicholas Cassirer and your uncle Jack in the past couple of days. Neither of them has been able to uncover any information about the intruder."

"What does that mean?"

"It means the man is a ghost. Jack has been working things from this side of the Atlantic, while Nicholas has been speaking to his contacts in Europe. Nothing has emerged."

Julia drank more coffee. "I suppose if the man is a professional, he'd try to keep a low profile. If he's good at what he does, he won't get caught, which means he wouldn't have a record."

"That was Nicholas's assessment as well."

"Gabriel, I hope this doesn't mean you're planning on keeping us in Miami indefinitely."

"No." Gabriel stopped the stroller and moved to the side. He caught the toy bunny that was dangling from its leash and placed it on the tray in front of Clare. She grabbed it and hugged it. "Rebecca says she wants to go back to the house, but I asked her to wait for us."

"And what did she say?" Julia felt into step with Gabriel as he continued pushing the stroller.

"She relented. I think she misses us, but since we aren't there, she's content to have a longer stay with her son. Although it sounds like he isn't home much, because he's working."

"She's probably spoiling him with her cooking."

"No doubt." Gabriel helped himself to his own (hot) coffee, which was resting in the stroller's (pretentious) cup holder. "How are you doing with Wodehouse's reading list, now that Rachel has sent you your books?"

"It's coming. I think if I work on it every day, I'll make progress. It's when I skip a day that I run into problems, because I forget where I am and have to reread passages. How about you?"

"It's coming along." Gabriel's features brightened, as they always did when he had the opportunity to talk about Dante. "What do you think of the river of Lethe?"

"Um, I don't know. I think it's the river of forgetfulness in Purgatory, right?'

"Correct. There's a debate in the literature as to how much forgetfulness it bestows on a human being. Some commentators argue it's a river of oblivion."

"I don't think that's right. The souls in Paradise have memory. So whatever the role of the river, it can't be complete forgetfulness."

"Exactly," Gabriel agreed excitedly. "This is one of the things Rachel has been struggling with. She picked up this notion that the blessed in Heaven are entirely removed from those of us still on earth—as if they'd forgotten about us or can't be bothered about us."

"Paradise has to be better than that. However, there is that strange passage in *The Divine Comedy* where Dante can't remember what Beatrice is talking about and she says it's because he drank from Lethe."

"There's the conundrum. That's part of what I'm trying to work out for my lectures. Beatrice says the waters will affect his sad memories."

"And the three virtues say he's faithful to her after he's drunk from the river. I think that's strange—that he needs to drink of forgetfulness in order to be faithful."

Gabriel wiped his mouth with the back of his hand. "I'm not sure that's what's happening. In any case, he hasn't lost all his memories. He asks for Beatrice in the next canto. And in the canto after that, she exhorts him to leave behind fear and shame."

"Fear and shame." Julia froze. "Can we sit down for a minute?"

"Are you all right?" Gabriel crowded close, his hand going to her lower back.

"Yes, but I think you've said something important. Is there a place to sit?"

Gabriel looked around. "Just past the church, there's some trees and a low wall; we can sit there." He grabbed her hand and piloted her forward.

When they reached the wall, he positioned Clare under the shade of the trees, facing him, and he and Julia sat down.

He placed his hand on her knee. "What is it?"

"I was just thinking about what you said about fear and shame. When I look back on my life, there are a lot of things I was ashamed about. And I'm still afraid of things."

"Julianne, you don't need to be afraid. Not anymore."

Julia entwined her fingers with his. "When you heal from a wound, you're supposed to move on. You should remember the lesson you learned, but not focus on the pain. I think that's Dante's point about the river Lethe. We need to forget the pain and put aside fear, and shame, and guilt, but remember the lesson."

"I think that's in line with what he's trying to communicate. But his exchanges with Beatrice are puzzling. After he drinks from

Lethe, he says he can't remember being a stranger to her. But we know he reacted to her scolding with shame in a previous passage."

"Lethe takes away the shame."

"But the memory of inconstancy seems to be gone, too. That's the problem I'm having. I think your account is healthier, but in canto thirty-three he says he doesn't remember the estrangement, nor does his conscience trouble him."

"Yes," Julia conceded. "That is a problem."

"Since we're on the subject . . ." Gabriel toyed with the ruby-and-diamond trinity ring he'd given her after Clare's birth. "Beatrice uses the allusion *if smoke is proof of fire* to argue that Dante's forget-fulness is evidence of a fault in his will."

"Smoke isn't proof of fire."

"Exactly. Smart girl." Gabriel touched her ring again. "There's a puzzle there—a puzzle inside a puzzle. Someone reading quickly would pass over Beatrice's remarks, finding nothing wrong with them. But if you stop to think about it, smoke isn't proof of fire; it's evidence of fire, perhaps, but not proof. Smoke could be caused by other things."

"Rarely, but yes."

"I think Dante wants us to dig a little deeper to excavate the al-lusion to forgetfulness and Lethe. And that's what I'm working on as part of the lectures."

"I hope you figure it out." Julia smiled. "I have no clue."

"Sure, you do." He admired her manicured fingers, evidence of her trip to the hotel spa. "You're my muse. You help me see things I can't see. And you propel me to be a better man as well as a better scholar."

"It's funny to hear that since I'm still a student."

"Wise people are always students. It's when you think you're be-yond learning that you're really in trouble." He leaned forward and brushed his lips across hers.

"Happy anniversary, darling."

"Happy anniversary."

Clare threw her bunny over the side of the stroller and stared in dismay as it dangled out of reach. She hadn't figured out yet that she could pull on the tether to retrieve it. She pointed to the bunny and made an indignant noise.

"Princess Clare commands me." Gabriel mock sighed. He retrieved the bunny and had it kiss Clare on the cheek.

"Lunch?" he asked. "I suppose we should have Italian, given the theme of our conversation."

"I was thinking of sushi, since Dr. Rubio banned me from eating it for so long."

"We need to go through her list of banishments and indulge in all of them. There's one in particular I have a craving for." He paused, and hurried to clarify, "Next week, of course."

"Yes, please." Julia's stomach flipped in anticipation.

Chapter Fifty-Nine

January 28, 2013

N ow is our chance." Gabriel took Julia's hand after sunset, fairly dragging her through the living room of their suite and out to the balcony.

On this occasion, he'd switched off the lights inside the pool as well as those on the balcony. Candles were positioned around the pool and the Jacuzzi, offering a low, warm illumination.

He'd chosen Latin guitar music again but kept the volume low so as not to wake the baby.

"Our chance for what?" Julia noticed that the daybed hadn't been made. Instead, Gabriel had placed their bathrobes on the bed, along with a stack of towels. In a dark corner of the balcony, the Jacuzzi hummed and bubbled.

"A midnight swim, before midnight." He tugged her toward the edge of the pool.

"I need to change." She tried to pull away, but he kept her close.

"You don't need to change."

Without words, he divested himself of his shirt and trousers until he stood barefoot in his boxer shorts. Then he waited.

Julia inspected their surroundings, just to be certain no one could see. She stood near him, as if he were a shield, and pulled her blouse and skirt off.

"May I?" He wrapped a hand around her waist and drew her closer.

She nodded.

He unfastened her bra and dropped it to the deck. Out of chivalry, he dropped his shorts before tugging her underwear down her shapely legs.

Taking her hand, he walked her to the edge of the pool and step-by-step down into the water.

He descended below the surface completely and when he emerged, he wiped the water from his face and smoothed back his hair. Water droplets clung to his shoulders and across his chest, glistening like little jewels atop his tattoos.

Julia decided to mimic him, and she, too, descended below the surface. When she emerged, he was standing in front of her.

He touched her face, an illegible expression on his own. He pulled her so they were flush against one another, the water rising to the tops of her breasts.

He kissed her.

It had been a week since they had loved one another and so his embrace was urgent, his pace quick.

Julia lifted her arms to his neck, clinging to him in the water. She kissed him back.

His hands slid down her arms to her shoulders, his palms smoothing across them. He reached below the water to cup her breast. His fingertips traced her nipple.

She reacted with a sharp intake of breath. She pushed her breast into his hand.

He passed his fingers over both of her breasts and brought his mouth to hers.

She leaned against him and he took her weight.

When he broke the kiss, he took her hand again, leading her back to the staircase. "It's warmer in the Jacuzzi." He gave her a dazzling smile.

He helped her up the stairs and down into the swirling, foam-capped water.

The water felt scalding against her skin, but once she submerged herself, she found herself enjoying the warmer temperature.

She gazed over at Gabriel expectantly.

He lifted his arms—an invitation.

She crossed to where he was seated and sat on his lap, legs dangling under water on either side of his.

His hands smoothed down the curves of her waist to where her hips flared. He squeezed, making an eager sound, and urged her closer.

Her breasts brushed against his chest as she felt him rise between her legs.

His hand passed over her navel and moved down, down. He lifted his head so he could see her eyes, just as his finger made contact.

Julia gasped and rested her hands on either side of his neck, leaning forward.

He continued to touch her, his hand jostled by the hot, swirling water. Then he slipped a single finger inside.

She lifted herself up, allowing him more room.

He moved in and out, gently stimulating her, his thumb pressing up against her.

When she was close, she pushed his hand aside and gripped him firmly. She lifted up and, guided by his hands on her hips, slowly sank down until she rested on his lap.

Gabriel groaned.

She used his shoulders for leverage and lifted herself up before slowly, slowly sinking down.

His fingers dug into her hips as she rolled forward on his lap. Then she was ascending and descending, up and down, her gaze dropping to the image of Jacob's ladder on his chest.

Gabriel's hand left her hip to lift her chin. His blue eyes seared into hers.

Up and down. Her gaze dropped to his mouth. His teeth bit into his lower lip as she rolled forward once again.

Ascending and descending. His hands began to lift and pull down, over and over. She ground herself against him.

He reached forward and kissed her neck, drawing the flesh against his teeth.

Julia rolled forward just as he thrust up, lifting his hips. His hands were a vise, keeping them joined.

She moved back and rolled forward. He jerked and pulled her closer, continuing to thrust up and in.

She felt him begin to lose control and bemoaned the fact she'd lost him. But then his hips shifted and she felt it, the glorious crescendo as every nerve in her body came alive. Pleasure raced along the nerves and she lost the ability to move.

Gabriel moved for her, his hips snapping forward.

Her head fell forward as he stilled. She felt him inside her.

His body tensed and relaxed.

And then his mouth was at her neck again, whispering kisses over the wet skin. "That was worth waiting for."

"Yes." She hugged him and rested her chin on his shoulder. It took her a minute to catch her breath. "Let's just stay here."

He kissed her nose. "All right. But I think eventually we'll start to cook."

"Well, let's get out before that happens." She toyed with his hair, winding the strands around her fingers.

His hands slipped slowly up and down her back, massaging her. "I'm not finished with you. Yet."

"Oh, really?" She sat back, searching his eyes.

"Really. More delights await you, if you get out of the Jacuzzi."

"Such as?"

"Such as one of the activities Dr. Rubio expressly and closed-mindedly forbade." Gabriel brushed his nose against Julia's. "So let's dry off and move to the daybed."

"I—I don't know if I have another incredible orgasm in me."

Gabriel's eyes narrowed with the focus of a dying man. "I'll take that as a challenge."

He lifted her out of the water and carried her up the steps and onto the deck. Then he placed her atop the daybed, wrapped her in a dry towel, and proceeded to best his challenge.

Multiple times.

Chapter Sixty

Julianne hadn't left the light on.

In itself, her choice was almost inconsequential. There was a night light in the wall nearby. There were lanterns that housed flameless candles in the hall, illuminating the path to the nursery, where Clare was sound asleep in her crib. But Julianne had switched off the lamp on her nightstand when she retired for the evening. By the time Gabriel joined her in bed, after a long evening spent in his home office making his own translations of Dante from Italian into English, the master bedroom was dark.

Gabriel hovered in the doorway, surprised by the sight.

Rebecca was asleep down the hall. She'd been working tirelessly since she arrived from the airport to make the house ready for them.

And she'd made lasagne for dinner, which was one of Julianne's favorite dishes.

Aaron and Rachel had joined them, speaking enthusiastically about their new jobs. Rachel had brought a stack of Dunkin' Donuts gift cards for Julianne, who accepted them gratefully.

And Leslie, their eagle-eyed neighbor, had greeted them with a homemade apple pie and tales of a very quiet but very alert Foster Place. The upgraded security system on the Emersons' property seemed to have accomplished its goals.

Nevertheless, Gabriel was surprised that their first night at home after the break-in, Julianne would be sleeping so soundly, in the dark.

He approached her side of the bed and as he did, he nearly tripped over that damn pink flamingo. Julianne had posed it like a guard dog beside her bed and she'd dressed it in an *I love Miami* T-shirt.

The Professor skirted the lawn ornament with distaste, but he allowed himself a restrained chuckle. If Julianne was making jokes, she wasn't mired in fear. And that relieved him. Greatly.

He kissed the top of her head and caressed her hair. Then he crossed to his own side of the bed and turned, admiring the repaired painting by Henry Holiday as it hung proudly on the wall opposite the bed.

He placed his glasses and his phone on his nightstand. He opened the drawer, simply to check that the memento mori was still there, after he'd unpacked it that afternoon. He closed the drawer, slipped into bed next to his wife, and succumbed to sleep.

Chapter Sixty-One

April 8, 2013
Magdalen College, Oxford

The wintry days of February and March soon gave way to spring. Graham Todd emailed the fall schedule of graduate courses being offered at Edinburgh and volunteered once again to speak to Cecilia and the chair at Harvard. Julia assured him she would handle it.

On April 6, the Emersons and Rebecca arrived in London and traveled to Oxford so that Julia could attend the Dante workshop organized by Professor Wodehouse.

Gabriel had to return to London the day Julia was to deliver her paper, on the first day of the workshop. He was to record a series of interviews and commentaries on Dante for the BBC. The producer had indicated he only need be in London for three days, which meant he would return before the end of the workshop.

Even so, Julia missed him and the support his physical presence gave.

As she entered the conference room at Magdalen College, she saw it was empty, save for one person. The man in question was six foot three and had dark eyes and dark hair. He was casually dressed in a button-down shirt and jeans and carrying a jacket that had *Saint Michael's College* emblazoned on the back.

"Paul." Julia greeted him shyly. Although he'd sent a card and a gift when Clare was born, this was the first time they'd seen one another since the last time they'd both been in Oxford.

After that, Paul had written to her saying he didn't want contact. Julia could still feel the sting of her friend's rejection, almost two years later.

"Jules!" Paul raced toward her and picked her up in a bear hug. "How are you? It's good to see you."

"It's good to see you, too." She laughed and begged him to put her down.

"Uh-oh. Is the Professor around?" He looked over her shoulder.

"No, he's in London until Thursday."

"Good. He won't punch me for hugging you." Paul embraced her once again before taking a large step back. "How was your trip?"

"It was good. Clare stayed awake almost the entire flight, but we kept her entertained. I'm still jet-lagged." Julia smoothed her hair behind her ears. "How about you?"

"Oh, fine. I arrived yesterday. Professor Picton met me at the train station. We had dinner last night."

"That's great. How are your parents?"

Paul jammed his hands into the pockets of his jeans. "They're fine. Dad is doing less and less on the farm, because of his heart. I help out when I can. You look good. How's the baby?"

Julia retrieved her cell phone from her messenger bag. "Can I bore you with a picture?"

"It won't bore me. I'd like to see her." Paul peered down at the screen. "She's getting so big. And look at all the hair."

"She was born with hair. I've been styling it." Julia showed him a few more pictures, including a photo of Gabriel holding Clare and smiling.

"That's the happiest I've ever seen the Professor." Paul marveled at the sight. "Clare has her father's eyes."

"She does. I thought they would change color and match mine, but they're as blue as his." Julia touched the screen absently and put the phone away.

"Listen, before everyone else gets here, I'm sorry about that email I sent. I was a jerk."

Julia lifted her head. "I'm sorry things were so weird."

Paul flexed his arms self-consciously. "I take it back, okay? I want us to be friends, if we can."

"Of course we can." A feeling of lightness settled over Julia's body. "I've missed you, Paul. I don't have many friends."

"I'm sure that isn't true." Paul changed the subject. "Gabriel must be pretty excited about the Sage Lectures, huh? Are you going with him?"

Now Julia looked over her shoulder. "I want to, but Professor Marinelli hasn't signed off on it. I'm going to ask her again sometime this week."

"What's her beef?"

Julia slung her messenger bag to the floor. "I'm still in course-work at Harvard and she doesn't want to accept transfer credits from Edinburgh."

"That's stupid."

"Tell me about it."

"Why are grad students always at the mercy of their professors?"

"Because we like pain." Julia sighed the sigh of the underdog.

"Do you remember her? Professor Pain?"

"Yes. I'd like to forget her." Julia looked around the seminar room. "Can you believe it was almost four years ago that we were in Gabriel's seminar in Toronto?"

"No, I can't." Paul appeared as if he were going to say more but lifted his chin toward the entrance. "Here come the others. Do you have plans for lunch?"

"No."

"Good. We can eat together in the Refectory." Paul grinned.

Julia nodded and turned to greet Professor Wodehouse and the rest of the workshop attendees.

She smiled at Cecilia but didn't rush over to her. Julia stayed close to Paul, finding a seat next to him when Professor Wodehouse went to the lectern to inaugurate the workshop.

Paul quietly slipped her a note.

Julia unfolded the paper in her lap, reading it surreptitiously.

Professor M. is an ass.

Julia had to cover her mouth to smother her laughter.

But she was careful to rip up the paper discreetly, lest it fall into the wrong hands.

❧❧❧

Forty-five minutes later, Julia finished reading her paper and opened the floor for questions.

"Why should we think St. Francis of Assisi traveled to the circle of the fraudulent at all?" a professor from Rome asked Julia. "Guido was a liar. He made up the story. It's clear."

"It's clear he's fraudulent, but we know from historical sources that some of what he claims is true. He had a pact with the pope. He became a Franciscan. The problem is that Guido blames others for the fate of his soul. And he mixes truth with falsity. Sorting out the two is the challenge. So although it's possible St. Francis never appeared and that it's complete fabrication, given the other parts of Guido's account, it's more likely the story of Francis is partly true, partly false."

The professor nodded and Julianne moved to the next question, which was from a younger professor from Frankfurt. "I enjoyed your paper. But what about the passage at the beginning of the *Inferno*, where Beatrice asks Virgil to guide Dante? She does this because she can't. So I'm wondering if the same force that prevents Beatrice from wandering through Hell would also prevent Francis from appearing in the circle of the fraudulent. In other words, Guido is lying when he says Francis appeared after his death."

"It's possible he's lying, yes," Julia replied. "But again, the rest of his speech is a mixture of truth and falsity. The point about Beatrice and Virgil is a good one. She asks for Virgil's help, but she also says she has no fear of Hell's flames, and that she longs to return to Paradise. So perhaps it's the case that she can visit Hell but only for a short while, which is why she can't guide Dante. If St. Francis is in a similar situation, perhaps he, too, can visit Hell briefly, but cannot stay."

"There are a lot of *perhaps* in your answers," a professor from Leeds joked, but he did so good-naturedly. "I can see why Professor Wodehouse was eager for a workshop in which to explore them. Thank you."

Julia reddened a little. She breathed a sigh of relief when there were no further questions and everyone clapped.

She sat next to Paul as Professor Wodehouse returned to the lectern to deliver his own paper.

"Good job," Paul whispered, giving Julia a discreet thumbs-up.

"Thanks. I'm sorry you've heard that paper before," she whispered back.

"It was even better the second time." He winked and turned his attention to Professor Wodehouse.

Chapter Sixty-Two

Gabriel stood looking out the window of his room at the Goring Hotel in London.

It was past midnight. He'd missed a FaceTime call from Julianne and Clare earlier. He'd been out for dinner and drinks with Eleanor, the BBC producer; Maite Torres, the television presenter; and the rest of the academics Eleanor had gathered for the documentary.

Like a cross between Survivor *and* Antiques Roadshow, he thought, *except the antiques are the academics.* Save himself, of course.

He tasted his tea dutifully, wishing it were Scotch. He wished he were crowded into the small rooms Julianne and Clare were sharing at Magdalen College, rather than the luxury of the finely appointed space at the Goring.

He adored luxury, of course, but it was empty without them. No toys on the ground, inspiring him to call down curses when he tripped over them at night. No burping cloths.

He sniffed the air. No diapers.

And yet, for all the luxury that surrounded him and for all the fine dining in London and the (admittedly) interesting conversations with world-renowned Renaissance specialists, Gabriel would have eagerly traded the lot of it to be able to tuck Clare into bed at night after reading the (not terribly) profound *Goodnight Moon*.

Here was the transforming grace of the family. Here was his legacy and his future.

Nothing could replace the contentment he felt in the presence of his wife and child. Although he knew there would be times in his life when they had to be parted, he resolved to keep those times as short as possible. Because without them, his luxurious, pretentious, scholastic life was empty and small.

Perhaps it was this realization that caused Dante to pen *The Divine Comedy*. Having had so great a love, his life was small without it. So he had to write a magnum opus in order to describe adequately his experience.

Gabriel put aside his tea and strode over to the writing desk that sat on the opposite wall. He picked up his cell phone and did something he'd sworn once he'd never do: He took a self-portrait. And he smiled gently in it.

He put on his glasses and with a few flicks of his fingers across the screen, he attached the photograph to an email he addressed to Julianne. He told her about his day and evening and wrote a very specific greeting to Clare,

> Daddy loves you, Clare.
> Be a good girl for Mommy.
> I'll see you soon.
>
> XO

Gabriel pressed *send*. As he readied himself for bed, he thought about Julianne opening the email in a few hours. He thought about her showing the photograph to Clare, and Clare pointing to the picture and recognizing him.

He was Clare's father, and perhaps that was Professor Emerson's most important title of all.

Chapter Sixty-Three

T he next couple of days were the longest of Julia's life. Or so it seemed.

She enjoyed the workshop and felt she was gathering lots of ideas for her dissertation, but Cecilia remained cold and distant toward her, especially when in the presence of Katherine Picton.

Julia spent most of her time during the day with Paul and Graham, when she wasn't running back to her rooms to feed Clare. Julia was grateful for Rebecca, who took Clare for walks and picnics and visits with her godmother, Katherine, who excused herself from a session or two in order to accompany the baby around Oxford.

On this day, Gabriel was due to return from London on the afternoon train. They'd kept in touch via emails and FaceTime, but he'd been busy during the day and evenings.

Gabriel described the other academics as something akin to what one might find in the British Museum. In fact, he hypothesized that a particular professor from University College London predated the Rosetta Stone.

And Cecilia had announced suddenly during the morning coffee break that she'd be returning to America the following morning, which meant that Julia could no longer wait. She had to ask Cecilia again for approval of a semester abroad at Edinburgh. So it was with great trepidation that Julia stood outside the door of Cecilia's temporary office in the New Building at Magdalen College on Thursday afternoon.

Julia took a deep breath and knocked.

"Come in," Cecilia called.

Julia opened the door. "Do you have a minute?"

"Certainly." Cecilia gestured to a nearby chair and Julia sat. The office was small but cozy, with a window that looked out onto The Grove. Nearby, a herd of deer were quietly nibbling grass. One could see the college's white buck standing proud among them.

Cecilia's desk was covered with papers and books, and her laptop was open. She appeared to be in the middle of writing.

She waited politely for Julia to speak.

Julia rummaged in her messenger bag, which had been a gift from Rachel and Gabriel several years ago. She retrieved a piece of paper and handed it to Cecilia.

Cecilia gave her a questioning look. "What is this?"

"This is the list of graduate courses in Italian Studies that are being taught in the fall at Edinburgh."

Cecilia's expression grew frosty. She skimmed the list and returned it to Julia. "Graham Todd's course in Dante is fine. But I don't see how coursework in modern Italian cinema will contribute to your program."

"There's a course on the influence of the Bible on Renaissance literature," Julia protested quietly. "There's a course in medieval poetry."

"The coursework offered at Harvard is more extensive, and more appropriate for your research. I'll be teaching a comparative course on Virgil and Dante that you should take." Cecilia's demeanor was implacable.

Julia looked down at the list of courses and slowly stroked a finger across one of the titles. "You won't approve a semester abroad for me?"

"No."

Julia searched Cecilia's expression, looking for any hint of equivocation. There was none. Resignedly, she placed the list back in her messenger bag and closed it.

"Thank you for your time." Julia stood and approached the door. "I enjoyed working with you."

"It will be all right." Cecilia proffered a small smile. "Many academic couples commute. You and Gabriel will be fine commuting for a year."

Julia looked at the doorknob, which was well within reach. She turned back to face her supervisor. "I'm not going to commute with my husband. Professor Todd's course looks interesting and he has invited me to be a teaching assistant for one of his undergraduate classes."

Cecilia removed her spectacles. She looked angry. "I've just told you I won't approve the transfer of those courses. They won't count toward your program, which means you won't be able to take your general exams in the winter."

"I understand. I'm going to call Professor Matthews and file paperwork to switch supervisors."

Cecilia blinked, as if Julia's response was unexpected. "Who will you work with?"

"Professor Picton. She looked at the Edinburgh coursework and agreed to supervise me. Her appointment at Harvard begins in August."

"You went behind my back." Cecilia's tone was accusatory.

"Only as a last resort."

"I won't serve on your committee." Cecilia switched to Italian. "You're short-changing yourself by forgoing the courses we are offering in the fall for the paltry offerings at Edinburgh. I won't read your dissertation, and I won't write a letter of recommendation for you when you try to get a job."

Julia recoiled. In the air, Cecilia's words were just sounds strung together. In Julia's world, they were arrows designed first to threaten and then to harm. Prospective employers would notice Cecilia's nonappearance on Julia's dissertation committee. They would notice the absence of her letter of recommendation in Julia's dossier. Beyond prospective employers, scholarship committees and grant-awarding agencies would also notice Professor Marinelli's lack of endorsement.

As Julia analyzed her professor, it became obvious Cecilia wasn't bluffing. Her arrows would find their target and their target was Julia's reputation.

She felt attacked. She felt wounded. She and Cecilia had previously enjoyed a very collegial relationship. Cecilia was the one who'd encouraged her to take a maternity leave. Now everything was unraveling.

There was a time when Julia had been the target of another professor's censure. Before Gabriel knew who she was, he'd met with her in his office in Toronto and told her their professor-student relationship wasn't working. She'd left the office humiliated. (And she'd left him an unintentional surprise under his desk.)

But Julianne was not that shy, awkward young woman anymore. And she would not allow herself to be a pawn in someone else's chess game of academic egoism.

She and Gabriel had survived months of separation and no contact before they were married. As long as they lived, Julia would do everything in her power to ensure that they were never separated again.

SYLVAIN REYNARD

She would do anything to protect Gabriel from himself, so that he wouldn't feel the need to reject the lectureship just to stay with her in Massachusetts. She would assert herself to Professor Marinelli, even if it meant accepting her unjust censure.

"I'm sorry you feel that way, Cecilia. I wish you the best." Julia held her head high and exited the office. She would not let Professor Marinelli see her dismay.

Chapter Sixty-Four

The Cloisters of Magdalen College were incredibly picturesque. Julia leaned through one of the open archways into the airy space, searching for the small stone carvings that ran along the walls. C. S. Lewis, the professor and author, had been inspired to incorporate those same carvings in *The Lion, the Witch and the Wardrobe*, one of Julia's favorite books.

On her first visit to Oxford, she and Gabriel had stayed in the college. And she'd sneaked out of bed late at night to look at the carvings. But she wouldn't dare set foot on the exceptionally manicured lawn in daylight, for fear of being evicted.

Her conversation with Cecilia replayed in her mind, over and over. Julia wondered if she could have handled it differently. She wondered if she hadn't broached the subject earlier, if Cecilia would have been more amenable.

Working with Professor Picton was an honor, of course, but Julia had enjoyed working with Cecilia. She had considered her a friend.

Their acrimonious parting was sure to haunt the rest of her graduate studies, and now her career. Even the power of Katherine's magic couldn't prevent Cecilia from speaking derisively about Julia and her project, if she so chose.

Academia was a good deal like a fiefdom.

"Looking for Aslan?" a cheerful voice called to her.

A tall, broad-shouldered man approached her from the side. Julia looked up into the face of Paul Norris and instantly felt gratitude. "I wish."

Paul's cheery demeanor changed when he saw her watery eyes. "What's wrong?"

"Cecilia wouldn't approve my semester abroad in Edinburgh. When I told her I was going to switch supervisors, she said she wouldn't serve on my dissertation committee and that she wouldn't write a letter of recommendation for me for the job market."

"Shit. I'm sorry." Paul moved so that he was leaning into the same archway as Julia. He stuck his hand in the pocket of his jeans and produced a tissue. "Here."

"Thanks." She took it gratefully and wiped her nose.

"I don't suppose Cecilia will change her mind?"

"She was pretty adamant."

Paul cursed. "It's ridiculous. You're in your last semester of coursework. Edinburgh has a program in Italian, and Graham is there. What's Cecilia's problem?"

"It's a long story, but basically I think she's upset she was passed over for the Sage Lectures. Our dean gave her some heat and I think she's taking it out on me."

"That's bullshit."

"Grad students are pawns. Or rabbits."

Paul gave her a quizzical look.

"Don't you know the parable of the rabbit and the typewriter?" Julia asked.

Paul shook his head.

"The rabbit is in her warren, typing furiously on a typewriter. She types for days and nights and finally, when she's done she emerges with her project. And there's a lion seated outside her warren, who has been scaring everyone away."

"And the lion eats the rabbit," said Paul.

"No. The lion protects the rabbit, so she can get her project done."

"You've lost me, Jules. I think you need to sit down, have a cold drink."

"The rabbit is the graduate student and the lion is a good dissertation director."

Paul searched Julia's eyes for a minute. "That's some bullshit right there. Who wants to work with a lion?"

"The point is you have to have a director who is strong and powerful enough to protect you from all the other animals that are trying to attack you."

Paul rubbed his forehead. "I am so glad I'm not a student anymore. I thought working with Gabriel was bad. Which lion will you work with now?"

"Katherine Picton."

Paul grinned. "She's a lion, for sure. The story of her calling out Christa Peterson and telling her she wasn't invited to the Oxford conference is legendary. Someone made a meme of Katherine yelling, 'Codswallop.'"

"I'd like to see that."

"I'll send it to you. I know Cecilia does great work, but Professor Picton is better. I'd choose Katherine over Cecilia in a heartbeat."

"I love Katherine, you know that. But I don't like to quit."

Paul bumped her shoulder amiably. "You aren't quitting. You're moving on to bigger and better things. There's a difference."

Julia smiled weakly. "Thank you."

"What are you going to write your dissertation on?"

"I'm still putting together the proposal, but I'd like to write about Guido da Montefeltro, St. Francis, and the death of Guido's son. I'd like to do a comparison between the two death narratives."

"I like your reading of why Francis appeared. You could bring in some of the hagiography of Francis, as well."

Julia's smile widened. "That's what I was thinking. I could talk about Franciscan spirituality and contrast that with Guido's political machinations."

"This workshop is perfect for you."

"It's been great. And people have been kind. I've had a lot of suggestions of books and articles to look up. I feel like I'm making progress."

"Good." Paul turned sideways so he could see Julia better. "Did Professor Picton agree to supervise you?"

"Yes. I still have to get the approval of my chair and Katherine has to sign the form. But she can't do that until she joins the faculty at Harvard, which happens in August. So for the time being, I'm without a supervisor."

At that moment, Paul's cell phone rang. The ring tone was "Guantanamera."

Julia eyed him curiously. "Cuban music?"

Paul's color deepened. "A friend of mine chose her own ring tone."

"Huh." Julia wanted to ask about Paul's friend but decided the subject might be too delicate.

Paul seemed to read her mind. "Her name is Elizabeth. We work together." He stopped abruptly and declined the call. "It's complicated."

"Sometimes complicated can turn out great." Julia gave him an encouraging smile.

"Sometimes." Paul put his phone back into his pocket. "Are you happy? With your life, I mean?"

"You've caught me at a bad moment, but in general, yes. I've come to the conclusion that falling in love is easy; it's life that's complicated. But I wouldn't trade my life for anyone else's, even though it hasn't always turned out the way I hoped."

"I'm glad you're happy." Paul looked down at his shoes. "You deserve to be happy, Rabbit."

"Thank you. You've always been a great friend." Impulsively, Julia leaned against his shoulder.

In return, he took her hand and squeezed it.

It was an intimate exchange, to be sure, but one born of true affection and friendship. Paul knew in that moment that Julia loved him. And although her love for him was not romantic, it was affectionate and it was deep. And it was the kind of love he hoped would continue through their lives, even as he pursued a different love with someone else.

They moved apart at the same moment, smiling shyly down at their shoes.

Footsteps sounded from nearby, and Julia saw Gabriel striding toward them, pushing Clare in her stroller. She was barefoot and kicking her feet happily, a toy bunny hugged to her chest.

Paul leaned toward Julia and whispered conspiratorially. "I see my rabbit was a hit."

"Don't mention it in front of Gabriel, but it's her favorite toy," Julia whispered back. "She won't go anywhere without it."

"She has great taste."

When Gabriel reached them he greeted Julianne with a kiss. Then he extended his hand to his former student. "Paul."

"Professor Emerson." The two men shook hands.

The Professor hesitated, his blue eyes evaluating the other man. Seemingly satisfied, he said, "You should probably call me Gabriel."

Julia's mouth dropped open.

Paul appeared surprised but quickly recovered himself. "Gabriel," he repeated dutifully.

"When did you get back?" Julia asked, hugging her husband extra tightly.

"A little while ago," he replied. "I went straight to the rooms to drop my luggage and then brought Clare to find you. Don Wodehouse said he thought he saw you over here."

"Paul, this is Clare." Julia leaned over and kissed the baby on her head.

"Hello, Clare." Paul reached out for the bunny. He wiggled it in her arms.

Clare pulled the bunny away from him. "Bababa," she replied, as if she were scolding him.

"I won't take your baba. I promise." Paul straightened. "How old is she?"

"Just over seven months," Julia replied. She spoke to the baby, asking how her morning was. The baby chattered in return.

"Katherine has invited us all to dinner at All Souls," Gabriel announced. "We're supposed to arrive at six thirty. Appropriate dress is required."

The Professor resisted the urge to stare at Paul's casual clothing of a button-down shirt and jeans. However, he adjusted the collar of his own pristine white shirt, possibly subconsciously.

"Great. Thank you." Paul pointed in the direction of the library. "I need to look up a few things before tomorrow's seminar. And then I guess I need to change. I'll meet you at All Souls tonight."

Gabriel nodded formally.

"Thanks, Paul." Julia gave him an appreciative smile before he departed in the direction of the Magdalen library.

"And thank you." She hugged her husband once again. "Thank you for being nice to him. He's been supportive of me all week. I was so grateful he was here, especially since Cecilia has been giving me the cold shoulder."

"Something has changed in Paul." Gabriel gazed into the distance. "He relates to you differently."

Julia shut her eyes and opened them. "I can't imagine how you could tell such a thing within a few seconds of seeing him."

"Call it a husband's instinct." Gabriel focused on his wife. "What is happening with Cecilia?"

Julia scratched the back of her neck. "I went to see Cecilia a little while ago. I ran into Paul after I left her office."

Gabriel pulled Julia's hand away from her neck and held it. "What did she say?"

"She said what she said before—she won't approve a semester abroad."

Gabriel pressed his lips together. "And what did you say?"

"You'd be proud of me. I told her I was switching supervisors."

"I am always proud of you." Gabriel's eyes met hers. "But are you sure you want to do that?"

"Absolutely." Julia leaned closer. "She was spiteful. Spiteful and vindictive. I wasn't even going to tell her who I was going to work with. I simply thanked her and tried to leave, but she pressed me for details. When I told her I was going to work with Katherine, she said she wouldn't serve as a reader on my dissertation committee. And she said she wouldn't write a letter for me for the job market."

"That's absurd!" Gabriel sputtered. "You've been working with her for over two years. She should give you a letter on those grounds alone."

"She won't." Julia's spine straightened and her eyes flashed. "That's when I knew I was making the right choice, not just for you and me, but for my career. I don't want to work with someone like that. I don't want to have to walk on eggshells for fear she'll drop me at any moment. Katherine would never do that."

Gabriel tugged Julia into his arms, burying his face in her neck. "So you're coming with me to Edinburgh?"

"Yes. I need to call Greg Matthews and explain the situation to him. I'll update Katherine over dinner."

Gabriel's arms tensed around Julia's back. "I'm furious with Cecilia. Are you sure you don't want me to talk to her?"

"No, I handled it. Even if Cecilia hadn't been spiteful, I wasn't going to allow her to keep us apart. I just wanted to give her a chance to do the right thing."

"Patience is one of your greatest faults."

"I thought patience was a virtue."

He pulled back to make eye contact. "In my case, definitely. In your case, not even close."

Julia laughed.

"The University of Edinburgh has offered us a row house on Drummond Street, near Old College," Gabriel announced enthusiastically. "There's a brilliant coffee shop on the corner, and good sidewalks for the stroller."

"We'll have to childproof it. Clare will be walking by then."

"Really?" Gabriel ran his fingers through his hair. "So soon? That's marvelous. We'll be able to explore the city together and the rest of Scotland as well."

"I think you're going to be busy being the lecturer in residence. And I'll be taking courses, and serving as Graham Todd's teaching assistant, if he'll still have me."

"He'd be fortunate to have you. We'll travel on weekends. And holidays." He picked her up and lifted her toward the ceiling.

"Put me down!" Julia shrieked, clutching his shoulders. "Professor Wodehouse will see us and kick us out."

"I doubt it. I'm sure Don has twirled pretty girls in the Cloisters a time or two in his past." Gabriel's laughter matched her own.

Clare made noises in her stroller, demanding attention.

"Hi, Clare." Julia waved at her. "Mommy and Daddy are talking right now.

"What about our house in Cambridge?" Julia asked, when her feet were finally on the floor. "What about Rebecca?"

"I'm hoping Rebecca will come with us because we'll need the help," Gabriel said firmly. "What would you think about having Rachel and Aaron house-sit while we're away? They can keep an eye on the house and it will save them rent."

"I think that's a great idea." Julia closed her eyes, momentarily distracted by all the things she was going to have to do in order to prepare to move to Scotland.

Gabriel caught her hand once again. He thumbed her wedding band. "I'm so grateful we will embark on this journey together. I know we'll be busy and I know it will be an adjustment. But I think living in Edinburgh will be an adventure." His blue eyes shone.

"And here I thought you were a hobbit, who liked to stay in his warm, safe hobbit hole in Cambridge, and disdained adventures."

Gabriel sniffed his dissatisfaction. "I look more like Aragorn than a hobbit."

"Yes, I suppose you do." She kissed away his frown.

"We haven't a moment to lose. You should call Greg Matthews immediately." Gabriel took hold of the stroller and pointed Clare in the direction of their rooms. "I'm going to call one of the kilt makers in Edinburgh and order a kilt for Clare."

"I didn't know the Emersons had a tartan."

"They don't, but there's a Clark tartan. She'll dress in their plaid, in honor of Richard and Grace. And there's a Mitchell tartan, too, I think. We should have a kilt made to honor your father."

"I'd like that." Julia took hold of his arm. "But as we plan for Scotland, there's still one more thing."

"Anything."

Julia smiled sadly. "The memento mori. Before we invite Aaron and Rachel to house-sit, shouldn't we be sure the thief won't come back?"

Gabriel looked down at Clare, who looked up at him. She smiled, exposing her gums.

Gabriel grinned back.

When he turned to Julia, he was somber. "We still have the object. We still have a sketch of the intruder. As far as the Cambridge police are concerned, it's an open investigation. I won't give up making inquiries, but so far, I've found nothing. I'm inclined to think that the thief would have returned to the house by now. Either he couldn't find a collector for the artwork we have or he's been deterred by the security system."

"So Rachel and Aaron will be safe?"

"By the time they arrive, it will be September. The break-in was back in December. The chances of the thief returning would be very small indeed."

"Good." Julia touched his biceps. "Maybe we should keep the memento mori, just for a while. Then donate it anonymously to Palazzo Riccardi. I'm sure they'd be happy to have it."

"Yes, they would." Gabriel began pushing the stroller, with Julianne at his side.

Clare turned around in her seat and pointed a chubby finger at Gabriel. "Dadadadada."

Gabriel practically tripped over himself, he stopped so fast. He came around to the front of the stroller and crouched in front of Clare.

"Dada." He pointed to himself. "Dada."

"Dada." Clare repeated. She moved her head back and forth. "Dadadada."

"That's right, Principessa." He pointed to himself once again. "Dada."

"Dadadada," Clare repeated. She clapped her hands and grabbed her bunny and began to chew on it.

Dada, Gabriel whispered. It was more of a prayer than a name.

"I've been trying to get her to say *Mama* first." Julia touched Gabriel's shoulder. "Of course Clare, like her father, has her own ideas."

"I think Clare, like her mother, has her own ideas." He ruffled Clare's hair and straightened.

"That was intense." He pressed his lips together for a moment. (And if you had said his eyes were watering, he would have told you it was his allergies.) "Where are we going? I've lost track of what we were doing."

Julia took hold of the stroller. "We're going to our rooms so I can call Greg Matthews. And then I'm going to take a video of Clare calling you *Dada*. We can save it for posterity and send it to our families."

"Perfect." Gabriel fell into step with Julia and the stroller, keeping a watchful eye on Clare.

In that moment, with his family, with the name his beloved daughter had blessed him with, and with the prospect of a new adventure in Scotland together, Gabriel had never been happier or more hopeful. No matter what challenges or dangers he and Julianne faced, they would do so as a family.

And that was Gabriel's promise.

Fin.

Acknowledgments

I owe a debt to Cambridge, Boston, Selinsgrove, Edinburgh, London, Cologny, Zermatt, Miami, Florence, and Oxford. Thank you for your hospitality and inspiration. All quotations of Dante's *Divine Comedy* are from Henry Wadsworth Longfellow's translation. All quotations of Dante's *La Vita Nuova* are from Dante Gabriel Rossetti's translation.

I am grateful to Kris, who read an early draft and offered valuable constructive criticism. I am also thankful to Jennifer and Nina for their extensive comments and corrections.

I've been very pleased to work again with Cindy Hwang, my editor, and with Cassie Hanjian, my agent. I'd like to thank Kim Schefler for her guidance and counsel.

My publicist, Nina Bocci, works tirelessly to promote my writing and to help me with social media, which enables me to keep in touch with readers. I'm honored to be part of her team. She is an author in her own right and I heartily recommend her novels.

I am grateful to Erika for her friendship and support. I also want to thank the many book bloggers who have taken time to read and review my work.

I especially want to thank you, readers, for your tremendous enthusiasm. This book was written for you, with my gratitude. While I was editing this novel, I learned that Tori, a longtime reader and supporter, had passed away. Tori was my first reader and she shared her affection for the Professor with her family and friends. She was kind and encouraging and is greatly missed.

I want to thank the Muses, Argyle Empire, FS Meurinne, the Fox Den on Facebook, the readers from around the world who operate the SRFans and TMITBS social media accounts, and the readers who recorded the podcasts in English, Spanish, and Portuguese devoted to my novels. Thank you for your continued support.

I am also thankful to Tosca Musk and her team at Passionflix, who will be bringing *The Gabriel Series* to film.

Finally, I would like to thank my readers for continuing this journey with me. We form a diverse, supportive community that spans the globe. I am so grateful to be part of this community.

—SR

Keep reading for outtakes from Sylvain Reynard's novels

Gabriel's Inferno

and

The Raven

Available now from Berkley!

Outtake from *The Raven* by Sylvain Reynard

WILLIAM, PRINCE OF FLORENCE

We'd missed St. Valentine's Day.

I first met Raven in May and soon after, she captured my heart. Our future was uncertain, threatened by enemies both inside and outside the city of Florence. For these reasons, I determined to live each moment with her to the fullest. I would not wait until February for a grand display of my affection.

Raven entered our bedroom at the end of a long day working at the Uffizi Gallery. I noticed she was leaning heavily on her cane, which meant she was tired. No doubt her disabled leg was causing her pain.

"Welcome." I bowed, speaking in English because she'd taken a shine to my Oxonian accent.

She smiled, like the rising of the sun. Then she stopped short, taking in the changes I'd made.

I'd positioned a high-backed chair at the foot of our bed, like a throne. Before it, I'd placed a silver basin with steaming water, a pile of clean towels, and a few other accoutrements.

She limped toward me, curious. "What's this?"

"A surprise." I bent and kissed her firmly on the mouth—a greeting. I put her cane aside and escorted her to the throne. Once she was seated, I pulled out a low stool and sat at her feet.

"I don't understand." She smoothed her black hair behind her ears and rested her green eyes on me.

I'd already lost myself in their depths. Raven's eyes mirrored her soul and were always full of feeling, courage, and compassion.

"This is a gift." I placed my hand on her knee, slipping a thumb under the hem of her dress. She shivered in reaction.

"Relax," I whispered.

I draped a towel over my lap and lifted one of her feet, carefully unstrapping her shoe and removing it. I repeated the same procedure with her other foot, allowing myself the luxury of touching her skin, trailing up the back of her calf.

She sighed, a hazy look on her face.

I fought back a smile.

I placed her feet in the silver bowl, which was filled with warm, soapy water. The scent of roses lifted.

"Too warm?" My eyes sought hers.

She shook her head. "It's perfect."

She leaned forward and placed a hand on my shoulder. "Am I dirty?"

I blinked. "Don't you know the story of Mary Magdalene? Washing Jesus's feet with her tears? Drying his feet with her hair?"

She sat back. "Is that what this is?"

"My hair isn't long enough to dry your feet." I winked at her and she laughed.

I liked the sound of her laughter. I adored it.

"You're washing my feet," she remarked, her voice filled with wonder. "I'm not a Christ figure, William."

"How do human beings express love?"

"They write poems. They kiss. They have sex." She smiled knowingly.

"Love and lust can be confused."

"That's true."

"Washing feet can't be confused with lust." I squeezed her ankle.

Her right foot was part of her disability and it turned unfortunately to the side. I cupped water with my hand and poured it over her foot, using my fingers to smooth over the flesh.

"You can see it." She gestured to her leg.

"Yes." I withdrew her feet from the basin and rested them on my lap.

Our eyes met and she looked away.

I took my time, rubbing the cotton towels gently over her skin.

"It doesn't matter to you, does it?" Her green eyes darted to her injured leg.

"It troubles me because it troubles you." I leaned over and pressed my lips to the top of her foot. "But because it's part of you, I embrace it. Fully."

Raven inhaled deeply. A small droplet escaped the corner of her eye, coursing down her cheek.

I reached up to catch the tear with my sleeve.

She took my hand and kissed it, closing her eyes and pressing my palm to the side of her face.

I pulled her into my arms and she buried her face in my neck. I felt the wetness from her eyes and went still as she took her long, black hair and dried her tears from my skin.

She'd given me many gifts in our time together, but the greatest gift was her love.

"Thank you, *Cassita*," I whispered, holding her to my heart.

Outtake: "Richard and Grace"
from *Gabriel's Inferno* by Sylvain Reynard

The scene takes place after Julia separates from her boyfriend,
Simon, while studying at Saint Joseph's University in Philadelphia.

Grace Clark sat at her dressing table in her bathrobe, brushing her long hair and thinking. She was upset. She was worried. But she didn't know what to do.

"Come to bed, love."

She took her husband's outstretched hand and followed him to the bed, divesting herself of her robe in the semidarkness and joining him naked between the sheets. She positioned herself on her side, running her fingers through the light dusting of chest hair that decorated his upper body.

"My love." Richard grabbed her hand and kissed it softly. "Tell me what's bothering you before I make you forget your troubles. You're driving me crazy."

Grace laughed. He knew her so well. She would absentmindedly glide gentle hands over his still muscular body in order to help her think better, but it had the opposite effect on him.

"Sorry, dear. I was thinking about Julia."

Richard sighed and waited for her to elaborate, but he knew what was coming.

"She won't return my calls. She won't return Rachel's calls. Tom says she's holed up in a tiny apartment near campus and she'll barely speak to him. I was thinking about driving up there to see her tomorrow and taking a care package."

Richard was a thoughtful man, a quiet man. He gave his wife's words his full consideration as she waited to hear his opinion. They were that attuned to one another. They were that much in love.

"I don't think that's a good idea. If she's retreating, it's because she's afraid. If you go to her home, you'll be upsetting her in the one place in which she feels safe."

Grace rested her hand on his heart. "You aren't a psychiatrist."

"That's right. But we both know Julia is withdrawn and timid. If you threaten her security, you will be threatening her coping strategy. And then she's going to have to find something else."

"So what should I do?"

"Why don't you write her a letter, expressing your concern? Give her some time to process things and respond. And then wait and see what happens."

Grace rested her head on her husband's shoulder. "I can do that, but I wish she'd talk to me—let me know what happened that made her want to hide from all of us. And then I could help her."

"Rachel mentioned something about her boyfriend."

Grace flinched. "I never liked the way he looked at her. He was proud of how she looked on his arm, but there was something in his eyes." She reached over and planted a light kiss on her husband's lips. "He never looked at her the way you look at me."

Richard smiled at her and caressed the naked curve of her hip with his fingers. "No one looks at anyone the way I look at you because no one loves anyone the way I love you."

Grace's worries were momentarily interrupted by a passionate kiss and a pair of strong hands stroking her lower back.

"Julia would have been vulnerable when she started seeing him. Her mother had died, she was away from Selinsgrove. She likely tolerated whatever he was willing to give to her. And gladly." Richard sighed deeply. "She's a dreamy romantic, I think, not unlike her mother."

"Don't mention that woman to me. She nearly ruined that little girl. When I think of what she exposed her to and—"

He leaned over and kissed her again. "I know, my love. But there's nothing we can do about it now."

"I feel helpless," Grace whispered. "She's suffering and she won't let me comfort her. I promised Julia I would be her mother. But she won't let me."

"She'll come back to you when she's ready."

"You said that about Gabriel. He never comes home."

Richard shifted uncomfortably. "He *has* come back to us. He's clean, he has a good job, and if we're lucky, he'll meet a nice girl and she'll straighten him out. You lit a candle for him. Why don't you light a candle for Julia?"

Grace kissed her husband, but her sadness over her eldest son radiated through her touch.

"Things will work out, my love. I promise. We'll find a way." Richard softly kissed her.

And when their contact grew more heated, he looked down at her and traced the soft line of her earlobe, pausing to touch the sparkling diamond in her ear, a gift from long ago.

"You're upset. You're sad tonight. I don't think that we should—"

"Making love with you comforts me, darling. Please."

He had never denied her any good thing. He could not deny her this. He hovered over her, staring deeply into her eyes. There was no need for words; their gazes said it all.

It was a slow, easy rhythm, the effortless, intimate coupling of a man and a woman who *knew* each other. The kind of lovemaking that could last for hours or even a lifetime.

"I worship you," he whispered against her neck, as she arched her back, her hands urging him deeper.

"I love you," she whispered. "Always."

The wave crashed over both of them, leaving them breathless and contented.

Grace's last thought was a silent prayer that one day Julia and Gabriel would each find love.

And then she fell asleep wrapped up in the arms of her beloved husband. . . .

Sylvain Reynard is a Canadian writer and a *New York Times* best-selling author of nine books, including the Gabriel's Inferno series and the Florentine series. Passionflix has optioned the rights to the Gabriel's Inferno series and will be bringing the books to screen.

CONNECT ONLINE

SylvainReynard.com
𝕏 SylvainReynard
📷 Sylvain Reynard
f AuthorSylvainReynard